Black Widow

The Detective Reynolds series, Volume 3

Ryan Holden

Published by Ryan Holden, 2023.

Also by Ryan Holden

The Detective Reynolds series
Burnt Blood
Murder on the Waterway
Black Widow
Secrets in the Bones
The Cursed Knights

Watch for more at www.ryanholdenbooks.co.uk.

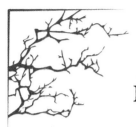

BLACK WIDOW

Ryan Holden

Edition Number: One/2023

1

RUDE AWAKENING

Our world had changed irreversibly, and I couldn't help but ponder how those around us would react once they saw my face covered in human blood. We faced a tough choice, one that none of us envied. The blood moon's events had cast a long shadow, leaving us to navigate a world now requiring a delicate balance. Michael and I had survived, but the fallout had only been postponed, not prevented. The impending challenges weighed heavily on my mind, but for now, I had to endure the confines of Locke's office, bracing myself for whatever fresh horrors the day would bring.

On a scrap piece of paper, a list of places caught my eye - "Cotswolds, the Shropshire hills, Peak District, and the Pennines" - all rural open spaces. Why did Locke have that list? Was it a potential getaway plan for his family, assuming he had one? Little else could be deciphered from this cryptic puzzle. Glancing over my shoulder to ensure Locke's absence, I toyed with delving deeper into the matter, but not by examining the tape.

Allowing my red eyes to flash, I regretted it immediately. Small traces of cleaned blood lay near Locke's chair, serving as a chilling reminder of the ordeal Michael had endured. It had been meticulously cleaned, only detectable by someone like me or a U.V. light. Tiny droplets led to the bookcase against the wall. But the faint heat signature piqued my curiosity even more - a heat source that couldn't be attributed to a radiator, especially considering the significant size discrepancy.

My curiosity had been awakened, pushing aside the fatigue that had gripped me earlier. Yet, guilt settled in as I realised Locke would never expect a sneaky, inquisitive werewolf searching his office. How long ago had the blood been there, and whose was it? The hidden heat signature raised more questions, as there appeared to be no obvious door to access its source.

Inhaling deeply, trying to distinguish the type or where from, I caught it again, only stronger with a strange, rancid tinge reminiscent of spoiled meat. Could it be coming from somewhere else? My heightened senses since the previous night made me consider the possibility that it could be the lingering stench of a forgotten, decaying lunch in the staff fridge. However, my neck hairs stood on end, suggesting there might be more to Locke and the excessively cleaned floor than met the eye.

That's exactly what I procrastinated when the door flung open, dragging the scent of 'Armani' aftershave with it. 'Think of the devil, and he shall appear.' My nerves frayed from sleep deprivation and a deluge of worries.

"Ah, Georgie, you look like shit, and I imagine a little punch drunk. This couldn't wait, unfortunately. My apologies." Locke dropped into his seat, showing signs of wear and tear. I could smell the fear—most of all, the desperation tinged with sadness. What was to come was more than a little personal. It was horrific, and he painted a picture of doom.

"Punch drunk? I feel like my arse got handed to me by Holyfield. What's so desperate that I can smell it dripping from you?" I surprised myself with the flippancy of my response. A lack of sleep and many worries take their toll on a man.

"Ooh, somebody crawled out the wrong side of the bed this early morning. For that, I apologise. What I need to show you isn't, as I'm sure you've gathered by now. For the usual detective," he said with an irritating smirk that had me shifting uncomfortably in my chair. He enjoyed having that over me.

"About that. Where do we stand?" I had to know if I would be dangled on a hook whenever the spooky stuff popped up.

"You keep doing what you do. Nobody needs to know, but you must keep Michael at your hip. I knew you were different the day we met. The how or why is unimportant just now,"

"No hanging us out to dry." How he could know from when we met made no sense. Adding weight to us, thinking he was different.

"I promise. We're all in this together, and far more than you will expect. It seems there's enough strange stuff to go around. With this being the latest," his shaky hand retrieved a light brown file from the satchel. The waver in his throat was full of emotion.

"What's got you so bent out of shape?" I could see sweat bubbling around Locke's forehead.

"A guvnor in Westminster works parliament and diplomatic protection unit. Is dead." Locke's voice softened; this was personal.

"Ok, a friend, I take it?" Locke handed me the file. I flicked the cover, and a spoonful of sick shot into my mouth. I couldn't even say what I was looking at. It belonged to a horror movie. The guy was in a full police uniform, but his face was withered, drained of life. As if he'd been dead for over ten years or more.

"You could say that. He'd been seeing my sister for a while. She worked as a P.A. To some MPs in and around that place. At least she did until she quit suddenly. They broke up soon after, but we remained friends." Locke took his turn to shift uncomfortably in his chair. His hand slid the VHS through his fingers. The weight of a man that's been handed a steaming turd after a nightmare case, and he's watched it. Any nightmares he was anticipating had just been made worse.

"And this picture is him?"

"Yep, you want to know how long it took to look like that?"

"Would usually say over ten years, but you are going to drop a bombshell,"

"One hour. One fucking hour. This tape arrived by courier. The killer filmed the process in ten-minute jumps." In sixty minutes, a guy is drained to death; skin sucked and stretched across the bone. Interesting that the killer knew who to send it to.

"Any idea how?" I couldn't see any visible markings in the picture, although it's only a headshot.

"Yep. Not that they can be seen. There are two small puncture marks on the carotid artery. So far, the Westminster M. E thinks it is similar to embalming, draining the fluids first," aside from the family connection and doing favours, I didn't see how this concerned us.

"Not speak ill of the dead. I don't know why we're involved?" Locke didn't answer. Instead, he took the tape from its box and slipped it into the VCR.

The image flickered to life, revealing a white adult male in uniform, appearing to be in his mid to late thirties with short brown hair. Slouched in a chair, he seemed drugged, struggling to keep his eyes open as his head bounced back and forth. The tape jumped ten minutes, and a decade seemed to age him.

Another leap in time, and the colour drained from his skin. It was sickening, but Locke wasn't watching the grotesque transformation. He focused on me, anticipating that something on the tape would seize my attention.

"What's his name?" Locke's ears perked up in time with his erratic heartbeat, sensing my interest.

"Inspector Nicholas Bamford," I replied.

The jumps continued until the tape reached the sixty-minute mark, precisely sixty and thirty-eight seconds. Inspector Bamford had transformed into a skeletal figure with dead skin stretched over every contour of his bones. Locke was waiting for a specific moment to unfold, and I suspected what it was. There was a way to confirm, but I hesitated to reveal it in front of Locke just yet.

"Rewind, please," Locke snapped to attention, having briefly drifted into thought.

"Saw the little shadowed flicker? It pulls from the neck," I explained.

"I'll get a better look, but you can't freak out," Locke nodded in agreement, his expression full of concern. He rewound the tape a bit.

I flashed my eyes at the right moment, zooming in. Locke played it slowly, and I observed something thin with a pincer at the end—a shadow on the neck. The best way to describe it was with a fork. Yet, it seemed implausible. Was it really possible?

"It's a damn tongue," I concluded, hoping Locke had reached a similar thought. His face revealed enough worry to suggest I was on the right track.

"Seems like it. Now you see why this falls into our jurisdiction?" Locke questioned.

"I do, but it doesn't make much sense," I responded.

The inspector was murdered, and not conventionally. Any disgruntled suspect would opt for a quick method, like stabbing or shooting. This was a gruesome act of torment, meticulously recorded to convey a message. But what was the motive?

"What do you mean?" Locke inquired.

"Why him? You don't just randomly pick an inspector from the Metropolitan Police and think, 'Sod it, you'll do.' There has to be more to this."

"Well, he wasn't exactly the confrontational type. And he's stationed in the wilderness of Parliament protection," I noted.

That part of Westminster was tightly secured, with three barriers just to enter the first section of the grounds near a car park. Security measures were stringent and operational nearly all the time.

"Exactly my point. Somewhere, it was heavily guarded and out of the way. A job officers take for an easy life, not to end up murdered. I need to see the body."

I scrutinised the details closely. The facts weren't aligning unless my sleep-deprived brain was overlooking something crucial. It was time to confront the dead, metaphorically and perhaps literally.

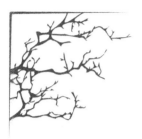

2

FLYING SOLO

In the eerie mortuary, morbid hues of blue and grey, laced with a faint whiff of disinfectant, clung to the walls, heightening the unsettling atmosphere. My feet hesitated in the hallway, resisting the pull forward as if sensing the swarm of thoughts in my mind. I didn't want to be in a place so saturated with death.

Beyond the overpowering scent of antiseptic, the unmistakable odour of decaying flesh lingered. The clock on the wall to my left ticked loudly, my mind drifting to the previous night's events. The thought crossed my mind — we could have been lying on a cold metal table, locked away in the depths of this place.

In those initial minutes, fear gripped me, a sensation I rarely experienced. I shouldn't fear anything, not with the abilities I possess. Yet, I couldn't help but shudder, feeling a chill no different from the frigid air outside. Despite being alone, the information regarding the case weighed heavily on my mind.

Or rather, the lack thereof. It was as if they had dumped a barren file in my lap. Crime scene photos, polaroids of "Nicholas," and a cause of death labelled as "syringeal punctures to the carotid artery" — "drained of all body fluids." The information could have fit on a Post-it note. Including the VHS tape was a new and unsettling element for me.

I believed it could only be one of two things: a warning or a display of prowess. Perhaps both. By the ten-minute mark, Nicholas had not only aged rapidly, his body withering, evident from the yellowing eyes and thin skin, but signs of organ failure were apparent. Any individual capable of such a gruesome display with their tongue is undeniably dangerous. I sensed Locke was holding back, and I wasn't pleased. Recent events have taught us that half-truths were insufficient.

An instinctual feeling told me this case concerned Nicholas's job or workplace, spun to be handled by an average officer. Yes, the tape revealed more than could be easily dismissed. So, what had frightened Locke enough to bring this to me? I may possess claws, fangs, and red eyes. Still, I'm far from being the all-knowing supernatural being he sometimes perceives me to be.

As I pressed forward through the sombre corridors of death, desperately wishing I could be anywhere but here, I couldn't shake the rising fear or, rather, the mounting dread. It felt similar to what I experienced at the stick factory last month. The spirits were present again. But this time, I couldn't discern if they were drawn to the corpses on the ice or those who had met their demise here. There were so many of them, aimlessly drifting with no apparent purpose.

Unlike the spirits in recent cases, which seemed drawn to me, these were different. They didn't pay me any mind, unsettling me even more. Was this a shift in the game's dynamics? I had seen a few spirits at the warehouse last month, but this was different — a crowd gathered in this small space. The rest of the hallway existed in a strange limbo between a hospital and a funeral parlour, a macabre realm mirroring the real world.

However, the receptionist defied my expectations. She didn't embody the image I had imagined — instead, a middle-aged woman, donning smart office wear and casually filing her nails, her complexion a vibrant rose-red. She didn't appear fazed by the deathly surroundings.

"Excuse me, I'm DC Reynolds; a body was brought in recently, a strange mummified one. Could I look and speak to whoever is in charge?" The receptionist snapped to attention, dropping the file she was working on before straightening herself. I couldn't help but notice a slight increase in her heart rate, showing she was spooked. The filing had perhaps been a welcomed distraction. But why would the presence of one body have her so on edge?

"Finally," she said, her face turning serious with a hint of scorn as she furrowed her eyes. "Mr Nicholls said he has been calling you a lot for a few weeks now." Suddenly, I felt slightly thrown off.

"I think there's some confusion. A murdered police officer has been brought in. From what I gather, it's being hushed up. Still, it's not the usual type of case," I explained, detecting a rapid acceleration of panic in her heart rate.

"Oh, I know that. Only he's not the first to come in like that. There have been at least six others." A detail was held back, and her breath turned hoarse, as if recalling the gruesome details. I guessed that she had been privy to the condition of those bodies.

"Not that being dead is a condition; it's the endgame. But the way Locke described it, and based on what I saw on the tape, I certainly didn't want to end up like that — a shrivelled shell in just sixty minutes."

"At least six? And all in the same way?" I probed further.

"Not exactly. Not in the beginning, but I'll leave that for Mr Nicholls to explain. I'll call him for you." She knew something. The thought seemed to scare her. I stood there, observing her angst, attempting to decipher what could be worse than a mummified body.

"Mr Nicholls, I have a detective here to see you."

'Ahem... yep.'

"He says he's here for the police officer. Wasn't expecting the rest."

'Ah, yep. I will let him know.'

Mr Nicholls's voice came through the phone, vibrating with urgency. 'About bloody time,' he grumbled. He seemed well-spoken but with a monotone quality, likely because of dealing with corpses all day.

"Mr Nicholls will be down in a minute; just checking if the room is still freezing," the receptionist informed me, causing me to jerk my head back in confusion. It was cold enough outside; I couldn't fathom a coroner's office being any colder.

"Excuse me, the room is freezing? What does that mean?" I asked, unsure what answer I would receive or if I truly wanted to know.

"It's a fucking igloo upstairs. The first two turned to bloody dust, and then we realised that the only way to slow it down enough for investigation is with a cryo-thingamabob," she explained, her voice laced with a mixture of frustration and fear.

"Like cryostasis, but for the deceased?"

"Something like that. Nicholls knows more."

So, it wasn't just the draining and mummification of the bodies; they were deteriorating at a cellular level until nothing was left but "dust." I must have looked dumbfounded because, while my mind drifted, the receptionist had to shake me to get my attention.

"You Okay?" she asked, her tone soothing, as if I had hurt myself.

"Yeah, sorry. It's been a busy few days, and I didn't think death could get any stranger," I replied, momentarily thinking about the other case that had thrown my world into turmoil.

"Well, my dear, I'm short-selling it," her voice remained steady, and she was persistent in making that point.

As if things weren't bad enough, now we had to worry about Michael and what might become of him. Would he even transform? And now, there was someone or something out there that could kill, with bodies disintegrating to where there would be no evidence left to convict. Not to mention, we were already six bodies deep.

"Thank God... it's a disgrace, I tell you. I've been trying to get someone to come down here for three weeks. But as soon as an officer dies, hey presto, here you are," a voice came from behind the receptionist.

I looked past her shoulder, beyond the bobbed brown hair and the exuberant red hoops for earrings. It was a man in his late fifties dressed in morbid grey coveralls. He was slightly shorter than Michael, with a round, peach-shaped face framed by a bushy mass of grey hair, giving him the appearance of a "crazy professor." Yet there was an unmistakable aura of the Grim Reaper about him. He sounded angry, and I knew I had to steel myself. Six deaths were no laughing matter.

"It's surreal to think that I used to be the kid they wanted dead, and now I'm the man in a world of strange and danger that everyone needs — at least for the time being. Mr Nicholls had a point — nobody had been interested until an officer died."

"Well, it's the first I've heard of it. I'm part of a murder task force dealing with another killing spree. Who did you speak to previously?" I inquired, hoping to understand why this had been overlooked.

"Anyone who would listen. I even went to a police station office. All I got back was, 'This time of year and the cold weather, there are quite a few sudden deaths.' I tried to explain, but the more I spoke, the more it sounded like the bodies had been there for a while," he recounted, frustration apparent in his voice.

"Perhaps it's just too strange for them to grasp. We discovered a connection between the recent body and a videotaped recording that was sent to the police," I explained, noticing the receptionist's face buried in a newspaper, trying to conceal her eavesdropping.

"A tape, you say? That's unusual," he remarked, pulling out a small notebook from his pocket, reminding me of Michael.

"That's not all, but I need to see the body if possible," I said, preparing myself for the freezing temperatures.

"Well, you're lucky I figured out how to slow down the degradation when I did. Otherwise, you'd have made a wasted journey," Mr Nicholls said with a smile. It wasn't a big smile, but enough to show he was human, albeit one that revelled in his genius in this macabre field.

"Yes, your lovely receptionist told me they turned to dust," I replied.

"We have three left, including yours. The only way to slow down the process is with liquid nitrogen. I hope you're not squeamish, Detective." Mr Nicholls seemed to relish the morbid game we were about to embark on; little did he know, I had already seen enough to make his toes curl. But the curtain had been pulled back briefly, and he seemed different.

"Well, Mr Nicholls, let's just say I'm made of sterner stuff," I replied, a little intrigued by using liquid nitrogen. I sensed we were about to step out of our comfort zones again. Meanwhile, the sound of impatient foot tapping told me that Mr Nicholls wanted to get a move on.

AS WE MADE OUR WAY toward the double doors of the morgue, white clouds billowed out from underneath, fogging up the windows. I wasn't looking forward to what awaited us inside, and Mr Nicholls seemed to enjoy that fact. A barrier of grey stood between us and another wave of the weird.

"Where do you think you're going?" a gruff voice behind us challenged. There was no keeping the old boy down; I only hoped he was in the right mind for what lay ahead.

"Mr Nicholls, this is D.S. Dalton," Michael interjected with a smirk, seemingly unfazed by the day's events. "How are you feeling, Michael?"

"Good. Locke briefed me, but judging from all this white stuff, he undersold it," Michael replied, exuding confidence. However, his racing heart and the smell of lingering cigarette smoke showed that he had likely chain-smoked his way through at least three cigarettes before coming in.

"Just a tad. I'll fill you in on some details later," Mr Nicholls conceded, his monotone voice carrying an undertone of excitement. We were about to delve into the unknown depths once more. Yet, despite the sound of impatience in Mr Nicholls's foot tapping, the older man didn't show any signs of wanting to rush ahead.

"It's surreal to think I used to be the kid they wanted dead, and now I'm the man in a world of strange and danger that everyone needs — at least for now," I mused to myself, realising the absurdity of the situation.

"Well, my dear detective, you best put these on," Mr Nicholls said, handing us heavy overcoats and thick black rubber gloves.

As we stepped out into the stiff arctic breeze, or at least that's how it felt, a wall of white greeted us. Three gurneys lined up side by side against the wall, each adorned with a black body bag. Tubes connected to the gurneys pumped in extra nitrogen, and the tips of faces could be seen poking out through the zipper cracks. If you could even call them face, — withered skin stretched over bones.

"Your boy is on the right," Nicholls informed me, noting the temperature gauge before inspecting the bodies.

"So, this is Inspector Bamford?" Michael inquired, sketching away in his pocketbook.

"Who are the other two?" I asked, leaving Michael to carry on with his observations.

"The one on the left is a local M.P., Martin Powd."

"And the middle one?"

"Patrick Ellis, Chairman of the Board for Transport for London," Mr Nicholls replied.

So, we had an inspector working on Westminster protection, an M.P., and the Chairman for Transport. It all felt too political. But that was only knowing about three of the bodies. Michael and I still had much to discover.

"And the others?"

"I don't know. I didn't get to that point with them. By the time we realised what was happening, they had already begun deteriorating. The bodies turned to dust," Mr Nicholls explained.

We needed to understand how the killer could drain a body and dissolve the corpse within hours. I took a deep breath, but it only made me regret it. I picked up on just enough to cause concern.

"Did you find any marks on their bodies?" I asked, noticing the puncture marks over the brachial artery area.

"Not sure. Your one has small marks on the neck, but the skin has decayed too much, making it difficult to evaluate. As for the other two, nothing is visible, but they're also too fragile to handle, as we would with a fresh corpse," Mr Nicholls responded.

So, the puncture marks weren't limited to the neck. The question remained - where were they, and how intimate? And what could make these individuals targets?

"Are you smelling what I'm smelling?" Michael whispered, his words catching my attention. I nodded in agreement.

"Can you retrieve anything from these bodies if drained?" I asked, hoping we wouldn't find ourselves at another dead end.

"The best we can hope for is tissue samples, but we also hope that the liver hasn't deteriorated already," Mr Nicholls replied, his gaze narrowing as he focused on the same spot I had been observing. The body before us had turned a sickly yellow-brown shade with a frosty blue tinge. The inspector's skin appeared crusty and decayed even before its time. It strained against his bones, emitting audible crackles and snaps as the tissue was pulled apart. Then came the crushing - I could hear the rib cage compressing in on itself.

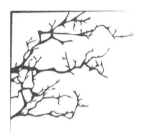

3

HOW MANY DEAD ALREADY?

We didn't have much time. The cold had only slightly slowed down the deterioration. We needed a closer look inside to understand better what was happening. But I couldn't risk it with Mr Nicholls lingering around.

"It's getting worse. Can you look inside now?" I requested, noticing a slight jolt in his throat.

"Alright, but I'll warn you. Seeing the insides of someone is not for the faint of heart," he replied, his lips curving into a half-smile that annoyed me. If only he knew what we had seen. He would tremble in fear.

"Be honest. Have you ever come across anything like this before? How does this connect?" I inquired, searching for any insight he might have.

"No, nothing like this. I'm afraid it's up to you to find the connections. However, for politics, it's always a shitstorm. Take last year, for instance-"

"-what about last year?" I interrupted, wanting to get to the point.

"Wow, don't they have news in the glamorous world of detectives?" he snarled, rolling his eyes as if to say, 'Is this necessary?'

"Well, we're busy with other pressing matters and don't have time to get caught up in mediocre press rants. Besides, I'm fairly new to this," I retorted, wondering where this conversation was leading.

"I vaguely remember hearing about a scandal, but I didn't think much of it," Michael chimed in, clearly just as puzzled.

"Well, 'scandal' is an understatement. They were throwing parties when they shouldn't have been. One of them got out of hand, and a few interns claimed sexual assault. One of them died. It was big enough to make head-lines in 'The Times' and other major publications," Mr Nicholls revealed.

"What happened afterwards?" I asked, realising we were far more out of the loop than we thought.

"It was hushed up. They claimed it was just excessive drinking, and one of the interns' boyfriends supplied drugs to liven things up. Of course, all parties involved denied it," he explained, a hint of cynicism in his voice.

"And that's it? It just dies off like that?" I questioned, feeling a sense of frustration. Corruption seemed to be not limited to the police force; politicians were equally guilty.

"What did you expect? Money and power make the world go round. Especially when influential families are involved, think of all those who end up burnt and swept aside. But eventually, the damaged fight back," he replied, his smirk annoyingly persistent.

"The Royals? Are they involved somehow?" I speculated, concerned about the potential for public scrutiny.

"Think even seedier," he answered, his smirk growing wider.

"Could it get any seedier than them?" Michael quipped, peering at the body in the middle and making additional notes in his pocketbook.

I continued monitoring Michael's heart rate, ensuring he remained in control. There was no telling when an outburst might occur or if his body would accept the transformation. My knowledge of the subject was limited, and the books I had read didn't provide much insight. They only mentioned that some shapeshifters are born while others can be made, and even then, it's a risky proposition. It depends on the person's inner nature. Stories about shapeshifters being able to turn into wolves from a simple werewolf's bite were not always true.

After all, as I looked at Michael's healed throat, it occurred to me I may have saved his life; I wasn't the one to shred his neck. For our sake, I hoped he wouldn't change into something like a Kanaima or anything equally dangerous.

"Ooh, it can. I don't know who. Only that there are a few. The type not to be messed with. Fingers in many pies. Now, are you ready?" Mr Nicholls held a scalpel inches away from Inspector Bamford's decayed stomach.

With only a nod from us, Nicholas pierced the crusty, cold flesh. The crackling of the shiny silver blade cut deep with precision, as if he had done this countless times before. His calm demeanour revealed the experience of a man who had endured such sights for many years.

The first incision caused Michael and me to cover our noses as a rush of putrid air wafted toward us. We fought hard against the urge to gag while Mr Nicholas remained oblivious. If the smell was that bad, I could only imagine how gruesome the insides must look. The grating incision ran from the chest bone to the naval.

"Oh my God," Nicholas said, his jaw-dropping open in surprise. To shock someone like him, the sight must have been truly horrifying. The stench filled the air—a sickening combination of rotting fruit and death. It was overpowering, and I hesitated to step forward. Even Michael, who was usually unflappable, seemed hesitant. Whatever was coming next might overwhelm him.

"What's wrong?" I dared to break the tension.

"It'd be easier to list what's right. The organs are present, but that's about it, and even that's minimal," he said, poking around inside with the blade while the sound of popping resonated. I could see Michael shudder in sync with the pops, as if feeling them.

"Well?" my impatience shone through. Nicholas liked to build tension, but human interaction wasn't something I had the luxury of now.

Nicholas cleared his throat, swaying his head from side to side while curling his mouth to the left. It seemed like he was preparing to share the most accurate description, matching the stench assaulting our nostrils. After a few seconds, my mind drifted to the story he had spoken of – a party, sexual assaults, drugs, alcohol, and death. It sounded like a typical night out in 'Essex.'

But now, a year later, these bizarre murders were happening. My heart desperately wished it was all a coincidence, but my weary brain told me otherwise. We needed to start by investigating the circumstances of that fateful night. Since forensic evidence was highly unlikely, we had to use anything we could find.

"All the organs have been mummified, tightly wrapped in a grey webbing. It's slowly crushing them, squeezing the life out of each one while simultaneously releasing a gas. As soon as the gas touches the body, it triggers rapid decay. Bloody hell, we need to get out of here,"

Mr Nicholas's face turned pale, and he frantically sliced through the flesh, collecting samples and hurriedly sealing the bag. He looked genuinely scared.

"Why? What's wrong?" Michael asked, unaware of the situation. But if my suspicions were correct, it was the gas. Once released into the air, the nitrogen would cool it down, change its density, and allow it to travel. Who knows what would happen to anyone or anything that came in contact with it?

"The gas is too dangerous. We must leave this room, turn on the extractors, and let them disperse it. We might lose the bodies, but these samples could still be helpful," said Nicholas, sweat dripping down his forehead as he looked at the vented trunking above our heads that led to the outside. That the water droplets outside were freezing showed his concern.

Michael's expression mirrored his unease, and he was already a step ahead of us, his heels tapping the pathway behind.

"Can you take care of all that?" I asked, curious since Ellena was currently tied up.

"Possibly. If not, I have a colleague or two who could help." The smile vanished from Mr Nicholas's face, and he appeared determined.

I lingered by the door momentarily, observing the gases emanating from the organs as they picked away at the skin. A yellowish surface that crumbled into a deathly brown and then black. 'Death to dust' in no time at all. At least now we had some clue how these murders were being committed. The bigger question was, how did these events connect?

THE SCENE SHIFTED TO the cold case file storage in the basement of the Westminster Police Station at noon on the 1st of November.

We found ourselves in a musty twenty-foot square room filled with many files. The atmosphere was anything but welcoming; the files felt more than just cold; they felt dead – kept in storage until the higher-ups deemed it time to dispose of them.

They became apprehensive when we explained the reason for our visit to the station's staff. You'd expect us all to be on the same team. But the moment I asked to speak to someone in charge of the investigation into the Houses of Parliament party, the staff grew uneasy.

The civilian staff member I talked to seemed to know what I was referring to. He fidgeted nervously in his chair, desperately trying to create distance even though there was nowhere to escape. At one point, he nearly toppled over. So, what caused their anxiety? What had them on edge about a simple request? Michael and I explored independently, as no one came to see us. Another basement awaited us, but at least this one was brighter and devoid of chains, though it still felt eerie.

We weren't entirely sure what we were searching for. It felt like we were grasping at straws. If the bodies were turning to dust, we needed to find a connection, anything that could shed light on why a board member, an M.P., and an inspector had been murdered. Not to mention the three deceased who had crumbled away before the coroner could examine them.

"Have you found anything?" Michael asked, flipping through a stack of grubby registers. Every file kept in storage had to be registered with a date and crime number before being assigned a location reference. Without that information, we would search unthinkingly.

"I'm afraid it's up to you. It seems we're not lucky enough for it to be straightforward and waiting for us on some shelf," I said, glimpsing a face peering through the window of the door.

"Well, we could be here for a while. On the bright side, thanks to you bloody saving my life, my eyesight is like that of a teenager again," Michael remarked.

"Oh great, I guess the hormonal surges are next," I chuckled, causing a smile to appear on Michael's usually focused face. The same face peered through the window for the second time in a few minutes before swiftly retreating.

"Piss off. I won't let you forget that," Michael responded.

"For saving your life?" I asked.

"No, for making that joke," he replied.

"Well, if you refrain from murdering anyone else, that would be great. But jokes aside, you're in for a rough ride. Christ, all of us are," I said, concerned about what lay ahead.

"I gathered that much. Let's hope the strength in numbers helps."

"Promise me that if anything weird happens, like spontaneous bleeding from your nose or anything of the sort, you'll let me know," Michael said, his expression filled with concern.

"Why? What does that mean?" I asked, puzzled.

"In case your body rejects the bite. I read it might happen, and there's no guarantee that you'll become a wolf. Add to that the fact that I have a demon in me, and it's like a spooky lucky dip," he explained.

"Yeah, sure. Fuck, I'm just glad to be alive. So, anything goes, except turning into a rat, mouse, or pigeon. Imagine being a were-pigeon," we burst out laughing until I noticed the face peering through the window for the third time.

"Oh God, that would be something. We're being watched, by the way."

"They certainly haven't rolled out the red carpet for us. We need to get this done and leave as soon as possible," Michael said, his serious tone causing my anxiety to rise. Things weren't going well for me either; I wasn't having much luck with my search.

Meanwhile, Michael's search hadn't been yielding many results either. Don't get me wrong, there were plenty of dusty files. I found the correct month and year, but flipping through them and searching for a specific crime type yielded nothing. While sifting through the pile, I discovered two thin folders slipped together, almost going unnoticed until I spotted them attached by a paperclip to another case.

"I think I found something, mate, but it doesn't make sense," I said, setting the two very thin folders free next to the open register that Michael had been examining. The two file numbers matched entries three-quarters of the way down the page – penalty notices issued to Sally Turnage and Collette Newton.

It was perplexing since the alleged victims of the scandal were women. Yet, these records were for drunk and disorderly conduct. There was also a third entry with no name but a case number. The numbers were sequential, meaning three files were created that night. Two didn't fit the gossip, and one was a mystery. So what the fuck happened that night, and what's the missing crime?

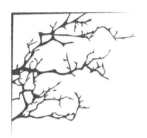

4

UNWELCOME

As we pondered, the head popped up at the window one last time, and the door swung open, revealing a short man in his thirties. Short black curls framed his head, a black moustache adorned his face, and he was decked out in a white shirt with a striped tie—a typical suit brigade member. Finally summoned the courage to confront us, he appeared unfazed, not realising we were old hands chasing lost causes. Armed with two new names and a series of deaths turning to dust, we were still missing the crucial connection between them. Stationed in the basement, he seemed as unwelcoming as the staff upstairs, bothered by our intrusion.

"What do you want? Maybe I can save you the trouble of being here," he said sternly, tinged with annoyance. Before I could respond, Michael beat me to it, his irritation apparent. Hospitality wasn't his forte.

"Well, I don't know. Maybe a red carpet or coffee on a silver platter. Or perhaps you could enlighten us about this missing file," Michael snapped, closing the folder he held and turning towards the door.

"What's it to you? This isn't your bloody borough," the man retorted. I waited for some territorial display, but it seemed to rile up Michael, whose heart rate increased slightly. He shifted from side to side, eyeing the man.

"Sorry, I'm just looking for the bloody high horse you seem to have ridden in here on," Michael quipped, almost making me laugh. No qualms about getting under each other's skin—this situation reeked.

"I believe D.S. Dalton mentioned that we're investigating a murder possibly linked to last year's fiasco in parliament. Does that ring a bell?" I watched closely, noting the nervous gulp and the twitch at the corner of his mouth. The man was stalling, and the slight bump on his temple betrayed his increasing unease.

Curiously, I could sense more—a gale-force wind through hairs on his neck standing like bristling trees and beads of sweat rolling down his cheeks. My senses awaited the cascade of lies. But in the back of my mind, worry lingered about Michael, the potential transformation, and Locke's cryptic mention of the bloodstain.

"Vaguely. You have the penalty notices, don't you? It should be fairly self-explanatory," he replied condescendingly, raising my blood pressure. Arrogant little prick. He stuck to the cover up narrative, but the change in his voice pitch indicated we were pulling the right string.

"Cut the crap. We're interested in what isn't here. The third crime with no details. Care to explain that?" I whispered to Michael, keeping it low. He had what he needed, but there was more the man wasn't sharing.

"It's probably just a duplication error, or two officers got their wires crossed trying to report the same offence. I'm sure you've seen it before," he replied, gaining confidence. But I wasn't buying the nonsense.

"Don't think so. No title, which could've been marked as an error. Yet, there are only two thin files here, considering what we've heard happened," I added, catching a small cough from Michael. He got what he needed, but I wasn't done; something was being withheld.

"If it's not there, I can't help you. If you're done here, don't go digging in someone else's backyard," he retorted.

"Why not? That's where all the skeletons are buried. If we find your station complicit, we'll involve professional standards. You wouldn't want old bones uncovered, would you?" I fuelled my determination.

"The nerve of you dictating what gives you the right?" he replied angrily. Michael's face turned red, ready to tear the man's head off. I intervened, placing an arm across Michael's chest. This was my confrontation, and I wasn't about to be easily brushed off, not when the body count was rising.

"The death toll overrides your authority. We have six deaths now, the latest an important figure. While you play with your secrets, remember this: the truth will come to light, along with your sins. You've just given us more reason to make your life uncomfortable," I stated firmly.

"Do that, and you'll only be shooting yourself in the foot. Career suicide, some would say," he replied, a hint of fear in his voice.

"I'd rather fight for the dead than protect a pen-pusher more concerned with getting drunk and assaulting women. What comes next is out of my hands," I responded, my voice steady and unwavering.

As we stepped forward, he retreated, reaching for the door handle. He intended to run off and inform higher-ups about our confrontation. Fear and adrenaline pulsed through my veins, and something ominous emanated from him. It was the right track; at least I connected one dot to the dead.

Even if it was a tenuous connection, we had to start somewhere. I hoped that if more bodies dropped, our grim reaper of a coroner could stabilise them.

"Well, the dead won't pay your bills when you're out of a job," he sneered as he walked away, returning to the station's main area.

Sure, we overstayed our welcome, but it was unlikely the red carpet would be rolled out soon. A different borough, but the same underlying issue remained—corruption. I couldn't say if the man was involved, but the vibes were anything but good.

SALLY TURNAGE - 6 ENNISMORE Mews, Knightsbridge, the penalty notices read. To say we were surprised would be an understatement. Knightsbridge was posh, filled with immaculate townhouses. Number six, a two-tone red brick building with pristine white windows, stood before us. Michael's furrowed brow expressed the same thoughts running through my head.

"This seems peculiar," he said.

"I know, matey. When is anything ever straightforward?" I replied. Approaching the black front door, I noticed spasms and cramps in Michael's body. Something bothered him, and the last thing we needed was a loose cannon—a new werewolf. I already had enough on my plate.

"Remember what I said. It can be challenging. And I'm still learning," I reminded Michael as we prepared to knock on the door. No cars parked outside, but judging by the double yellow lines, street parking wasn't permitted.

"Hello, how can I help you?" greeted a man in his early fifties, maybe late forties. He was smartly dressed but wore a suit, greying hair, and a confused expression as he took in our warrant cards.

"Afternoon, sir. This is D.S. Dalton, and I'm DC Reynolds. We were wondering if Sally Turnage lives here. Don't worry, she's not in any trouble," I assured him, hoping to put him at ease.

His discomfort was apparent as he quickly shifted his weight. He knew Sally; given her age, she was likely his daughter. There was more to this story than met the eye, and we had to approach it tactfully.

"Talking to the police isn't exactly on our wishlist after what my daughter has been through," he replied, a touch of bitterness in his voice.

"We're not like the others. I stumbled upon your daughter's case while investigating a murder. We wanted to talk to Sally, hoping she could help us," I explained.

"My daughter was treated like a convicted murderer, while those bastards did whatever they pleased." Mr Turnage's face turned red with anger. There was more to this story than just a sleazy party. Perhaps the missing piece is connected to a motive for murder. The question remained: who was responsible?

"Let's be frank, Mr Turnage. It sounds like you and your daughter were treated horribly by a bunch of arseholes who should know better. We're here to rectify some mistakes and hopefully gather some information about why there's suddenly a wave of murders all connected to the den of iniquity they call parliament," Michael chimed in, surprising both Mr Turnage and me. Michael's way with words was like a machete, cutting through the underbrush and making an impact. Hearing the summary spoken aloud was sickening. All we could do was hope that Sally hadn't been too traumatised and that she could offer some clues.

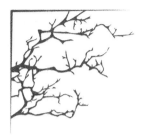

5

THE TURNAGES

It felt like a cosy family home with group photos on the mantlepiece and a neatly thrown blanket on the sofa. A beach-themed coffee table displayed a fruit bowl with at least one banana past its "eat by" date. The air carried a strong, sweet fragrance.

Despite the warmth, the place seemed wrongly tangled in a cover-up. Mr Turnage was deeply conversing with a woman, likely his wife, both engrossed. Meanwhile, Michael hung his head low, struggling to make sense of the overwhelming sensory onslaught.

The assault on my senses was almost unbearable, urging me to escape the constant noise. Yet, I had to endure it while eavesdropping on Mr and Mrs Turnage's discussion, seemingly gripped by fear.

"She's only just started feeling normal again. She's only just been able to look at the world without breaking down, for God's sake," Mrs Turnage's words flowed non-stop, punctuated by the loud crunch of her chewed fingernails. Each crunch made Michael flinch.

"They claim they're different. There have been more deaths. How can we stand by and do nothing?" Mr Turnage's reference to "more deaths," caught my attention. Was he talking about the incident at the party?

"It's not just Sally, remember? The others went through it, too. Do we want to dredge it all up again?" Mrs Turnage's voice conveyed concern and worry, her constant nail-biting emphasising the tension.

"I understand that, dear. But should they have to live with the stigma of being social pariahs? Branded as liars, women trying to use their bodies to climb the career ladder? The pressure becomes too much, and they make up stories. Is that fair?" Mr Turnage questioned.

"No, but... tipping over the edge isn't right either," Mrs Turnage admitted, her voice trembling.

"Let's try to get Sally to talk. I have a feeling about this. No nonsense, no BS. We need to be straightforward. Maybe we can all find some closure," Mr Turnage suggested.

"Alright, I'll talk to her. But if they push too hard, or if it feels like it's her fault, then it's over. I can't go through that again," Mrs Turnage agreed.

The protective instincts of the Turnage parents were admirable, driven by pain and fear. They felt like powerless pawns in a world of privilege. While the Turnages may not be on the poverty line, they couldn't compete with the "silver spoon" types.

As I listened to their conversation, a growing sense of disgust came over me. Covering up an allegation was one thing, but what about the aftermath of the victims who stood firm in their truth? How many times could one be beaten against a wall before the bleeding became too much?

The weight of Mr and Mrs Turnage's concerns felt all too real, and I couldn't help but wonder what had transpired that night. While Locke might view our presence as a waste of time, perhaps he would understand that we couldn't rule out any connection, no matter how tenuous.

"Look, I'm sure you've noticed that this hasn't been a walk in the park for us. So I must ask, as a father... do you have children?" Mr Turnage's question jolted me.

Memories of what could have been flooded my mind. I couldn't relate, but not for lack of trying.

"I'm afraid not... Almost, but he died during childbirth. Both of them did," I replied with raw honesty.

While I couldn't share the experience of fatherhood, I knew the pain of loss. Mr Turnage's fear was palpable, stemming from the thought that his daughter might take her own life. The anguish of a father fearing for his child.

"Sorry to hear that. You know, the idea of having a child is borne out of the belief that everything is going right. You'd do anything to protect them. This is what it's like for Sally and us. She's our only child, trying to become a teacher. But now, she might as well be a social outcast," Mr Turnage admitted with tears in his eyes.

Mr Turnage's struggle to contain his emotions was clear. We had unwittingly walked into someone else's storm, which was awkward. The discussion about children reminded me of what I lacked, cutting me to the bone. The redness around Mr Turnage's eyes, where tears had welled up but not yet fallen, spoke volumes about the depth of a father's love and concern for his daughter. It made me wonder what he would do to protect Sally.

"Mr Turnage, taking the law into your own hands would only compound the pain for you and your family," I cautioned, sensing the anger simmering beneath the surface.

"Taking the law into my hands? I'm not sure what you mean. Please, just be gentle with her," he replied with a hint of frustration.

As we continued to engage with the Turnages, Michael noticed something amiss in the air. He whispered to me, "Georgie, there's something off. I can smell it. There's a mix of pain and anger in the air. Are you getting that?"

I nodded and replied in a hushed tone, "Keep listening and act normal. We don't know who or what is causing this, but we must stay composed for them."

'SALLY TURNAGE,'

'Come on, love; it's okay,'

Mrs Turnage called gently, trying to coax Sally out of the hallway. Sally's heart raced with panic. She fidgeted, cracking her fingers and grinding her teeth. I could smell her fear when she glided to the glossy white doorframe. It enveloped her.

Sally was of average height, slim, with light brown hair cascading below her shoulders. She appeared to be no larger than a size ten, and her looks could have opened doors in the academic world. But then, I noticed her scars—more than the ones hidden behind her hazel eyes. Two sets were on each wrist, with one set overlapping the other, suggesting attempts made at intervals of three to four months.

Additional scars marked her forearms, likely the result of self-inflicted pain as a distraction from her true troubles. It was apparent that she had subjected herself to immense suffering, compounding the torment she had already endured.

"Sally dear, these are detectives working a murder case, and they'd like to ask you about that night," Mrs Turnage explained.

Sally paused, her lips pursed and her eyes darting around as if searching for an escape route. Her fight-or-flight response took hold, and I had only a few seconds to steer the situation in the right direction.

"Sally, we're not here to cause trouble. We need your help. And if we can assist you and bring those responsible for your suffering to justice, we will."

Sally took a hesitant step forward, glancing at her parents, who nodded reassuringly.

"Why... why now?" Sally stammered as she continued to move forward. I had yet to win her over completely.

"We only recently learned about your case or the incident. We're part of a murder task force currently occupied with ongoing cases. Our latest investigation led us to an incident where you received a penalty notice last year. It didn't sit right with us; something seemed concealed at the police station. We want to understand why and what happened?" I explained.

Sally lifted her gaze, and her heart steadied. She crossed her arms to hide her scars. As she settled into her chair, I briefly focused on my hearing outside. Whoever had been watching was still there, lingering and possibly listening. It made me wonder if they were acting like guards. But why?

"What they said, what the papers reported, it wasn't true," Sally declared.

Her eyes pleaded with us to believe her. She would undoubtedly struggle to recount the painful memories. Still, from the atmosphere in the room, there was a story we needed to hear, a story that could shed light on the situation.

"Why don't you tell us what happened? We're here to listen."

Michael appeared more at ease, his earlier twitchiness giving way to a semblance of calm. He jogged his chair back, occasionally glancing at the window as if he were both inside and outside the room, trying to maintain his composure as his other self loomed within. I, too, was transforming, but the fear of transitioning from a normal state to something more primal was a daunting prospect.

"Please, what I'm about to say is the truth. I didn't know about the other stories until one of my friends told me later," Sally began.

"What stories? How many of you attended this party?" I inquired.

"Blackmail, insider trading, and fraud involving pharmaceutical companies," Sally explained.

"Sorry, what?" Michael's interest was piqued. He had a penchant for conspiracy theories, particularly involving companies in the pharmaceutical industry.

"Susan, Alice, Maria, Francis, Grace, Selene, and me. We were all invited, though initially, just four of us interned with Parliament members. Susan got close to a man with a red briefcase," Sally recounted.

"The Chancellor?" I interjected.

We couldn't simply demand the truth and expect the world to reset. Life didn't work that way, and the truth didn't unveil itself so easily. It would be our responsibility to show Sally that the truth could be brought out of the shadows and make a difference. Even if occasional, small victories built up into a broader quest for justice. Since my awakening, I have witnessed corruption, greed, pain, and the destruction that power could wreak in the wrong hands.

No, we didn't possess a magic wand, but we served as a bridge between two worlds. It was high time that the "silver spoons" tasted the medicine they had long avoided.

"That's him and his friends. Don't be fooled by appearances: Susan, me, Alice, Maria, Francis, Grace, and Selene. We all had a good time. None of us could have foreseen how that night would unfold. Now, only Alice, Grace, Maria, and I remain. Empty shells, fighting to regain wholeness. A battle we're losing."

Sally's voice was heavy with pain, the words escaping her throat like a groan. Her eyes drifted, closing as she recalled the night forever altering their lives. If I had understood correctly, Susan, Francis, and Selene had died. Francis Collyer, the name on the other notice, was a life reduced to a mere penalty. Was it worth it?

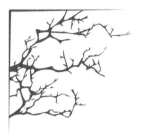

6

'4 O'clock- 6 Ennismore Mews,'

'It was a Halloween Masquerade party. I realised how odd it was to cele-
brate a birthday on such a superstitious night. I used to scoff at supersti-
tions, but now, well... Let's just say that the events of that night made me reconsider. I can't be sure if it was the drinks or something else, but one thing
was clear – none of us knowingly took any drugs. We would never do that,
and there was no one delivering any. Our boyfriends were out of the picture.
I heard they later accused Susan of smuggling in her drug-dealing partner.
Still, given her hectic schedule, it didn't seem plausible.' -

- 'We first gathered a modest group of four coworkers at Maria's place.
But we soon got word that 'the more the merrier' was the motto. It was
around 4 o'clock, and we thought a few glasses of wine would help calm our
nerves. After all, we'd be rubbing shoulders with 'well-to-do' folks. We didn't
go overboard, just enough to boost our confidence.' -

- 'The plan was to meet at Parliament by 7 p.m., where there was ample
hall space. So, we assumed it would be a simple affair... Oh, how wrong we
were.'-

-'Limousines awaited us. A person donning an elegant masquerade hood
and a tuxedo ushered us inside. The doors locked as soon as we sat down, and
a blackout screen concealed the driver. The windows were equally opaque.
Panic coursed through me, but Susan reassured us. As the car moved, I mon-
itored the clock. It was 8 p.m. when we finally came to a stop.'-

-'Francis and Selene showed no concern and dived into the mini-bar,
getting a head start on the drinks. When the car doors opened, I noticed
the trees, dim yellow lights, and a distant white glow. My high heels clacked
on pebbled gravel, and I thought it seemed rather fancy. But only when we
stepped outside did I realise how abundant it was.'-

-'A grand structure stood tall and wide, with bay windows on both levels. It was a cluster of three buildings with sides at an angle, their base adorned with elegant white pillars. Four pillars on each side framed five marble steps, black and white. Two imposing men, much like the one who greeted us at Parliament, stood at the entrance, their masquerade hoods ensuring anonymity. I got the masquerade theme, but this felt like something from a spy novel.'-

-'Grace, the intellectual of our group, had everyone fooled with her blonde hair and fair complexion. Beneath her appearance, she was sharp and loved to analyse everything. She seemed worried as we were handed a selection of masks that emitted an odd scent. Within five minutes, my head felt lighter, and my body seemed to float. All eyes were on Alice and Selene, who were known for dancing and flirting. Selene had a knack for captivating crowds of men with her long, dark hair and penetrating dark eyes that seemed to read minds.'-

- 'The room's lights dimmed, and the music grew louder as a mesmerising red glow enveloped the space. Drinks flowed, and about an hour in, the atmosphere shifted. The men in the room resembled predators on the prowl. We weren't the only women there, but we stuck close together. As the night wore on, the strange smell from earlier gave me a headache, and I felt increasingly dizzy.'-

- 'I stepped out of the room to clear my head. Susan and Selene were missing when I returned, along with the man with the red case. My head was spinning, but something felt very wrong. The atmosphere was shifting, and my sense of unease grew. As I felt disoriented and that strange smell lingered, fragments of the night began pounding in my brain. Everything felt off, and fear set in.'-

- 'Gradually, the others woke up, confused and disoriented. Then came the pain. Our bodies ached, adding to our confusion, and a searing pain radiated from between my legs, unlike anything I had ever felt before. Beastly faces with fangs filled my vision, and I felt helpless to escape. Susan, Selene, and Francis were nowhere to be seen. My head was spinning, and I slumped into a chair, gasping for breath, which only led to blacking out. My memory became foggy, with only glimpses of waking up in a small, dark room with a red glow on a bed and a white light flashing in my face, followed by a clicking sound. It seemed like they were taking pictures.'-

- 'Hands pulled at my body, and I couldn't move. Everything hurt, and those beastly faces continued to haunt me, albeit in a blurry, nightmarish haze. Susan, Selene, and Francis were nowhere to be found. My head spun, and I eventually blacked out. Worried cleaners woke me up. We were back at Parliament, on a sofa in a hall. I said we but Selene was missing. Still in a daze, struggling to remember what had happened, I soon realised the cause of all the concern. In a corner lay Francis, with vomit covering her mouth and a large bottle of vodka cradled in her arms. She never drank vodka.'-

- 'My heart raced, and it felt like someone had reached inside and ripped out my stomach. I watched as the crowd tried to shake Francis, but there was no response. The world moved in slow motion. I knew Francis wouldn't wake up. Her skin had turned a dull grey, and her lips were stained with vomit. Susan was still unconscious but pressed against me; I could feel her breathing as she inhaled and exhaled.'-

- 'I turned my head, and reality sank in. The hall was dimly lit, with an artificial appearance, as if a party had taken place, and we were the last to leave. My ears were still ringing, and that strange smell from earlier lingered, causing fragmented memories of the night to assail my brain. Everything felt off, and I was scared. The others slowly regained consciousness, feeling similarly confused. As the pain set in, our bodies ached, adding to our bewilderment. We all felt the same: me, Alice, Grace, Maria, and Susan.'-

- 'Alice took one look at Francis and panicked. By this time, more footsteps were approaching. Alice was screaming, and I tried to calm her down, but her cries only added to my unease. Someone grabbed my arm, and I panicked, shoving my arm out. When I turned around, I saw uniformed police officers. They were no older than their early thirties, with neat and clean uniforms. The officer frowned at my attempt to lay a hand on a police officer.'-

- 'He had furrowed eyebrows, and his wrinkles deepened as he glared at me. My peripheral vision remained fixed on Francis, who was still surrounded by a pool of yellow vomit. My head couldn't help but wonder how this could have happened or how it had happened, with so much of the night now a chaotic jumble of fragmented memories. I felt groggy, unable to reconcile the hazy recollection with the limited number of drinks I'd had—only four.'-

- 'The chaos escalated when two men in suits suddenly entered the room. I couldn't recall seeing them at the party. Their purposeful stride set them apart as they approached from a doorway about twenty feet away. Their direct path led them straight to Francis, who had her dishevelled hair facing away from them. How could they know to go directly to her?'-

- 'Their faces quickly contorted in reaction to her condition. Something about the situation didn't seem right. Susan, Alice, Maria, Grace, and I found ourselves at the centre of it all, with Selene missing. I tried to explain to the officers that we needed help and couldn't remember much of the night. Alice's behaviour was becoming increasingly erratic.'-

-'A whispered conversation with one officer led to a sudden and alarming change in the situation, if possible. Grace inquired about Selene's whereabouts, but heads shook in the background, and an arm pointed at Susan, who had raised her tear-streaked face just in time. Mascara ran down her cheeks, her lipstick smudged, and her face twisted in horror as an officer pulled her from her seat, clutching her arms. I attempted to reach her, but I was blocked.'-

-'Maria received a slight push to her upper chest as she tried to stand and speak with an officer. The puzzle pieces were coming together, and we were in trouble. Trouble we couldn't quite figure out. Soon, everything became a blur as we were separated, and more police and ambulance staff arrived. I was taken to a hallway, where words were spoken, but only a few registered with me. My focus remained on Francis and the surrounding people. My head swirled as I searched for clues and details to remember where Selene could have gone.'-

-'Before I knew it, a piece of paper was thrust into my hands—a penalty notice for drunk and disorderly conduct. My pleas of innocence were incoherent, and the world felt like a never-ending nightmare, one horror after another. We were escorted away from the premises, leaving us with the sense that we had done something wrong. Alice also received a ticket, but Susan's face was a picture of anger.'-

-'Maria was distressed, running her fingernails through her goosebump-covered skin. I felt as if something lingered on me, something invisible and unknown, tormenting me while my mind remained clouded.'

"What the hell, those bastards? Did they take you to the hospital or offer any aid?"

Michael spoke up first; I couldn't. Speechless. My mouth couldn't engage. The thoughts were there, but nothing came. Michael's face showed horror. Sally had been brave so far, but the tears were falling. Her mother, too, Mr Turnage, had rage on the brain, and it was brewing on his face, turning it a shade of crimson.

I wanted to know how much more Sally knew. She could clam up at any moment, and I didn't want her to break. Her pale, scarred frame had been through enough already. Were we beating a path down a blind alley? The connection wasn't clear yet, assuming there'd be one.

"We weren't believed and didn't receive any help,"

"What do you mean? Surely, they checked for the pain?"

Sally slowly opened her mouth, her head drifting forward a little while her eyes bounced left to right, seeking reassurance from her parents. Her heart raced. There was more to the story, and it was uncomfortable. I had a feeling it involved her friends.

7

THAT FATEFUL NIGHT

"We stood on the pavement, and it must have been a little after 7 am. The world had got brighter, slowly getting busier as the night had disappeared in the blink of a disturbing eye. Huddled close, feeling the chill that alcohol had held off, we exchanged glimpses of memories, trying to piece together a tale."

"A particular theme formed, centred around that strange smell from the masks and the pain we were left with. Tears poured; it was almost a state of confused limbo. We had one friend dead and one missing, yet we didn't know what to do because it hadn't sunk in yet. The truth didn't feel real; buses whizzed by, leaving diesel fumes to cut into our lungs. The first sign was that it wasn't a dream, but a living nightmare."

"Susan was nearing the point of speaking, trying to recall a memory, when two officers came running. We all thought they had realised the gravity of the situation and that we needed help, but Susan was pulled to the side. We couldn't hear what was being said out of earshot, but Susan looked worried, and the officer was aggressive. They weren't helping."

"Susan's look of worry turned hysterical; streaks of mascara ran down her cheeks as one officer, a short and tubby guy, gripped Susan's wrist and placed her in handcuffs. It was a defining moment that made me think things would only worsen if we hung around. We had to find somewhere safe to regroup, think, and make calls. With one friend dead, one missing, Susan arrested, and the rest of us hanging on by a thread, Maria grabbed my arm, her face pale, and asked, 'What the bloody hell did we get mixed up in last night?'"

"My mouth moved, only to catch smoggy air as no words came out. Susan was dragged past us like a 'walk of shame.' All she could muster were the words 'Insider trading.' What that meant at that moment was anyone's guess as the girls and I exchanged confused looks. However, we later learned that Susan was being blamed for using her closeness with the chancellor to feed political details to a rival 'party.' Black market, pharmaceutical information."

"Yet, as we stood on the pavement, growing colder, observing our friend being taken away and the number of people dwindling, we had to savour the sour taste in our mouths as nobody came to tell us anything or offer help. Blue-white tape stretched across the gate entrance, and in the distance, press vans hurtled toward us. We knew we had to leave; the looks between us were filled with the urgency to fight or flee, but we were still clinging to the notion of not leaving Francis. Then we had to defend Susan."

"The dilemma tore us apart, but our minds were made up for us the moment the 'press' charged out of their vans and headed our way first. Reluctantly, we collected enough to hurry down the road and hail a taxi. I told Mum and Dad we went home first while the girls phoned their parents. My dad couldn't go to the local stations until he found out where Susan was, so I could inform her parents. The hard part was figuring out how to handle 'Francis.' Her phone was busy, so we went to her home."

"I'll never forget the look on her mum's face. We made it into her hallway, but watching her turn pale, stumble backwards, and slump on the steps was horrific. Her tears started ours again, and making matters worse was that we couldn't explain simply between us. Behind all of that, my brain kept searching for the last sighting of Selene, praying to God that she was safe and had just slipped out with a guy."

"Susan was released that evening on bail pending further investigation. After a lot of soul-searching and sobering reflection, we got together once Susan was home, trying to piece everything together, including why she was arrested. Before that, we looked for Selene—not at her home since her parents hadn't seen or heard from her, and we were her only friends. One suspicious moment her parents remembered was a phone call in the early hours. They said heavy breathing sounded like a man."

"They assumed it was a drunken crossed wire, but Selene never came home—that day or any day since. The police finally took a missing persons report, but no sooner had Selene's parents done so than the newspapers somehow got hold of our addresses and began hounding us."

SALLY STOPPED AND HUNG in shame, even though none was to be had. Her hands trembled in time with her bottom lip. I had listened and watched every micro expression and every word. Sally didn't skip a beat. So why were my hackles whipping up a storm? The dad moved forward and away at certain points of the story, edging to Sally's left shoulder to offer reassurance.

Comfort was one thing, but then why not stay by her side? Unless his presence was reinforcing what had been said. The mother couldn't look at our faces, choosing instead avoidance and unrest. She kept fidgeting. The story was heartbreaking, but something was off.

"Did you hear what caused 'Francis's' death?" Michael said, tilting his head to actively listen while his eyes were on the photographs on the mantelpiece.

"Ecstasy overdose."

"What? Really?"

"No... I mean, she wouldn't knowingly take that."

"The smell from the masks. How would you describe it closest?"

Michael was fishing, using his years of experience and, more than likely, a past life to narrow down what it could be.

"Um, 'Black Jacks,' that sweet liquorice but a little different, I guess. Now that I think of the first drink, too."

"What do you mean?" I said as Sally recalled details that didn't come easily initially—elements of truth when someone delves deep. But I was listening to the exaggerated tales. The elevation in her throat as panic mixes, as she hopes its believable. There was a moment in the 'sofa part,' but I couldn't grasp what.

"When we entered, someone stood with a tray of drinks for us to take as we passed. Seemed like champagne, but the aftertaste was different."

"What happened with the hounding?"

It happened again; Mr Turnage came to Sally's shoulder. I watched intently as his right hand dropped on her bony frame. His wiry black fuzz bristled on his knuckles as they curled inward, pinching her left rotator. A large gulp thumped down her throat, and a gasp escaped her lips just in time for Sally to clamp it shut. Her eyes widened.

I heard it—the raft of neck hair blazed to attention. My eyes homed in on Sally's. There was more to this 'well-to-do' wronged family than we were told. I could see her pupils dilating. Then, a blink—a black pool of fluid was in the corner of Sally's left eye. Mrs Turnage noticed in time as a small trickle rolled free. Sally felt it and moved quickly to scoop it away.

There was more to know, but I could sense we were about to be blocked from getting further details. My sixth sense told me Mr Turnage wasn't as he seemed, and more happened to Sally than was being let on.

"Okay, what about the other girls? Are they okay?" I attempted to gather what I could before we were shown the door. Michael couldn't take his eyes off the photos. My seating angle only produced a sheen of window light across the glass, so I couldn't see what had him so fixated.

"I think that's enough now. Sally has suffered enough," Mr Turnage said, stepping forward to stand near Sally and make his point. Sally raked at the scars on her arms, then lurched forward.

"Susan killed herself. Selene is still missing, and the rest... We don't talk anymore."

It was her eyes; they kept darting toward Mr Turnage. We had nothing else to push the issue, but I had a troubling niggle that the murders and that night were connected.

"Damn, one last thing. What's Susan's last name?"

"Westlake."

"It's time to leave now before Sally gets upset," Mrs Turnage uttered through a trembling croak.

We stood to head to the door when the house phone rang, and Mr Turnage sprinted to answer it.

'Hello?'

'Yep, I know.'

'Ahem,'

'It's in hand. No problems.'

'I told you it's all good.'

'I know what it means; I have to go.'

The conversation was ominous and tense; the voice on the other end was hard to understand, but it seemed modulated. This was a daunting 'string' we had to pull on to find the 'devil in the details,' at least before another body dropped.

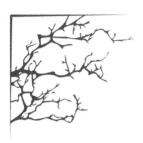

8

A DARKENING GLOOM

The door slammed behind us, and the atmosphere changed. Michael's face revealed a dilemma, as if he carried the weight of the Turnage family physically—troubling, heavy, and painstaking, much like the angry wrinkles clapping in the breeze.

Despite appearing somewhat fresher since the bite, he grappled with his path. Experience and scorched shoe leather painted a nightmarish picture of discontent as we pounded damp concrete into our car. My hackles rose in the darkening grey gloom. That eerie feeling returned. Somebody was watching.

Static crawled up and down my spine, a foreboding sensation. Though I couldn't pinpoint its source, people doing their business looked ordinary. Yet, it was the smell we knew too well. Death, wrapped in tormenting toxicity and, above all, pain. I couldn't discern if it was a man or a woman; I only sensed their silent suffering.

"What did you see, Michael?"

"The pictures didn't fit."

"What do you mean?"

"Mr Turnage didn't seem the same. A close fit, but not quite him. This process makes me doubt my instincts a little."

"Don't doubt them. Something's off. The story felt genuine but mixed, and when pushed, Mr Turnage, or whoever he is, controlled her cues. That phone call felt off. The voice on the other end was modulated."

"And what's been watching?"

"I don't know, but the black trickle from Sally's eye could be another story."

The image stuck in my head—black with a glimmer coating. The masquerade party hinted at something more. We needed to uncover what was laced in the masks. Michael's doubts required a cautious approach. The next full moon was in three days—an ordeal I found the hardest to endure. There was no telling how he'd take it.

"There's more to this, matey, and my gut is kicking me in the arse, telling me things didn't go down as clean as presented. As for the control freak... Let's just say I heard alarm bells loud and clear."

Michael was more in tune than I realised. If he felt that way, more dots needed to connect. Selene was missing, and the news was scarce. I wasn't even aware of something happening in parliament. The cover-up was effective and ongoing. Another question lingered—how many seedy layers were this wrapped in, and what's the connection?

"Do you think Guvnor was involved? Or the M.P.?"

"I think it's bloody uncanny that a year ago, there was a party at that place, and the shit hit the fan but got covered up. Fast forward a smidge, and we have a dead inspector who works there. M.P.S. that hideout there is also dead... It won't take a rocket scientist to draw a line between them."

"So, now the question is to what?"

I commented, having heard Michael summarise the connections. We had one significant incident in which important people wanted to be buried, and now a series of sock murders that could only be revenge.

"Which one?" Michael blurted out, surprising me.

"He must've been reading my mind."

"Which one what?"

"Which of the girls still alive do you think are doing it?"

Michael had suddenly given me food for thought as we stared at each other across the car roof. Muddled expressions prevailed as Michael reached for a cigarette from his pocket. Meanwhile, I kept sniffing deeply for that stench of 'death,' which had now disappeared.

"What makes you think it's alive?" Even though it vanished in the light from that 'Kanaima' case, we had to assume the unexpected. Susan allegedly hung herself. Francis had an accidental overdose, and Selene was missing—presumed dead.

"What's got your tail in a twist, then?"

"Cheeky twat, no tail... yet. As for the other, I don't know. Did you get the impression Sally was at pains to highlight Susan Westlake killing herself?

Even though by that point, it was quite clear Mr Turnage didn't want her to divulge any more."

"Oi... remember it's D.S. twat to you. But you're right. I could hear the nails tearing across her scarred skin in surround sound before jumping forward to let that out."

Michael chuckled, putting me at ease a little over his condition. My eyes stared at his throat, picturing it ripped through again. It was gruesome enough for me to have to shake it off.

"Where next?"

"Alicia? She got the other penalty notice until another call came in. Dig a little into Susan?"

"Until she's told to be quiet."

Slumping back in my chair, there was a feeling that whoever we spoke to would sing off the same hymn sheet as Sally. They've had a year to practise any tale in need of telling. Behind it all, something horrible happened that night, and I doubted we'd heard it yet.

"Well, that's why you're the semi-human lie detector. Don't think I haven't noticed how you watch and listen to the micro-expressions and wavers in people's voices. You had me try it in there, but I'm not Georgie. Besides, you get all fidgety when you're onto something. What would you say that black shot from Sally's eye was?"

"Wish I knew. It wasn't blood. And I barely caught the slightest of smells. Metallic, not like copper. It could be a weird infection that I've never seen before. It's bothersome, for sure."

My brain spun into gear, going through what could smell like metal and making a silver-grey haze. I lurched toward iron or magnesium, but how? Why? What the bloody hell happened to that young lady? All became a blur of issues I didn't have answers for, to the point I faced a hazy dream of battered, naked trees through the windscreen.

A distant noise muddied my fixation, faint at first, gradually getting louder. And it wasn't a voice. 'Beep, beep, beep, beep, beep.'

The haze cleared, and the beeps were louder for Michael and me. I caught his face in time as a puzzled look turned to me.

"What the hell is that?"

Michael flung his head around, but nothing was obvious. The fact we both heard it was troubling. Our heads dropped to the floor in unison.

'Beep, beep, beep, beep, beep,'

We froze in our seats; neither spoke, but I could feel the wet pebbles ripple toward my sideburns. My heart sped up, and Michael roared. We were thinking on the same page.

My right hand hung helplessly in the air, the key protruding inches from the ignition. If what we were thinking was correct, then it wasn't a wise move to spark the beast into life. Anyone else would've already gone ahead, and perhaps 'boom.'

"Georgie, please tell me you hear that, right?"

"Yep."

"And it's not some dog whistle nonsense?"

Ordinarily, I would've been tempted to wind Michael up, especially being so close to a park. This time I couldn't; too busy crapping myself.

"Nope. Erm, you want to check?" I grimaced almost pleadingly.

"No. You?"

"No way."

"Together then?"

"Sure."

"Ok, matey. Count to three, and we both jump out, ok?"

"On three or after?"

"On. Unless you want to keep puckering that arsehole of yours for longer,"

Michael seemed more confident than I felt. An ejector seat would've been good at this point. Knowing my luck, I would've landed in a tree or something.

"One... Two... Three,"

'Click.'

The doors flung open, and we bounced out, getting clear. My body tensed, expecting something to happen. I couldn't figure out to what extent, but I expected all the same. Silence fell around us, Barring the passing traffic. I swivelled long on my heels; gravel churned beneath my feet.

Michael glared across a look of 'what the hell?' all an anti-climax, yet the beeping could still be heard. Michael heard it, too; the confused caterpillars on his forehead danced to meet at the bridge of his nose as he became curious. His head rocked from side to side, testing which end of the car it could be.

My heightened hearing is more attuned than Michael's, as he is still transitioning. I'm intrigued whether he'll become a werewolf or something else. Maybe even reject the 'bite.' An 'up yours' and 'thanks for saving me.' A perk without the circus. Either way, my ears twerked at every 'beep.' coming from the driver's side wheel arch.

My foot shifted forward; then, a thought crossed my mind—a test of sorts. Knowing where the noise emanated, I wanted to see how quickly Michael could home in on it. So, I'm putting on my best poker face...

"What are you thinking, Michael? Should we get the bomb squad, just in case?"

Michael calmly shook his head 'no' and brushed down his navy suit to present an air of calm and authority, even if his heart was anything but. Pretending I was uneasy with the situation, half-stepping back gave Michael the impetus to take over. This wasn't me being work-shy or anything. Lately, I've bulldozed my way through things as if I were the one with the 'D.S.' rank. With his head a little shaky, my thinking was to give Michael some direction to take his mind off the dark path ahead.

Unlike me, at least Michael could call Andy and me if it got too much. He'd chained us up on a full moon anyway, so Michael knew what to expect in that respect. Leaning his head down, Michael quickly got on track and circled the wheel arch like an over-excited cocker spaniel. Any moment, I expected him to cock his leg to Mark on the spot.

Michael's puzzled expression soon changed to more of a 'could it be?' with an air of confidence that hadn't been there when we first heard it. His hand reached under, and my hackles bounced with trepidation. Moving left to right until I saw the 'jackpot' smile before shoving his arm deeper.

The air filled with a vapour-clouded sigh of relief as Michael yanked his hand back hard. Plastic hit metal, and a short wire dropped free first. A light red flashing light beamed out—a dot on a black box about the size of Michael's wrinkled palm. Simple, yet I got the sense it came from 'sneaky bastard.' territory.

"A fucking tracker," Michael tossed it toward.

"Don't get these in Dixon's." It looked far too upmarket to belong to the average criminal. More to the point, 'What the hell?'

"This is high-end, long-range. Somebody wants to know our every move,"

"It could only have been since we were in the Turnages. We would have heard it earlier,"

"From that smell?"

Michael made me think. The stench of death and a tracker. It didn't add up. The two scenarios didn't seem likely. Now the question was, who is watching who?

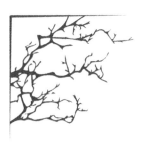

9

Alice Etherington

Michael spun the tracker in his palm, gauging its weight. It had lodged itself beneath an unmarked police car during our dive into a cover-up.

He located the off switch with a flick, and we prayed it wasn't accessible remotely. Unimaginable thoughts raced through my mind. Here we stood outside 46 Neville St., South Kensington—the address of Alice, another group member tied to that ticket incident. Like the Turnages' residence, rows of neat white townhouses lined the street.

"For Christ's sake, South Kensington wasn't the typical area for murder links. How did these girls get caught up in this? The white walls scream 'money,' unless it's all a facade. The kind that usually buys its way out of trouble. Why not last year?" I pondered.

"Do you reckon these people wipe their arses with pound notes?" Michael quipped.

"Begs the question, doesn't it?"

"I was joking, you know."

"No, I mean, how did well-off people get caught up in crap like this?"

"The other side already has more money than sense, or the repercussions of throwing a group of impressionable young girls under the bus were nothing compared to the bigger picture."

"That bigger picture being corruption and lies at the highest level?"

Curtains twitched as we approached. Mrs Turnage or Sally might be on the phone already, given Mr Turnage's peculiar call.

"What's the bet?" Michael asked.

"On?"

"They have a big family portrait above the mantelpiece, too."

"What's next, a corgi?"

Jokes aside, that was the reality. We were out of our comfort zone, and a single complaint could cost us our jobs. Michael was uneasy, humour acting as his mask.

Michael knocked on the door, then remembered to ring the bell. A man in his late forties, with scruffy hair and a few days of stubble, answered. The stench of alcohol engulfed us.

"What do you want? Making sure we've kept quiet? We don't need more reminders. Thank you," the man retorted with alcohol-laden brashness.

"Excuse me, who is it you think we are?" Michael retorted with cockney bravado.

"Them bloody bastards that have ruined our lives. Can't breathe without judging eyes." His words confused us, yet added another layer to my curiosity. Mr Turnage might not be on the 'up and up,' but that family shared the same theme as the man before us. Persecution.

"We're not here to ruin you. Quite the opposite. We're investigating a small spate of murders and came across an accident that happened last year."

"Alice, you mean. I'm afraid there's nothing we can say that would make any difference. They weren't believed then, and now we, parents, are left with shells of once-happy children. Those that are lucky enough to have a daughter still."

"Please, if we can help. We will." I pleaded; we had to learn more about who was putting pressure on these families and to what extent. With the tracker in mind, somebody was on our trail, and my senses were hyper-vigilant. The stench of death hadn't returned... yet.

A tingle flickered around my hackles, a feeling we were still at the calm before the storm. Enough to cause sickness in my stomach. Another body would soon drop. The last case taught me to expect the unexpected. With every conversation, I'm expecting the 'other shoe.'

"No chance I'm not risking it. Believe it or not, I used to be the head of the local council. Look at me now; aren't I the picture of happiness?" Mr Etherington stepped off his doorstep, affected by the dim skies. The light of day didn't seem too acquainted with him. Enough to paint a more damning picture of a troubled man than we first laid eyes on.

"Silence doesn't breed happiness, nor does self-pity. The only cure for those ills is to speak up. And know that we intend to take this seriously."

I attempted to shake some sense into Etherington, but he didn't flinch; we posed no threat compared to those already in his family's life.

"It may not; it sure as hell keeps us safer. If you don't mind, I have important business to attend to. Filling my glass."

"Does it help you sleep at night?" Michael was irked by the lack of cooperation. In some respects, I could understand the reluctance his longing for more alcohol watered down my sympathies.

"I may not sleep well, but my daughter is alive—more than could be said for others. I suggest you try poor Susan's parents. See if they share my enthusiasm. The Cliftons."

Before we could answer, Mr Etherington showed enough coordination to swivel on his heels. He darted inside, leaving the front door rattling against the frame.

"Do you think some have been made to sign NDAs?" A strange thought popped into my head; the fear might have been caused by a physical threat. It never occurred to us they'd been coerced into a legal contract not to speak of that night or at least tell anything of the truth. They may have been brave initially, but a flex of power cost Etherington his job.

"Fuck knows, matey. All I know is this stinks so badly, chasing dead ends."

'Any officers from the murder task force receiving?'

The radio crackled through our procrastination, breaking my gaze from the front door and the shadows twitching curtains.

'The murder task force receiving?'

'Go ahead; this is D.S. Dalton.'

'We've been directed to you. A body has been found on a bench at Speakers' Corner in Hyde Park. Believed to be connected to your current case.'

'What's the connection?'

'At first, they seemed to be a rough sleeper. Underneath the rags was a man in a suit. It's the Secretary of State for Business and Energy.'

'What the hell? Right, nobody touches it. Contact Mr Nicholls at the corner office as a matter of urgency. I need the body tented off and sealed. Tell Nicholls it's linked to the others.'

'Received, will show you assigned.'

The feeling had been there, but the controller's words didn't make me feel good about being right.

"It seems they're playing our song, Georgie."

Michael sighed, coating the already dreary sky with white clouds. Some say actions speak louder than words. The dead body of another M.P. is being dumped at Speaker's Corner. Screams.

A cold breeze cut across my face. Decaying leaves were swirling through the darkening sky as the first few street lamps blazed on. Their yellowed glow was enough to stand out from the purpling grey as heads bobbed in the distance.

A crowd was gathering, and the flashing blue lights drew them in like moths to a flame. From what I gathered, the corner was no stranger to crowds; deaths—were a whole new experience. A large white tent was being hastily put together with a square cordon wrapped around trees twenty feet further out.

Every whistle of cold air brought with it the smell of decaying flesh. Michael caught it, too. His face theatrically displayed disgust—a moment where the enhanced senses could be seen as a downside. This was different; the stench screamed at least ten years dead. We knew otherwise, much to our fragile constitution's delight.

Neither of us was in a rush to cut a path to the front; my brain was working through the best ways we could manage the body without getting exposed to the outdoors. In full view of the public, no less. Something like that would cause widespread panic and more than a few nightmares.

My feet moved in their mind, and Michael followed suit. We must have made it less than a few steps before it returned. My skin turned to ice on an already chilly autumn day. We were being watched. My head spun, searching for the unknown. Anything to give us a target instead of merely clinging to loose ends. All I got were the mindless 'gossip sheep,' looking to fuel their evening conversation.

Habits that even this neck of the woods wasn't immune to. Whoever this was wreaked pain and anger; we didn't have time to be distracted, but I nearly missed what was happening with Michael for a split second. Thin white claws were breaking free. They weren't long or 'full' enough to cause concern. Instead, I gripped his arm to usher him forward.

'Michael. Your hands, hide them,' I whispered, grabbing his attention. His expression was priceless, and for once, he didn't have his usual cockney banter. No, his heart sped up at the sight; the reality spooked him.

'Fuck. I was so focused elsewhere I didn't feel it. Now I do, and it bloody stings,'

'Breathe and focus on what we must do; it should ease up.'

The tent door whipped open in time for us to step through; the first glimpse of the body was horrifying. A navy suit clung to a frail frame. The face had sunken, and eyes popped out of the sockets with frightened, blood-shot ripples over the whites. There was no chance of knowing how he used to look, not now. The body was decaying rapidly. There was enough stretch in the throat skin to tell, though. Two small puncture marks lower, a couple of inches above the clavicle.

"I leave you alone two minutes, and you're already eyeing up another body,"

A voice came like a bolt out of the blue. My body shivered with static weaving through its hair. Their words caused my pulse to quicken and my throat to run dry. Michael smirked at me as my mouth involuntarily crept in-to a smile.

"Ellena, what brings you here?"

It was a welcome surprise, yet she was supposed to be getting checked out at the hospital for a while. To hear those words pass her pouting red lips gave a much-needed spring in my step.

"Well, I couldn't leave you boys to have all the fun now, could I? Besides, I got wind of what's been happening to the bodies, and I think I can help."

Ellena came with her confident sass, but something bothered me. Behind that bravado hid a little fear. She didn't want to go home to her flat near Mile End alone. I could relate, feeling an invasion of privacy. Ellena had been at-tacked and captured in her hallway, and I didn't know if her blood had been cleaned up yet. She hid it well, but betrayal from a friend cuts deep.

"Well, we're all ears, lovely. That sourpuss is happy to see you, really."

"Hey, Michael, I am. I'm just worried."

"I'm fine. Plus, I'm sure you're all in the same boat. You had to jump from one shitstorm to another without catching a breath. So why not me, too?"

"Yeah, but we have no choice; you could rest after having paralytic toxins injected into your organs,"

"What about me, matey? I had my throat ripped out, yet you couldn't give a shit. Made me search for a tracker and everything."

Michael chirped up, joking. His wrinkles painted down his cheekbones. It was crazy to see, though. His throat was wholly healed. Even his shoulder was moving freely now.

"A tracker? Really? All the more reason to keep you boys out of trouble. Anyway, I heard the body's decay quickly after being drained, and liquid nitrogen helped slow it down. So I jerry-rigged a little gadget. First, you two need to 'glove up'. And no, Michael, not what you're thinking. Get these on and control those bloody nails of yours,"

Ellena tossed a pair of thick, black latex gloves at us. They seemed stronger than usual, but we'd pierce them if the claws paid a surprise visit.

"So, lovely. What's this genius plan, and what the hell is that?"

Michael retorted with a confused frown; the pinging of rubber echoed through my eardrums while I wondered if we were still being watched. Ellena held a man-sized transparent rubber suit aloft.

"Our dead friend here has to play dress-up."

Ellena's timing couldn't have been any more perfect. Laying eyes on her beautiful smile reminded me of my feelings for her. I was still worried about how ready she was physically.

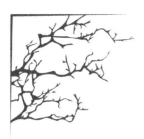

10

SPEAKERS CORNER

Considering how decayed it was, the weird thing about this dead body was that the joints and muscles were still kinda squishy. It was delicate, and I was worried about going Hulk on it. As for Michael, if those claws meant anything, the bite was doing its thing. He wouldn't get how strong he could get yet.

It felt like babysitting a grown-up toddler. I wished someone had given me the real lowdown from the start. Hiding stuff and throwing around half-truths doesn't cut it. Ellena was almost on tiptoes, holding the clear rubber suit like a fashion statement. She even found it a mystery, like everything else she does. It sucks you in and then blinds you with something special.

"How does this work, then?"

"As you can see, his limbs aren't stiff yet; we can wrap him up, seal any gaps, and blast this handheld nitrogen in, freezing everything that's falling apart."

Ellena left me speechless for a moment; she'd turned into a pro at body containment in no time. The theory was nice, but would it actually work?

"Ahem. What's the deal here?"

"Ah, Mr Nicholas. Looks like our forensic whiz, Ellena Walker, has some tricks up her sleeve. She's rolling with your idea."

Mr Nicholas didn't look impressed at all. I was checking his pulse and micro-expressions wrapped in a bundle of sweat beads. The guy was worried.

"Hold up. I tried that. The trapped air, nitrogen, and whatever is mixed with the toxin react in a confined space and go boom. The only thing that buys time is a super freezer. Sadly, we don't have one."

"Crap. Um, what about a meat wagon?"

Michael's brain was on overdrive. Mr Nicholas wasn't spilling the beans easily, and there was something he wasn't letting on about. Watching his face as he stared at the dead body, my money was on him having at least half an idea about the chemicals in the toxins. Or he had secrets.

"What do you mean?"

"You know, one of those butcher vans delivering frozen meats."

"I guess. But you know that only slows the process, and we can't crack him open."

"Mr Nicholas, we need at least one body to last long enough to find something useful."

Ellena seemed down; she came in guns blazing, not knowing any better. But she was trying to prove herself. I've been down the betrayal road, and Ellena was compensating for her shady past partner.

"Alright, but I need to work on him and others. There's a process, and I don't like what's happening now."

"Got it. Um, Michael. What the hell?"

"Hey, buddy... I know a guy who knows a guy with a van."

"I won't ask."

"Yeah... that's probably for the best."

"How long?"

"Twenty minutes."

"Ellena, Mr Nicholas, can you keep it together until then?"

"I guess so." Mr Nicholas was edging closer to the body.

Michael vanished to a payphone by a closed kiosk. I could hear the body creaking and cracking. The hair was more or less intact. Brown combed to the right in a side parting.

"Ellena, he's been drained. The toxin breaks down the body while mummifying its organs to build a gas that disintegrates it. Can we find a chemical breakdown from the hair?"

Clutching at straws, but it was all we had. No fluids and the body could soon be gone. If Michael gave the okay, Ellena could try reverse-engineering something.

"It's possible to find many things, Georgie; whether the path to the truth is among them remains to be seen."

Ellena's face lit up again; maybe a purpose more challenging than her original plan was the genuine spark she needed.

"Ellena, got a minute?"

"Sure, what's up?"

"Can you distract for a moment? I want to inspect. If Michael comes back, send him over, please."

"Ah, yes. Of course."

Ellena smiled and winked before scampering toward Mr Nicholas. That earlier feeling of being watched hadn't faded. Each breeze rushing through the tent carried their pain.

My notebook was soon out, and I got to sketching. A glance over each shoulder gave me the all-clear. A blink and the red haze came, highlighting many things unseen and a few I wished my eyes hadn't seen—each step we'd taken in varying strengths of heat. Yet, there was a set that intrigued me the most.

Smaller and cooler, each set was a foot apart and at an angle. They took their time around the body, pivoting and up close. Almost taunting and personal before fading away in the distance. There was more, though, all cooling but scattered over the upper body—the right arm and throat before reaching around the jawline. The killer was up close, checking on their handiwork.

One finger snaked and weaved over once thriving skin, circling the two punctures. Then, an 'sssshhhh' moment on the bottom lip. The forefinger rolled across mercilessly with lips pursed. These were seemingly the last moments of the poor man's life. Sins of the past notwithstanding, this was the end product of hate.

Michael approached quickly; I could feel his agitation and struggle to roll into one. He was losing his grip on himself as darkness drifted in—a half-moon night.

"Easy, Michael, breathe," I whispered in time with his steps, his pounding irregular heart vibrating through my ears.

"Slow down and take a moment. Remember, you're in control."

His pace slowed along with the heartbeats in time to bounce through the tent's entrance. His eyes blazed yellow but dimmed.

"Bloody hell. How do you cope with this?" He gushed, gathering himself.

"Think yourself lucky. I was going insane, remember? And being blamed for the murder. At least you have support now."

"Fair point. Still, it's no picnic."

"Well, come here and see what I see."

It was another teachable moment; they say, 'You can't teach an old dog new tricks,' but that's precisely what will happen. He needed to control his eyes and use them. Michael had to learn quickly on the job if the bite was as it seemed. He was teaching me to be a detective, and with werewolf experience of fewer than two months, I was trying to teach him to learn from my mistakes.

"How?"

"Stare at the body as if daydreaming, but try to look through him."

At first, it was only sporadic flickers. After a few tries and a deep breath of annoyance later, it finally worked. "Oh, my God. You see all of this?!"

"Yes. Now, look closely. Follow the heat patterns like infrared."

"The killer is a woman... She taunted him. Revelling at her work. Wait, the lips."

"Yep, she shhh him as he struggled,"

"No. Not just that. Look at the edge by the teeth."

Michael was right; my juggling of ensuring he remained in control and scanning the body caused me to miss a detail. Could it be a dot that connects?

"He bit his killer's fingertip."

"Do you reckon that lovely lady of yours could fit this in once she's done playing with hair?"

"She's not my lady,"

"Come now, matey. This old dog has been around long enough to see the signs,"

"Are you serious right now?"

"What? Come on, for Christ's sake; you can't play the wounded puppy routine forever. You two dance around each other like a pair of ballerinas. It's high time you blew away some cobwebs."

"Says the puppy himself. You need to concentrate on whose territory you're marking."

"Hey. I've been a priest for a while. Melanie left a stink that doesn't wash away easily,"

"A priest? Are you sure that's the right choice? You know what they get up to. Besides, I'm sure chemists medicate shampoo for that these days."

Michael furnished truth among all that; a line needed to be drawn between Ellena and me, whether anything could happen. She's dangerously intoxicating. How much wasn't apparent until she breezed to us with her idea? Ellena revels under my skin and enthralled my senses. Yet, she has only seen a fraction of my world. I'm not yet all-knowing, and we wouldn't know what's coming from one day to the next.

Subject her to that? Hand on heart, I couldn't say she'd be safe. Not that Ellena gives the impression she'd be bothered. A weight that could prove too heavy would rest on my shoulders. She came close last time, and we've yet to understand the tormenting danger lingering just out of sight. The upshot is that Ellena is a drug I need. The downside, what if I had to bite her too?

Michael already had miles on the clock, and I'd given the old boy a bounce to his step. Ellena is quite the opposite. There was more to Michael's words that kept my attention when he brought up Melanie. What else did she know?

Melanie's sins, at some point, will be laid bare, and she will finally be put through the wringer. But for now, Melanie projects an air of not being bothered. It makes me think she has an 'Ace' up her sleeve. A 'break glass in case of emergency' call. The smile stayed long after the cell door shut, unnerving me.

"You cheeky sod. You get what I mean, though, right? When we met, you were troubled and dragged through the mud. Trouble will always be there for you because of what you are. Does that mean you must spend your life miserable? I think not."

"You mean us? You're part of this, or at least on your way."

"Of course. How could I forget? I easily zoomed in on small details of a dead man's mouth. Hopefully, Ellena can get us something to work on."

"No harm in trying. Holy crap. A quick look below the neckline. Do you see what's slightly edged up on the decaying chest skin?"

I noticed a dangerous reminder of the past and issues we've yet to put to bed—no rest for the wicked. Michael looked as though he'd seen a ghost. He'd forgotten, too. His cocky smile faded, and fear became real again. Michael quickly rolled up his sleeve to show his arm. My turn for a surprise. His tattoo was gone. The branding he'd been given had healed. Yet the scarring lived in his mind.

"The freaking devil's circle. He's one of them. A top M.P. is part of a corrupt, low-life organisation that killed Andy's wife and God knows who else,"

We were looking at the partial outline of a forked serpent in a circle burnt into the skin. A haunting. If these were involved, then there's no telling what trouble awaits. This case just took a dangerous turn for the worse.

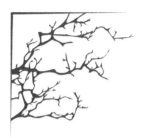

11

EMBANKMENT

Navigating central London's streets is usually chaotic, but catching the tail end of rush hour was just plain bad luck. Michael and I sat in our car on Victoria Embankment, stuck two cars back from the 'Butchers Van' carrying our dead M.P. Michael's friend clearly missed the memo, making it through the last set of lights and leaving us stranded. Catching up wasn't easy, with pedestrians risking life and limb to skip across traffic.

No words passed between us. The latest twists in the case had us absorbed. Another body was one thing, but that branding added a layer of mind-boggling we could do without. Michael, caught in his deep-cover role, had the healing branding presenting awkward questions. It would be a tough spot if the ones responsible called, demanding Michael's involvement. Forensic data was limited, and I hoped Ellena could work her magic on the partial fingertip. Between her and Mr Nicholls, they could I.D. the body, but trust had become a big issue since Charlie, Ethan, and Melanie. A coroner was the last thing I wanted to worry about.

Roadworks and a diversion forced us onto the stretch toward Cannon Street. The night deepened, and sparse streetlights made distinguishing one vehicle from another hard. As we exited a short tunnel, an unsettling sensation hit. Hackles rose, and my tiny hairs stood at attention as if caught in the car's vents. A ripple down my spine signalled something amiss. Michael shuddered, too, feeling the static. Every instance was new for him and me; we were still clueless about the demon side.

Exiting the tunnel into the purple-black night, a Mercedes van cut in front, going 40 in a 30 zone, followed closely by a rude tipper truck. Initially, I thought they were in a hurry, but something felt off. We weaved right to check on our makeshift morgue, and the tipper truck mimicked our moves. When we darted left, it did the same.

"Georgie, what the fuck is wrong with you? Can't you see I'm deep in contemplation? Do not disturb," Michael snapped.

"Yeah, you're right. You're disturbed enough already. When you're done, trust those instincts. I think something is up," I retorted.

"Ya, bastard. What's that supposed to mean?"

"That static you felt? That's a sixth sense. Our wolf, or whatever you are, senses kick in when they detect danger or anything out of the ordinary."

"There's me thinking I was getting a chill in my bones."

"The only thing in your bones is calcium deposits, you old git."

"Less of it. So what's with the driving?"

"The two vehicles in front. The second one is acting like a blocker."

"You sure?"

I wasn't certain, but it was the only reason I could think of for the tipper truck to mimic our moves. It wanted to block our view or create a direct route for someone else. My hair was buzzing like wildfire. Every bob and weave greeted me with flashes of red, for a change, not from my bloody eyes. Another ATS and more roadwork furniture were fast approaching up ahead.

Yet, there was something amiss that I couldn't put my finger on. Lots of bright orange, white, and yellow, but the layout looked weirdly clean and brand new. A hurricane was now sweeping around that wildfire in my senses.

"Michael, look. What do you see?"

"More bloody roadworks."

"What else?"

"Wait... Where's the bloody work? I get they take their time, but that's a joke. It's just furniture and a truck."

That was it, what I couldn't see. There was no roadwork being done. The driver of our morgue had gathered speed to make the lights, and the two vehicles in front did the same. We were heading straight toward the point of the roadworks, with amber lights, and I had sped up only for that truck Michael spotted to come flying into the road. There was no choice.

My foot jammed on the brake... Gripping the wheel tight, we veered sharply right... The truck covered the space, and I had no choice but to grind to a stop. Michael and I jerked forward, nearly hitting the dashboard.

"Charlie Whiskey, this is D.S. Dalton. Our current assignment has a problem. We've been blocked approaching Tower Hill. A white panel van and a roadworks tipper truck follow the body from the crime scene. Any units in the area?"

"Received by Charlie Whiskey, the same index you gave us for body transport?"

"Yes."

"Will circulate now."

There was nothing we could do until the truck moved. There was no turning I could make with no sign of lights or life. Michael and I got out to see what was causing the hold-up and get them moving. We found that only the driver's door was open, and nobody was inside.

"What the hell is going on here, Georgie?" Michael asked.

"I was just thinking the same thing," I replied.

"I'll move this. You keep the car ready. We have to catch up," Michael instructed.

Just as Michael went to jump in, the radio boomed out...

'D.S. Dalton receiving?'

"Go ahead," Michael reported gruffly, annoyed at the situation.

'A marked unit has your van just inside the Limehouse Link.'

"Everything okay?"

'Afraid not. The back doors were open, and the driver and the officer accompanying him were unconscious.'

"Damn... Received by D.S. Dalton. Can you let your duty officer know? We'll brief our ADI. We now have two more scenes to examine. I trust LAS are on it?"

"Will do, and yes. Marked units are en route to you."

"Received." Michael couldn't hide the bitterness in his voice any longer. His face reddened, and he was pissed. And so was I.

"Fuck... This shitstorm is about to get a lot worse. Stealing a dead body is bad enough, but an M.P. that's been murdered, that's another level of wrong."

That was the problem. Everything was escalating, and we hadn't noticed. What started as a strange, supernatural murder seemed part of a series, possibly connected to a party where many wrongs happened yet were hushed up. Our dead M.P. was now entangled in the devil's circle, and to top it off, his body was stolen.

My other worry was Michael. I kept getting flashes of his eyes changing, yellow glimmers at night. I inhaled the polluted air, checking for fear or heightened adrenaline nearby. I got overwhelmed by the hormones swirling around a nearby pub. It seemed to be a posh twat hunting ground. Cutting through the pollution and other rubbish drifting through the air was difficult.

It was made worse by the burgeoning redness in Michael's face as his wrinkles intensified. Yet, his changing appearance provided some solace. Elena and Mr Nichols had already gone ahead with some samples and the bitten fingertip. At least, I hoped they had reached their destination safely.

With no immediate urgency and further inquiries that could wait until morning, all Michael and I could do was check both vehicles, hoping to find something tangible we could use. It's a thread we could pull on to expose the sneaky bastards.

That feeling crept up on me again, the sensation of being watched. But it was different, no longer the aura of death. This time, I felt that powerful and malevolent gaze, as if some terrible people were watching us intently, waiting for the right moment to interfere. It was reminiscent of blocking a road with fake roadworks and a truck.

Those bastards lurking in the shadows were playing a dangerous game. On the one hand, we wanted to uncover the killer of these important people, but we had to keep the details quiet. The cunning nature of their actions made me miss the routine of domestic calls just slightly. Whichever way they envisioned this unfolding, they better brace themselves for disappointment.

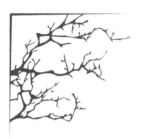

12

SQUEAKY CLEAN

The truck's cab was spotless, with no gravel dust under our feet. We'd nudged it for traffic, and a thought hit me. Unlike the last gig, no ghosts this time. Maybe the bodies stuck around, keeping the spirits tethered. I almost asked Michael, but I knew his reply.

'Ooh, I don't know, mate. The only spirits I know come from the top shelf and find their way down my neck!'

Not the classiest, but a pattern emerged. Restless spirits used bodies as anchors. Some haunted for kicks, others sought peace—find their killers, they move on.

No dust, no ghostly knocks on my door yet. Maybe the latest soul would hang around. I scanned for a heat signature—someone slight, but no glove clues. Smart move. Before I knew it, I was in the driver's seat, catching the reflection of our blue lights. A bounce tested the seats; my pockets dropped and changed into the car gap. There, a card, business-like but too slim for my fingers. I slid out claws and pinched the card.

The noise grated on my sensitive hearing, but I pushed down as far as possible when Michael's head popped up. He looked bewildered, as if I were mad. Even in my awkward position, my concern shifted to him. His eyes were wild, sweat formed—a primal urge to tear through flesh. We needed to get through the night or expose ourselves more than the world was ready for. With the card in hand, my long, sharp claws retrieved the prize. It remained to be seen as if it was worth the effort.

The weathered card had tears at the corners. On one side, a taxi number, nothing special. On the other, scruffy blue ink—a non-usual address.

'Unit 12C, Albert Dock Road, Custom House.'

The card rested for seconds before that familiar chill hit again. A shiver ran across my shoulders, coaxing my attention outside. My ears perked up, seeking movement, but I heard Michael shuffling before yanking the door open.

"You felt it, too?" Michael asked, his voice filled with concern and curiosity.

"Yeah, it keeps coming. I don't see anyone, though."

Michael shook himself free from his shudder, his lips gradually returning to normal. I wondered if we were being sought rather than seeking. The eerie mystery was on our trail without being seen.

"What's that you got there?" Michael looked around the cab, using his controlled eyes.

"That's it. Remember to breathe and focus, maintain control, and don't let any anger set in. As for this, well, notice how empty this truck is... All apart from this."

Michael moved his head, his bright yellow eyes lighting up his wrinkled face. I caught a glimpse—the first real clue that the bite had taken effect. Michael's facial skin rippled, phasing between a 'shift'. That inkling told me Michael wouldn't turn into a wolf. I must have shown surprise, because I felt his yellow stare pierce directly into me.

It's not like I had an instruction manual, only what I had read in books about myths and legends. An alpha bite can change someone, either gifting them or cursing them. I could argue for both. But what I saw fluctuating through Michael differed from what I had expected. And I didn't know how to break the news. The dear old Michael was a fox, a werefox.

"I'm quick and steady, you know, matey. Listened to your heart, too."

"That's good to hear, then."

"Don't worry. It's better than I expected."

"What's that?" I asked, but I could see where he was heading with this. I didn't need to tell him. He had already seen.

"I'm not a wolf."

"Yeah, but you are something different with its perks," "Matey, I kid you not. There are worse things I could be. A fox is wily and intelligent; it improves senses, speed, and strength. So I can't complain."

"Yeah, but all those years ago, Skippy was turned into a wolf, and now you are a fox, something we're unsure about. How do you feel?"

"Could do with a plate full of steak, raw. You know, really fucking bloody."

That one sentence told me that the same primal drive remained, regardless of the beast's form taken. We just needed to figure out if Michael could do anything different. I guessed he would be quite agile, but we hadn't had the time to explore what the demon side would do to me yet. Perhaps the resulting change reflects the person they are inside. And I knew firsthand just how cunningly sneaky Michael could be. So did the 'Devil's Circle' members, who I hoped would never come calling.

"And aside from that?"

"There's rage, a quick temper when things don't go our way, but it's manageable. So what's that?" Michael quickly changed the subject with his trademark cocky smile. He was right, though, pulling my attention back to the card. I had been juggling too many issues at once.

"Well, it has an address for a warehouse or one of those seedy units where you and your mates stash stolen VCRs. Maybe it fell out of the driver's pocket."

"Oi... I'll have you know I've got a good range of 20-inch televisions now! Fuck you very much. But you're right; this truck is too clean for there to be nothing. So, what's the plan?"

"That's my thinking. At worst, it'll be a wasted journey. We might stumble upon a group of bad guys sitting around a table playing cards. Okay, maybe that's a bit too much to expect. But it's worth a try."

Michael nodded, and we left the truck cabin, the doors banging shut and rattling in my ears. I glanced at the sky; even if not full, the moon still tormented us.

'LIMEHOUSE LINK.'

Much like the roadworks truck cab, we moved around in a mobile icebox. The freezing temperature wasn't helping my search for heat signatures. Any semblance of a track mark was too cold to determine.

So far, we were hitting brick walls. Michael's friend and the other officer regained consciousness but were blindsided by "all dark clothing." I couldn't even catch a scent. Michael was relying on his instincts, going about his business calmly.

We were proceeding quarter by quarter, and I overheard whispers outside suggesting we were losing the plot and wasting time. Fortunately, the ice vapour provided us with enough cover. However, that eerie feeling persisted closer this time. The pain and anger overwhelmed us, acting as a beacon reaching out.

"Coming up blank, are you?"

"Same. You wouldn't even know we had a body in here."

"Do you think it's related to the political side or your friends in the circle?"

"Since I saw that symbol on his chest, it's not a stretch to say they are the same."

"So, is it far-fetched to suggest they could have helped with the party?"

"With their resources, it wouldn't be surprising."

The more we thought and dug, the more the sense of battling against a wasp's nest grew.

"Michael, are you sensing that?"

"Yeah, and it's not a good feeling."

That eerie sensation suddenly became overwhelming, seemingly everywhere and nowhere at once. One, two, three, four, and five—I extended my claws, starting with my right hand, then my left, all the while my hackles were raised. My senses went haywire, and I saw Michael struggling against the partial shift. Everything turned bright red, and the stench was death—a scent of a thousand bodies.

"Be on guard. Something is coming, and it's coming hot. And it's the usual."

"Oooh, the dark and scary action," Michael replied.

I glanced at Michael's hands, noticing that his claws were longer and thinner, light brown. They resembled talons but straight. It was strange to be curious in the heat of the moment, but I guess forewarned is forearmed.

The van doors crept closer to closing, and the vapour was thickening. With each warm breath we exhaled, the vapour clouded our vision. The eerie presence was nearly upon us. Our fangs were fully exposed, with Michael's appearing different—shorter and slightly more pronounced. A haunting wind whipped through, causing the vapour to bunch up, momentarily obstructing our view of the doorway. But my neck hairs were on fire. And then it came...

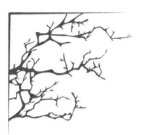

13

DEATH FILLED

The air in the van thickened, and the oxygen sucked away. Michael struggled, face red, gasping frantically. Powerless, claws dug, blood drops fell. Death filled the van, black smoke mingling with white clouds. Mouth watered at blood, stomach fought violent urges. Sickly sweet smell, fangs surrounded, air heavy. The world outside is oblivious.

Death had filled the van. A rush of black smoke swam with the white clouds. My mouth watered at the blood, while my stomach fought the urge to be violently sick. A ripe sweetness pooled around my fangs, and I didn't like it or could do anything about it. All the while, the world outside remained oblivious.

Nothing but pain and anger. How? A black cloud had us pinned, and my brain couldn't figure out how it was possible or the next move we could make. We were slowly asphyxiating, and I needed to think fast. The trouble was all my effort was being directed toward fighting. Michael, much the same.

"Why won't you leave it alone?" a voice, Velcro feeling, chill up my neck. The pitch fluctuated; there was no way of telling whether it was a man or a woman. The pitch was all over the place. To make matters worse, no pulse or heartbeat. Not that one was expected. A cloud that is alive. Then again, I wouldn't have thought there'd be a voice.

"Cuh, Cuh. Who...what...please stop,"

'You're all the same. How easy it would be to ruin you both, too,'

'Too' if I didn't know before, I knew then. This was who or what had killed before? How many were a different story?

"Why? Cuh Cuh, why ruin us?"

'Because you won't leave. '

"Leave what?"

'The natural order in the chaos,'

"Does that natural order include murder?"

The smoke began crunching into my chest, breathless enough as it was. This felt like something trying to burrow inside me. Michael was the same, pinned backwards. I could barely move my arms.

"Funny how it's suddenly become a problem,"

The voice was throwing me, my heightened hearing focussed deep with the octaves, slowing it down. It was more than one...

"Cuh, Cuh suddenly?"

'Don't pretend to care. You're all the same. Never bothered when it was needed,' squeezing continued, piercing my chest. Michael's glow flickered, faltering—deep pressure, shooting pain, simulating a heart attack.

"Never bothered? Who are you? Who let you down?" I demanded.

"Leave us alone, or you will follow," the voice warned.

The crushing sensation became unbearable, and neither of us could barely breathe. With the last ounce of strength, I delved deep within myself. I gripped onto all the pain I had endured over the past few months and before that. I remembered the breaking bones during the blood moon, each fibre of my being trying to shift entirely. Ellena had pulled me back then. I didn't have her with me now, but the image of her face gave me strength.

A spark ignited inside me, and a rush of heat surged through my body. My eyes blazed blood red, and that heat coursed through my veins. My muscles throbbed and grew, as did my claws. I felt different, an unfamiliar sensation akin to the blood moon. My body reacted, pushing back against the encroaching smoke, loosening its grip on my heart. Somehow, there was more than one presence, an entity of sorts.

The strangeness peaked when I began hearing a quick, chaotic flurry of voices. Not from outside, but emanating from within the smoke. They seemed at odds with each other, a jumbled mess that made it hard to discern the number or genders. It unnerved me, but my body remained in control, rejecting the smoke and allowing Michael's eyes to steady.

"Whatever you've done or are doing, stop before it's too late. Otherwise, you'll face consequences you can't live with," I warned.

My body was finally free from the smoke. I couldn't see anything beyond the black mist, but the pain subsided. I felt powerful, unlike the werewolf side of me. At least I could breathe again.

"Maybe living isn't on their agenda. This is your only warning, especially now that they know you're different, both of you," the voice echoed.

The smoke released its grip and rushed away in a blink of a blood-red haze. Cold air rushed back in as if a vacuum had been created. Michael and I slumped back against the icy sides of the van, a sense of relief spreading between us. However, I couldn't shake the unease I felt.

"Michael, are you alright?" I asked.

"They say smoking kills, but I never expected literal black smoke," he replied.

"But it's more than that," I said.

"Matey, it felt like my balls were in a vice, and my ex-wife was twisting the handle. It took my breath away," he joked, though I sensed he understood the gravity of the situation.

"Well, I thought I was about to have a heart attack. The pressure was squeezing my heart, toying with it," I added.

"To be honest, I wouldn't have minded so much. It's not like it was even a first date," Michael quipped, but I could tell he was contemplating the entity and its significance.

"Yes, well, I reckon it would've been one expensive date—three of you," I replied.

"Well, sunny Jim, you should know that this old dog has been there and done that. But this... this felt different," Michael said, his tone serious.

The chaotic voices I had picked up on would lead Michael in the right direction. How was it possible? It was like the "pot calling the kettle black." We shouldn't exist, and yet we did.

"How many?" Michael asked.

"At least three," I replied. "Don't ask me how, but while I was grappling with the excruciating pain, I picked up on varying pitches of sound."

"Modulation? Trying to deceive us?" he pondered.

"I don't think so. These voices were separate yet together, sharing a common trait—pain. Their pain resonated through me, feeding off it and fuelling their rage," I said, cutting him off. He was right. Their pain bonded them, but it wasn't directed at us. Otherwise, they wouldn't have warned us. They had more targets; it was just a matter of identifying who.

"Are we still heading to the warehouse, or does little old Georgie need his bed now?" Michael asked.

We could have called it a night and resumed fresh the next day. However, I couldn't rest with the address lingering in my mind.

"Steady on, old man. Won't they miss you at the nursing home? Isn't it medication time?" I retorted.

"You know what? Think of it as Viagra on tap. I'd be like a bloody kid in a candy store," he joked.

"That sounds about right. I can picture you teasing the grannies, chasing them around in your wheelchair," I said.

"Blimey, Georgie, I don't know what's worse—your imagination or the fact that you think I'd stoop to using one of those death traps on wheels," Michael replied.

Michael had regained his usual composure, shuffling through the icy debris on the floor and brushing himself off. I understood why. My chest still felt the residual effects of heartburn—persistent and irritating.

One thing was certain: I couldn't escape the smell of death. Not like before when I felt watched. This stench was inside me, clinging to me. It was a putrid, rotten smell of decaying flesh, gripping my lungs and nostril hairs. It made me think about the last comment we heard: 'Maybe living isn't on the menu, but you could be.' Were they already dead?

"9 pm, Unit 12C, Albert Dock Road," I read aloud.

The nighttime sky appeared like an endless abyss, with little noise or movement nearby. We braved a secluded industrial estate guided by the 'Taxi card.' Albert Dock Road stretched for quite a distance, far from any help or signs of life.

"Once bitten, twice shy, and all that," Michael said.

We had recently survived an onslaught of pain-ridden black smoke that could crush our insides and steal our breath. We pondered over the inside throughout the journey while Michael massaged his throat, still soothing the discomfort. It was strange how the case had led us to engage in activities we wouldn't typically bother with. Before we left Limehouse Link, Michael searched under and around the wheel arches, looking for another tracker. The one we found in the backseat needed further investigation.

Yet, there was no time for food or delving into the realm of the spy world. Michael suggested taking it to one of his dodgy friends in Romford, Essex. Seemed like Michael had more connections on the wrong side of the thin blue line than the right. If it provided us with a viable lead, I wouldn't complain. However, the whole situation left me on edge and slightly paranoid. We had been traversing different levels of London's social hierarchy throughout the day. We were pulled, pushed, tracked, and lied to, only to have a dead body stolen from us, followed by the assault of the black smoke.

High fencing to the left of the road isolated wasted, unkempt grassland. On the right, warehouses curved to the left, with extensive parking spaces in front. Many of them lacked names, which was to be expected in that part of London. I expected some were being used for "cut and shuts" or to break down stolen cars. I hadn't even stepped out of the driver's seat, yet the overwhelming stench of engine oil had already engulfed my senses.

"Ahead and to the left," Michael urged impatiently, reaching for his cigarettes. Despite the recent encounter, the old habit persisted.

"Tut tut. You may be healthier than ever, but do you have to kill your lungs all over again?" I quipped.

"Piss off. Can't a man indulge once in a while?" he retorted.

"Yeah, but what about indulging every twenty minutes?"

"I'm not that bad. Honestly, I'm trying to eradicate that lingering taste of death. It's wreaking havoc on my taste buds," he explained.

I didn't press Michael any further on the subject. He seemed edgy enough as it was. He had a point, though. Throughout the journey, I couldn't shake off the lingering sense of death. At least my heightened sense of smell allowed me to overpower it, as did my superior hearing. First, I picked up on Michael's heavy footsteps and the thumping sound of his movements on the concrete. A cat scavenging through a nearby bin caught his attention, and a fleeting yellow glint shone from his eyes before we continued.

"Yeah, it's overstaying its welcome, alright," I agreed.

The unease wouldn't leave me, but I knew I had to push forward. We neared the warehouse quickly, but I was already considering different scenarios and excuses. Perhaps someone had cut themselves on a piece of machinery. However, as we approached, I could smell the distinct coppery scent of blood. We couldn't avoid it, whether we wanted to. A pool of blood awaited us.

"Looks like somebody might be home. Do you think they would roll out the red carpet? It would be a pleasant change from the usual," I remarked.

"Unfortunately, you're out of luck. Although red is a possibility," Michael replied.

"Eh?"

"There's blood," I said.

A waft of the scent came on the breeze. No sooner had Michael mentioned the carpet than we both slowed down slightly. In my mind, I began counting and considering various scenarios and excuses. The weakest explanation would be that someone had accidentally injured themselves on some sort of machinery. Despite our reduced pace, we quickly approached the source. The smell of copper was overpowering, too strong, and too prevalent. A pool of blood awaited us, whether we wanted to confront it.

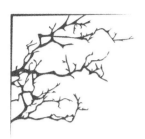

14

ANTICIPATION

From the angle we approached, I missed a faded red door to the right of the window. Just a few feet away, the overpowering scent of blood hit us. Michael struggled to maintain control. Thankfully, Albert Dock Road was deserted, but I feared a grim fate had found someone else. Michael, a beacon to werewolves—or, in his case, a werefox—still felt strange to classify. Anticipation had centred on his transformation into a werewolf.

Now, I questioned what that meant for pack dynamics. I recalled from books how a wolf pack operates, with an Alpha stronger due to the presence of betas. Michael was my sergeant, but in this dark world, I was his leader. Did it matter which form a shapeshifter took? I needed to know.

Time was of the essence tonight. Our shift had extended far past its intended duration as we chased our tails. We could have left the warehouse address for the next day, but I wasn't a fan of coincidence. Something about finding the card in an empty truck cab set off alarm bells. Now, the smell of blood justified our decision. A sense of impending doom settled in, making me feel sick. The stench was too strong, undoubtedly human.

My taste buds went into a frenzy. I hoped the allure would somewhat diminish. For now, it had lessened. Worrying about Michael's prey drive diverted my mind from what drove me. However, the hunger still lurked, waiting for a chance to taste flesh. I would never willingly indulge in such desires. Saving Michael had been an exception I hoped not to repeat. Besides the blood, human flesh didn't have much of a taste. It was more of a smell, tinged with soap and the salts released through dried sweat.

Michael clung to the shreds of his self-control, but I sensed his desire to cut loose. What awaited us on the other side of the shutter could either push him—or both of us—over the edge or become a welcome distraction. The bottom corners of the shutter were secured with sliding bolts and padlocks, and there was another bolt, roughly chest height, near a handle on the right side. At least it would be chest height for me, more like in the middle of Michael's face. A fleeting thought made me chuckle, eliciting a strange look from Michael as if to ask, "What's got you perked up?" It certainly wasn't the much-needed coffee.

Curiously, the door also had a latch. A silver latch flipped to the left, held in place by a bulky, worn-out grey "Yale" lock. It was likely silver at one point, but time had taken its toll—similar to my ageing knees and Michael's jowls. What struck me as strange was that the door was locked from the outside while the light was still on inside. My initial thought was that someone had left quickly, given blood. However, it would only draw attention. The average passerby wouldn't possess our heightened sense of smell. But I couldn't discern anything beyond that.

A quick, deeper inhale added another layer of worry. The scent of decaying flesh. The pieces didn't quite fit together. I almost connected the dots, but the blood was much fresher than the scent of decay lingering behind it. If I didn't know any better or had a propensity for conspiracy theories, I would say that this was a setup, that we had been lured here. It wasn't beyond the realm of possibility, given how the roadworks had been arranged and the two vehicles blocking our path before the truck obstructed the road. It all seemed meticulously planned. We could have easily fallen for it now that I reviewed the details.

Perhaps they knew we would latch onto the one thing that stood out amidst the chaos of our encounters with the fewer corpses. They might have thought they were doing us a favour by providing a trade. I doubted it would be of any use or benefit to the escalating situation we found ourselves in. It was too late to fully understand the implications of what the black smoke had done and could do to us. It had trapped us, suffocated us, and could have killed us, but it didn't.

How was I able to hear the chaos within it? Michael had caught onto the different levels, but I heard a discordant conversation as if I were standing among them. Something inside me fought back, and I was fortunate that it did.

"This isn't good, Georgie," Michael remarked.

"No shit, Sherlock. There's at least one decomposing body, and the scent of blood is fresh," I replied.

"Yeah, but it's locked," he noticed.

"When something feels too good to be true, it usually is," I responded.

"And what exactly does that mean?"

"It means, old man, we stumbled upon the one thing that shouldn't exist in an empty truck. The bad guys might as well have drawn us a map for directions," my pessimism surged involuntarily. I hadn't meant it to come out that way, but my nerves were thin.

"Okay, stroppy nuts. What do you suggest? We can't get an out-of-hours warrant based solely on the aromatic smell of blood and death that nobody else can detect. The bloody judge would laugh us out of the courtroom," he argued.

"What if we found insecure premises?" I suggested.

"Is there any CCTV?" Michael asked.

"I haven't seen any, and I'm not picking up on any interference," I replied.

"Alright, you want to flex those wolfy muscles and break the lock?" Michael questioned.

"No, not really. But we're already here. Suppose you devise a good enough reason for us to get back in the car and leave, then great. But I doubt it," I responded.

Michael looked like a constipated rabbit caught in headlights. I knew he had pushed boundaries many times throughout his long career. Still, the prospect of doing it for the sake of another dead body didn't seem appealing. We were in the same boat, but that boat was sailing up the creek, and we were devoid of paddles.

"Alright, wise guy, what about that alarm?" Michael prompted.

I noticed a recess near the roof, almost concealed by a drainpipe. I hadn't even considered looking up there, as my mind was preoccupied with confusion, misdirection, and a million pieces of a puzzle that I couldn't fit together. We still had many leads to follow, and Ellena was working her magic with Mr Nicholls.

The alarm was live. A dim amber light spun behind an opaque section of the alarm system. After Michael pointed it out, I half expected it to be a dummy alarm, but I noticed wiring drilled into the wall. This was another detail that puzzled me. It was a heavily alarmed warehouse, with a visible light that could be seen through the window by anyone who cared to look—robust padlocks reminiscent of Fort Knox and a disturbing stench emanating from the other side.

Were the owners of that "taxi card" hoping we would charge in and set off alarm bells, drawing attention to us and the awaiting chaos? Call me paranoid, but our recent luck hadn't been the greatest, and this situation seemed suspicious. Parked alone in the frost-covered car park, our car appeared to be the safer option.

"Well, old man, time for another lesson," I said, waiting for Michael's expression as if he had been slapped by a wet fish. His heart skipped a beat as he looked up, realising what I was about to suggest.

"You want me to climb up there?" Michael looked up, mouth agape, contemplating whether the crusty white pipework would hold his weight. I had already noticed that the bracket near the top, including the raw plugs, was partially torn from the wall.

No, he had misunderstood. My suggestion demanded far more athleticism from the wily fox. I had never asked if he was afraid of heights.

"No, you twit. I want you to jump," I replied.

"What the fuck, jump? Seriously? Look, I may have had a hormone transfusion, but that doesn't make up for the mileage on my knees," Michael protested.

"Hey, what do you do in your private life? I won't judge. But seriously, all you have to do is feel it. Picture yourself jumping that high, and you might be surprised," I urged.

"Oi, less of that, madam. I'm telling you, if I fall and break my neck, you'll be in trouble," Michael smirked and gave me a cocky wink. The cockney prince began limbering like an Olympian preparing to compete in the high jump.

"Don't worry. You won't fall, and you won't break your hip. Just breathe, imagine, and do it. And by 'do it,' I mean I need you to claw through the wires," I clarified.

With a glance, Michael bounced a few more times. He inhaled deeply before exhaling into the cold air. His eyes flashed yellow, and his claws extended with a flick of his fingers. On the final bounce, Michael propelled himself into the air, using a swing of his right hand to tear through the wires effortlessly.

He made it look easy, and the lesson was successful. Michael landed on his feet, his knees bending slightly before he slowly turned his head to face me with a satisfied expression.

"Hips, knees, and back intact, matey. Just in case you were worried," he quipped.

"Don't pat yourself on the back too hard. You might get winded. Besides, that was the easy part," I retorted.

I held my breath as we stood just two feet from the door, wanting to gather as much information as possible before entering. We had been betrayed before, which left me doubting and questioning everything. If my suspicions were correct and this was a setup, what else awaited on the other side? My mind raced, contemplating various possibilities, like a bomb ticking down. Perhaps that thought was extreme, but nothing about this case had been ordinary.

"So, while I had to jump, you just have to force open a door," Michael quipped, lightening the tense atmosphere. In reality, I think he enjoyed the thrill of it all.

My hand gripped the cold metal handle. It wasn't too late to abandon this place and leave it in our rearview mirror. I glanced at Michael, who nodded, offering his encouragement. With a deep breath, I turned the handle, exerting gentle pressure on my shoulder. The door burst open, the frame splintering, and some remnants of the lock clanging onto the floor.

The narrow space was only a foot wide, but the stench permeated beyond my expectations. It resembled the basement all over again—a strong, musky scent of decay that clung to the pores of anyone unfortunate enough to encounter it. I almost closed the door, but we wouldn't make any progress in our investigation or uncover the reasons for the missing bodies. Michael was already tagging along, his hand covering his face and becoming a hairy, clawed appendage in anticipation.

"Now it's time to pull up your big boy pants, Michael," I said, urging him to continue.

"Ladies first," Michael responded, pointing playfully while lingering behind.

"I could say 'age before beauty,' but we both know you have no intention of braving it first," I laughed, not as bothered as I made it seem. The door opened into a hallway, revealing a flight of steep stone stairs to the right, accompanied by a black metal fence.

The light seemed dimmer up close. The hallway extended for about twenty feet, leading to another faded red door on the left. That was where the smell was emanating from. The only other movement I sensed was the scurrying of rats nearby.

We proceeded cautiously, our heads swivelling, taking in our surroundings. We saw the open warehouse space through the doorway illuminated by distant, dim lights. Racks holding boxes were scattered around the perimeter, with additional pallets scattered throughout the floor. However, it was the horrors near the shutter that seized our attention. I could spot a dirty body bag partially opened on a table. Next to it, in a chair, sat a lifeless body.

As their back was turned to us, we couldn't see much besides the man's head drooping to the side. His left arm hung down, mere inches from the floor, covered in a river of blood. At the centre of it was a gun, with sulphur still circulating, making me believe it wasn't too old. What the hell was going on?

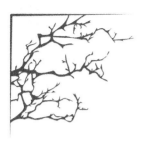

15

THE TURNAGES

The drool pooled as we neared. Blood used to make me queasy, but dealing with others' blood was an occupational hazard I'd grown accustomed to. A paper cut or pricked finger would usually go straight into my mouth, even though it tasted horrible.

Now, I only wanted to rinse it around my gums—the crimson tide rippling under the dim yellow light. The droplets raining down indicated this unfortunate individual hadn't been gone long. Michael hesitated, hanging back. I strained my ears, thinking someone might be approaching, but it was Michael who seemed to spiral. His heart roared, light brown fur sheets rippling across his cheeks, adding to his already greying stubble.

"Michael, are you okay?" I asked.

"No, I can't control it," he replied.

"The blood?" I inquired.

"No. Can't you hear it?" Michael's face twisted, showing pain. Claws and fangs were out, his face revealing the fox within.

"I can't hear anything. Can you point in a specific direction?"

"There, and it bloody hurts. But it's not mine. It feels like pain radiating towards me," Michael explained.

"Can't you block it out?" I suggested.

"No, it's coming in waves. My body feels like it's breaking," he replied.

"Is it coming from the bodies? And your body feels like it's breaking?" I asked.

"I kid you not. It's as uncomfortable as a prostate exam, except the doctor is shoving a tree trunk up my arse," he lamented.

"Was I just about to suggest that you glove up? Sounds like it could be a sore subject," I chuckled.

"Oi, you cheeky twat. I'll let you know I glove up constantly," Michael retorted.

"Thank fuck for that. The last thing we need is a mini psychopath Werefox on the loose," I joked.

"Christ, imagine another one like Melanie," he replied.

"Bad enough that we already have one mini psycho Werefox," I said.

"Oi, I'm not that short. But honestly, what the hell? It's easing a little. It felt like I could feel the pain from one of those dead bodies. Or both," Michael explained.

Michael's revelation added another twist to our story. I had another reason to watch him closely. His shifting had been unpredictable, and it wasn't even a full moon. However, I didn't plan to mention it to him. I didn't want the cockney prince getting carried away with himself.

But his unique ability raised questions. Whatever had just happened seemed connected to the dead bodies and the bloody pool. I stepped forward, and a small glimmer of colour caught my eye—the symbol on my wrist, a green triangle with a blue looping swirl.

It flickered like static, happening as I moved toward the bodies, particularly the body bag. It hadn't happened in a while.

I still didn't fully understand the meaning behind the symbol. It had been a month, and I hadn't had a moment to pause and scratch my head, let alone track down my potential birth pack of werewolves. So why now? Why in a warehouse with a body bag resulting from a horrific death and a lifeless man next to a smoking gun in a pool of blood?

"You're not the only one, Michael. Look," I shoved my arm toward him, and as I moved it away, the symbol disappeared again.

"I saw, just like before. I remember that day, too. When we found Chris's body, it was the first time I saw it."

"But now? With dead bodies?"

"Neither of us is a fan of coincidences. So, I'll say it's best to brace yourself."

"You know how to bring down the mood, you know that, right?"

We shifted forward, and Michael's eyes went bright yellow again. Mine went red, with claws sliding out of control. My body felt defensive, but this felt different. It was like we sensed danger, heightened by my hackles bouncing to life.

I couldn't pinpoint where the danger could be. There were no other heartbeats aside from ours. An eerie silence fell, our footsteps patter the concrete floor, and the smell grew stronger. The body bag was three-quarters open, revealing the decomposing body of a young woman with dirty, slimy chestnut hair. Her skin was a dirty grey with smears of dried blood.

As I scanned her decomposing body, I noticed my symbol was acting up. My arm lingered at rib height, and I could see both my arm and hers. Blocking out everything else around me, including Michael, our symbols pulsed in synchronisation. In that hazy moment, a sickly feeling of loss crept into the pit of my stomach, reminiscent of the pain I felt when I lost Helen.

Looking at this stranger with the same symbol, I couldn't explain why I felt this connection. A wave of overwhelming sadness washed over me. The emotions were brewing, and Michael appeared by my side as the haze slowly faded.

"Mate, this is weird. I can feel everything you're giving off. Your pain, but I can't see how or,"

"I don't know either. Only we have the same symbol and... And... I think we're related. I think she's my."

The words slipped out without thinking, but they finally put into words the rush of pain I had been feeling. I didn't understand how it was possible. What I knew was that the dead woman in front of us had something that reacted to my presence.

"But how? She looks like she's been dead for at least a year. Are you sure about the sister part?"

"I can't be certain. How could I? But the emotional pull was there, along with the pain of loss. I remember seeing pictures of another child at my parents' burnt home, a young girl. If this isn't her, then she must be related."

Facing these cold, hard facts, I couldn't ignore the more pressing issue: why? This added credibility to the notion that the "taxi card" was a setup. I refocused on the body, searching for clues to the truth and a connection to other pieces of the puzzle. That's when I first noticed something I had missed about her hands. She had claws, light brown and short ones.

I couldn't say she was a werewolf, but she was a shifter. My next point of interest was her face. She would have been attractive if not for her current state. Her long, symmetrical face with closed eyes and lips that couldn't shut, strained by something that had them bulging. I reached for my gloves, but Michael grabbed my arm.

"What are you doing, matey?"

"I have to know,"

"What?"

"Look at her hands. I need to know what she was,"

"While you're at it, I'm getting a whiff of dead blood from an open wound." I had been trying not to breathe, and the emotional pull interfered with my senses. Michael was right; the smell of dead blood was far more rotten than the pool on the floor.

A part of me screamed to leave it alone, but curiosity got the better of me. One of the amber lights above us flickered, adding to the surrounding horror. There was still more to uncover. We had been brought here for a reason, and it was more than just a family reunion.

My hands shook as I fought to keep my claws at bay. Even through the thin latex gloves, her skin felt cold and rigid. The sound of flesh pulling apart crackled in my ears as her receding gums revealed fangs similar to mine rather than Michael's. A wolf.

'Tick, tick, tick, tick,'

"Michael, do you hear that?"

"No, what?"

"Listen closely,"

"Tick, tick, tick, tick, fuck,"

"What do you think it is?"

"Nothing good, or are we just being dramatic? Maybe that guy has a watch on."

Michael had a point. Every noise made me jumpy in the silence, and I strained to see who the guy was. Michael spun his chair to face us, but neither recognised him—just an average bloke in his forties, serving some purpose. The front of his shirt was ripped open, revealing a message carved into his chest: 'the devil is in the details'. Blood dripped from his temple, a bullet hole.

The message was right because the gun couldn't have fallen and landed the way it had if he had committed suicide. Even if the muzzle hit the floor first, it would've landed in two ways. But the handle faced us as if someone right-handed dropped it in the blood.

"Top pocket, matey,"

Michael pointed to the guy's jacket, where a small folded note was found. Common sense told me to leave it be, but common sense had been screaming at me since we arrived. It seemed we may need to divorce common sense.

'Don't worry, Detective Reynolds, Patrick here. He was a wicked man and played a part in all this unfolding. Isn't he a peach? But that's beside the point because I don't think I sold the bad man enough. Let me make a more direct point. The attractive woman in front of you is Leila. She was a lot like you. I would say it's in the genes, and I don't mean your diesel denim. No, she had the same fiery red that runs through your veins. At least until Patrick had her chase her last ball.'-

'Now, let's talk about quid pro quo. We kindly got rid of the menace of Patrick, who was such a stain on society and ... your family. Ah, dam, there I go again, getting carried away. You two hadn't met yet. Well, our condolences. All's fair in love and war. So, yes, he killed her, and we killed him for you. So, you could say you killed him. At least, that's how it looks on the tape we have. But let's not stray from the details. We need you to make this mess disappear as if it never happened. That way, we'll know how good of a boy you are, and you'll get a treat. The location of more of your real family. And I don't mean the cemetery.'

'Just in case you're thinking, fuck this, we'll offer a further incentive. We're going to take your bumbling ordinary friend there. Don't worry, he won't be harmed... As long as you do as requested. You can investigate and make all the right noises, but ultimately, they'll all be futile. Tik, tik, tik, tik... anyone feeling sleepy...'

The note was sadistic, yet confident and controlling. How could they expect me to go along with their demands? Anger brewed deep within me. 'Patrick' allegedly killed 'Leila', who might be my sister, and yet they spoke of it so casually. A blip to them or a means to an end. Sleepy? What did they mean?

"You okay, mate?"

"It's bad. Listen carefully. I sense danger coming. They want you, Michael, to silence me and cover everything up. It's a cover-up. In return, I will find out where my real family is. That girl there is supposedly related, 'Leila,'"

"Fuck... that ticking is getting louder. I hear wheels approaching fast,"

He was right. At least two vehicles were rapidly approaching, and the ticking grew louder.

"It's coming from him,"

I moved closer to listen and search for anything obvious while Michael assessed our options. The ticking sound was relentless. Then a loud 'click' echoed around us. A vast cloud of pure gas burst free from 'Patrick', seeping from every orifice and gap in his clothing. The purple gas, fruity yet spicy, spread quickly through the air, forcing its way into our lungs. Michael began choking first, his veins bulging as he turned red in the face. He struggled to breathe, just like before.

Then, the gas started affecting me, too. It burned through my airways, causing my insides to feel like they were on fire. I struggled to keep my eyes open, feeling drained of strength and energy. Each breath I took was a fiery, chilling sensation, accompanied by the scent of sweet, fruity flowers and burnt wood. With every stumble, I was on the verge of hitting the floor. My body fought desperately, but the relentless effects of the gas overpowered me.

I flopped onto the cold stone floor, feeling its chill against my skin. My eyelids flickered, allowing me to catch glimpses of my claws retracting. In the distance, I could hear the echo of foggy footsteps.

"Don't worry, Detective Reynolds," a voice taunted. "We'll keep him safe. There's no use in fighting wolfsbane. Oh yes, we know. Now sleep." The voice faded into the distance as I lost the ability to keep my eyes open.

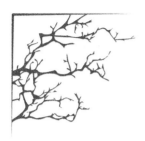

16

WAKE UP

Smooth, pale skin, a reassuring smile, and confidence in her stride—Elena approached. A bright light accentuated her long, perfectly straightened blonde hair. Her mouth opened, but I couldn't hear her. A faint sound reached my ears.

"Georgie, Georgie. Wake up."

"Come on, Georgie; it's time to wake up."

Her voice deepened, and my eyelids felt too heavy to open. The light shifted, alternating between shades of blue and red.

Panic swiftly took hold. I remembered what had happened and rubbed my eyes frantically. I was still at the warehouse, but now outside. Paramedics, a marked police unit, and ADI Locke, the owner of that voice, surrounded me. He hovered nearby, calling for my attention, while I kept glancing back into the warehouse. All inside was 'Patrick'—not even a hint of another body.

The bloodstained gun still sat in the middle, its scent reaching me from a distance, carried by the breeze. Mixed with the fruity-floral aroma, it left a nasty taste in my mouth. I returned to the table where the body bag lay, then to my arm, searching for that symbol. A tear rolled down my cheek, and emotions overwhelmed me. Was that truly my sister or someone connected to me?

"Shit, Michael."

I remembered his red face bulging as he collapsed to the ground. I quickly scanned the surrounding chaos, but found no sign of him. Locke's worried expression pierced into the side of my head.

"Georgie, are you okay?"

"Huh! I feel hungover as hell."

"What happened?"

"Michael? We need to find Michael."

"Why? Because of this?" Locke held up the note. I had almost forgotten about it.

"I'm not going to do what it says, but we have to stop them and find Michael before it's too late."

"Try to catch a scent, but you're heading home to rest. Plenty of units are on it, and I have an old friend who can take over for you."

"Who?"

"It's a surprise. Has the wolfsbane worn off?"

"The what now?"

"Wolfsbane. It's dangerous for werewolves and various types of shapeshifters. The smell was in the warehouse."

"You mean the purple gas?"

"Ah, the basic one. You're lucky they only wanted to hinder you."

"I'm not going anywhere. Michael wouldn't either, and we do not know what's happening. Wait, you mentioned 'incapacitate.' They also said they wouldn't hurt Michael and that they knew about my real family and me. Do you think it could be the suits? Could they have paid for information?"

There was no way I was leaving; we needed all hands on deck. Glancing at my watch, I noted it was approaching midnight, and I had been unconscious for nearly an hour. I wondered what other levels of this 'wolfsbane' existed. My senses had returned, and I was ready to analyse the events until we lost consciousness and decipher the note's contents. 'Your bumbling ordinary friend'—they didn't know that Michael was different.

"I wouldn't put it past them. This kind of operation requires money or power."

"Wait, how did you know we were here? And they don't know Michael is like me."

"Despatch. The address was in their possession, and when nobody could reach you, we sensed something was amiss. As for Michael, that could work to our advantage if he tries to escape."

That explanation made sense, but Michael lacked control, and his shifting was unpredictable. Another thought nagged at me—how did Locke know so much about 'wolfsbane' and the dried blood residue in his office?

He seemed to possess a wealth of knowledge, and I couldn't shake the feeling that there was more to him than met the eye.

"He doesn't have a proper grip yet, and things could go downhill," Locke remarked, reminding me of our missing Ds. I guess he had a point. Although I hoped it wouldn't come to that, as it would only attract unnecessary attention.

I pulled myself off the ambulance bed, ready to get going again, but the wolfsbane still slightly gripped me. I felt dizzy and stumbled a little, prompting a concerned look from Locke. The taste of the gas lingered on my tongue as well.

"About time you got up and moving, lad. Time's wasting," a familiar voice broke through the darkness in the distance. I couldn't fathom why Locke had involved him. He had come through for us once before, but now he was here just 24 hours later. It was my former mentor, Sgt Andrew Morris. He had been a werewolf for much longer than me, and there was still much I had yet to learn.

"I see you're enjoying some time off from the job," I commented.

"Well, somebody has to bail you out. Didn't think it would happen two days in a row," he replied with a chuckle, bulldozing his way towards us. Before long, his bulky form stepped into the light of a dim street lamp, and I saw his bright yellow eyes flashing in the darkness.

"Speaking of which, let's move on," Andrew said.

"I need another look inside the warehouse where he dropped," I stated. If I was going to catch any scent, I needed to know where Michael was last.

"Right, keep me updated. I'll have the others searching elsewhere and looking for CCTV points," Locke said, pulling his coat tighter before giving a smile and disappearing into a crowd of police officers to our left.

As we approached the open shutter of the warehouse, Locke took that as his cue to usher everyone away. By the time we crossed the line of shutter runners, the coast was clear for us to investigate further. Andrew had already begun, his yellow eyes shining brighter than Michael's.

"Alright, Georgie Lad, I need you to try something. Only an Alpha can do it—"

"—hold on a minute, Skip," I interrupted, looking at the table where Leila's body had been. I could feel the rush of emotions again, and the outline where the body bag had rested was still visible.

"What's wrong, lad?"

"There was a body here. Her name was 'Leila.' She was another werewolf, and... she was family," I explained.

"How do you know?"

"We both had the same symbol, and the note hinted at it," I replied.

"Holy shit, lad. I'm so sorry," Andrew offered his condolences.

"He killed her, allegedly," I pointed to the body in the chair, referring to 'Patrick.' The scent of the wolfsbane still lingered in the air, although it had weakened.

"So whoever this is knows who you are?"

"And where is more of my family? But they want me to wipe it all away, including the families," I said.

"Are they deluded? That would only raise more questions," Andrew remarked.

"Exactly."

I visualised the scene, moving on to where I had last seen Michael drop. His face turned red, veins pulsating in his neck and temple, as he clutched his throat and fell to the ground, only ten feet from where 'Patrick' sat.

"What were you saying, Skip?" I asked, attempting to steer the conversation back.

"Ah yeah, you need to look closer than ever. Being part demon will help, but you should be able to see remnants of where your pack members were—signs of their past actions. If you tap into Michael's scent, you might see," Andrew suggested.

He didn't need to tell me twice. I took a deep breath, closed my eyes, and pictured Michael as I had been doing. Then I opened my eyes again. Everything was tinted blood red. I saw Michael dropping to the floor, hands gripping him, and then Michael dabbing his fingers in his mouth and rubbing them on the floor as if writing.

Next, he was dragged away through the open shutters by a waiting car that didn't resemble the typical vehicles we would expect. It looked fancy, almost like a limousine. The car drove off, and the image faded. I was left stunned into silence. Michael was taken away in a limousine. How did that fit with the usual suspects? But it reminded me of Sally Turnage's story and all the talk of being whisked away in limos to mystery locations.

"Are you okay, lad?" Andrew asked, breaking through my thoughts.

"Let's just say Michael was taken in style," I replied.

"What?"

"They whisked Michael away in a fucking limousine. Oh, and he did something on the floor," I added.

"What did he do?"

"I believe he dabbed his fingers in spit and wrote something. I'm not sure what or why," I explained as I scanned the area. Almost missing it because of its faintness, I discovered the barely visible residue on the floor.

'Listen.'

Michael wanted me to listen. He expected trouble and wanted me to pay attention. It made me think that his skills and senses were highly attuned. The brief display of empathic ability was something new to me. I had never imagined that something like that was possible. But what did he want me to listen for?

"Skip, how far have you ever been able to hear something?"

"I'm not sure. Why?"

"Michael left a message—just one word. Listen," I said.

"Listen to what?"

That was the question. I didn't understand what Michael was trying to convey. Ghostly guidance had been lacking lately, and no one else seemed to have any particular insights. Especially not the note. Two things stood out to me: despite the effects of the wolfsbane, something Michael wouldn't have known about, he had the mind to leave a message. And second, everything he did had a purpose.

"Fuck. The bloody tracker," Andrew exclaimed.

"The what now? How out of the loop am I?" I asked, bewildered.

"No sooner had we taken on this case than someone planted a tracker in the car. Only we would have known with our heightened senses. It was like a high-pitched signal," Andrew explained.

"This case truly is a clusterfuck. So, what is Michael trying to tell us?"

"I think that clever bastard has the tracker on him and wants me to listen for it," Andrew concluded.

Michael had thrown us a lifeline, but they were already an hour ahead of us. A limousine in the middle of the night could easily cover 40-60 miles on the motorways. How were we supposed to hear something like that?

"There is another way, you know. If you roar, another werewolf will respond. Like how I heard you and swooped in to save your ass, wearing my metaphorical red cape," Andrew suggested.

"I didn't know what I was doing. It was just built-up stress, and it felt good. It confused me because I thought wolves howled. Oh, and in case you didn't notice, we have a crowd gathering," I replied.

"Well then, let's head to the docks. The acoustics there carry sound across the water. If that old bastard, whatever he is, hears it, Michael will naturally respond. Wolves howl, but werewolves bloody roar, and an Alpha's roar makes the blood run cold," Andrew proposed.

He put the image of his fierce Alpha roar back in my mind, the one where he had effortlessly grabbed Melanie by the throat while Michael lay bleeding on the floor within seconds of his life. The last thing we needed was to find Michael caught up in another deadly encounter.

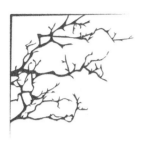

17

SILENCE

The body was removed once we finished. Andy drove slowly, passing signs toward the A406 or the docks. All the windows were down, and the night was eerily quiet, just a few straggling cars. I did what Michael asked, keeping my ears tuned for any sounds. Part of me wondered if he meant a howl or a roar, so I listened for those, too. But the most rational explanation pointed to the missing tracker; it wasn't in the backseat unless those bastards took it, too.

Eyes closed, the world disappeared, and for a moment, it felt heavenly. I was tempted to keep them shut, avoiding the trouble ahead. But I couldn't give up. I had to stay focused and determined.

Then, a faint beep, low and far away. I struggled to discern whether it was an alarm or a traffic crossing. But the timing was the same, a second apart. We had to try it. We could cross it off our list, even if it were nothing. Andrew's idea would have been easier, but hesitation swirled in my mind.

If Michael responded, it would inadvertently reveal him as a shapeshifter, putting him at greater risk. Panic could ensue, and there was no telling how his captors would react, especially if they were potentially far away. We had to approach this with caution. My instincts told me to head to the motorway, and Andrew seemed to feel the same since he was already heading toward the A406.

"You hear it too?" I asked Andrew.

"Just about, lad," he replied.

"Have you been talking to Locke since the fallout with Ethan?" I blurted out, an unconscious nagging needing to be addressed. Locke was reaching out to Andrew in a time of need — it made me curious, considering how reclusive Andrew had become afterwards. I also wanted to understand in what capacity he was back: as my sergeant or as a friend.

"Sort of. He's consistently reached out to me, as everyone else has. You sense there's something different about him, don't you?" Andrew responded.

"How did you guess?"

"The way your mind operates, Georgie. You ask one question to seek answers for a few other things that are bothering you," he explained.

"Yes, I can't quite put my finger on it. He seems to know a lot about certain things, like Wolfsbane. I did not know," I replied.

"Another reason I'm here is in an advisory capacity, especially regarding the wolf aspect. I have the sense that he's different, but he'll only reveal that when he's ready and feels comfortable sharing," Andrew said.

"There was dried blood in his office," I revealed.

Andrew fell silent, his expression showing surprise. It was an unexpected reaction. He would even approach Locke about it, bringing up another issue entirely. We had to observe and wait, ensuring that we could trust him. There was always another shoe waiting to drop.

In that silence, my mind wandered, reflecting on the past. Thoughts of the board in his kid's room and my parent's home made me wonder if he had discovered anything more about the rest of my family. Particularly 'Leila,' the name the symbol had led me to. There was a connection, and the emotional pull was strong. But with all the misdirection we'd encountered lately, we found it difficult to sift through the information and uncover the truth.

"Skip, in your search, did you ever come across the name Leila in relation to me or anything?" I asked.

"Not the name specifically, but family packs often have symbols. She likely was related if hers was the same and came and went. I'm sorry, lad," Andrew responded.

"What about your situation? Warren Whitlock has been quiet. Any word on your daughter?" I inquired.

"Has he? Who's saying he's not behind all of this, or at least a part of it? Money and sneaky bastard tendencies, not to mention the involvement of powerful people," Andrew mused.

"A bloody limousine, though. It seems a bit too on the nose, don't you think?" I added, pondering the peculiar choice of vehicle.

The beeping got progressively louder as we approached Oak Lake Farm in Brentwood, Essex. Surrounding us were country lanes and wilderness, with overgrown trees and bushes concealing potential eyes watching our every move. We reached the location, a small victory, but the real challenge lay ahead. The vastness of the land meant the properties would likely be set further back. If our assumptions about their organisation were correct, people would be stationed at the front door to keep watch.

The air was chilling, and without torches, visibility would be limited. For once, I was grateful for our werewolf's eyes. My hackles hadn't settled since we arrived. I couldn't help but question their true plan. What if we were the real targets all along? They could have taken me and left Michael, leading us into the middle of nowhere with nobody around. They knew who I was and the risks of transporting me, yet I had willingly come along. Michael would suffer through torture while they incapacitated me for a reason that remained unclear.

"Georgy, the front door is out of the question," Andrew acknowledged as if he were about to saunter up and ring a doorbell.

"I gathered as much. So, we'll take cover in the trees?" I suggested, scanning the area for the best route. Surely, there would be a surveillance camera at the main gate. It made sense to go over the fence and navigate through the trees.

"Yes, but something doesn't feel right," Andrew voiced his unease.

"I agree. There's more to their plan than we know. They were aware of what I am and expected my involvement," I replied.

"Impressive. Under no circumstances do we split up, lad. Are you listening? And only shift if necessary. We don't want to play into the hands of anyone recording the events. Knowing is one thing; having tangible evidence is another," Andrew advised.

"Agreed. If we encounter any cameras, we'll disable them." I nodded, fully aware of the precautions we needed to take.

The beeping from the tracker was the strongest it had been throughout our journey. The sounds of pain emanated persistently. 'Georgie, I can smell you. I'm in a basement. Hardly anyone has been here, but they all wore hoods,' Michael's voice echoed in the wind. He now knew we were coming for him, and the relief of knowing he was still alive washed over me.

"Are you alright? We heard your cries of pain. Have you learned anything about their intentions?" I asked, concerned for his well-being.

"It all went downhill when my eyes lit up. Their plans change then, a mix of panic followed by a calm demeanour as if it lured you in. There was mention of tests for a hybrid and controlling the situation," Michael explained, revealing what little information he had gathered.

"Can you sense any heartbeats nearby?" I inquired, hoping for further insight.

"Only three. I can also smell more of that gas-like substance they used before, the shocking person, and two further away. I suspect they plan to gas us again and then conduct experiments elsewhere," Michael responded.

"Save your strength. We're making our way inside," I assured him, determined to free him from their clutches.

"Be careful, you two. The place seems rigged," he cautioned us.

The other shoe had finally dropped, confirming our suspicions. We needed to proceed cautiously, infiltrating the premises without falling into their trap. It made me think of the girls from the masquerade. What if those who were killed were taken and subjected to experiments? Perhaps all of them were. That would explain the black fluid that Sally had experienced. We already knew the 'devil's circle' had a sinister history, with connections to powerful figures in parliament. They thought that having us again could solve more than one problem. But I had no intention of playing their game.

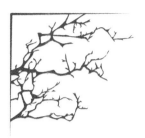

18

AIR OF SECRECY

Not so posh, up close, bigger and hidden—a place for nasty activities. Well concealed, probably unregistered, at least not to someone still alive. We huddled behind low, prickly bushes to the left of the property. The limousine was nowhere in sight, but a black Range Rover was parked at the front. Two burly goons, donning black hoods and dark suits stood guard at the front door.

Taking them out was an option, but Michael was right. Since our encounter with wolfsbane, I recognised its scent, filling the air with something else. Familiar with my parents' place in Surrey—a berry-like aroma lingering after the house was torched.

"How are you feeling, Michael?" I asked.

"Getting weaker, but not from the shocks. I feel bloody weird; that stuff we inhaled seems to be everywhere, but there's something else I can't quite figure out. They took my jacket, so don't rely on the beeping anymore. Just get me out of here; I'm dying for a cigarette and a pint," Michael responded.

A spark of concern rumbled within me. My sixth sense, learned and trusted, was back. Left me on edge, continuously looking over my shoulder. Andrew and I hid behind the bushes to the left of the house's wing. My gut told me that if we entered that house, there was no guarantee we'd leave—certainly not conscious.

Considering our options, I surveyed the gravel gutter line. The lower part of the house caught my attention; it didn't conform to typical construction practices. Michael had mentioned being in a basement, and some farmhouses like this one often had low windows. If the previous horrors I had experienced were any sign, storm doors could hide on the floor. We needed to determine the exact location without alerting the guards.

"Skip, we can't risk simply barging in," I said, conveying my concerns.

"I smell it too, lad. Lead the way; I'll follow," Andrew responded.

Everything appeared red as I assessed the heat patterns. Any temperature changes stood out, particularly the heat escaping the property. Michael's electroshocks had me speculating that a significant amount of power was used with accompanying wiring and cabling. The limited number of guards showed confidence in fortifying the run-down hellhole.

We followed a pipe that ran thirty feet to the left. The heat emanating from it was unmistakable. Michael was likely sweating profusely, intensifying the temperature even more. The house had more spots of heat leakage than a sieve rising into the air. I sought the area with the highest concentration, hoping to find a vent, window, or door.

"Michael, if you can hear me, hum or talk to your friend there. You're quite good at that," I suggested.

"Just wait. Karma is a bitch. There's glass high behind me; I don't know if you can get in," Michael replied.

"It may come down to you forcing your way free, and we'll drag you out because I sense we won't have the chance to leave once we're inside," I explained.

"I'll try it. The leather restraints smell weird; they might also weaken me," Michael said.

"Just picture that ice-cold pint. I'm sure it'll motivate him," I encouraged him.

"Picturing a pint—and many other things—has kept me going, matey. I'm strapped to a metal grid rigged with jumper cables and connected to some huge bloody batteries," Michael shared.

"In that case, hold on tight, old man. We're not far away," I reassured him.

The wing turned north, and right on cue, the humming began. I also picked up the rumbles of electricity. Michael wasn't exaggerating; it sounded like a feral beast. It's a bit like the old git we were trying to rescue. We had no plan and no idea of the surprises that awaited us. Our goal was simple: get Michael out alive so we could fight another day.

Sixty feet north and kissing the floor, I found myself face-to-face with a pane of glass. Sure enough, it was embedded with chicken wire, and I couldn't see a latch. The window was two and a half feet long and two feet wide. If he breathed in, we could pull him through.

"Georgie lad, I don't like this. Feels too straightforward," Andrew said, making me question if it was truly straightforward. Yes, it's guarded by the three wise men, but a house littered with a debilitating substance is hardly a cakewalk. I got what he meant, though. All this trouble for what? Was that shoe drop a false alarm, and the real one was yet to come? I couldn't shake that sickly pit in my stomach.

"I wouldn't say it's straightforward. Maybe the calm before the storm," I replied.

"Okay, genius, what are you suggesting?"

"We need to get him out, but he has company."

The gap around the edge of the window was hardly visible. The rumbles of electricity threw off any chance of listening for CCTV cameras. Nothing was visible, but there was too much that could conceal them. Our window of opportunity was almost non-existent.

'Michael, how's that strength coming along?'

'I'm okay, but my new wife here isn't easy for a divorce. He's hanging that close. He may as well be humping my leg.'

'You move fast, you smooth operator. I'm afraid Skip and I can be jealous fuckers, so you're going to have to break up unpleasantly.'

'Awww, I didn't know you cared. There's leeway on the straps; I need the opportunity.'

'You tall enough? I can't send for a stepladder, you know.'

'Piss off.'

Michael jumped and pounded against the window. Whatever this was, it had to be some supernatural rubbish. My claws tingled, and it felt off. I dug deep, and fire brewed, tearing through my veins. It was going to take everything I had. My eyes turned blood red, with a mist of blackness around the edge.

My body shook. It was coming loose, but the house had more to it than met the eye. Andrew was talking up a storm, and voices were getting raised. Time was running out for all of us. With one final yank, the window came flying off. I landed in a dusty heap, spraying a blueberry cloud. That fruity smell again. I'd inhaled a fair chunk and felt like a weight had been dropped on my chest. My energy was suddenly zapped.

Michael was jumping up and down. I crawled to the window. That smell was riding me hard. I threw an arm through to grip Michael's arm. The tank was all but empty. Michael used my arm as a rope, and his sweaty face finally appeared. With one last exhausted and desperate surge, I yanked Michael through.

"Georgie, Georgie, you okay?"

"The wood or window was laced with something. It drained me instantly."

Michael dragged himself up before pulling me to my feet. I stumbled, barely upright, but we had to get a move on. My energy tapped against the red, running on fumes without knowing how long I would feel this way. All I could do was direct while Michael kept me moving.

'Skip, we're moving.'

I didn't hear anything back. All we had now been hope. My eyes and ears were working overtime while Michael had me moving like a puppet. We made it to the fence line, but still no sign or sound of Andrew. There was no jumping for me. I leaned forward and let gravity do the rest. As Michael landed on his feet, I slumped on my back, gasping for breath.

"At least buy me dinner first," I said as Michael rooted for the car keys in my pocket.

"Come on, wise guy."

The car door flew open, and I crawled into the back seat, relieved to feel the door slam shut. Michael had the car purring quickly, but still no sign of Andrew. The clock thumped in my ears. My pulse was a bass drum.

Voices were still raised in the distance, with a flirted background of snapping twigs and frosty grass crunching. It could've been rabbits or several animals living in the wild, but my prayers were for someone else. Silence fell between Michael and me. Our anticipation and fear were at their peak. Loud stomps beat a path in our direction. Who was it going to be? Friend or foe?

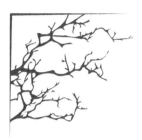

19

SAMARITANS

That's what I heard. Distant, heavy breathing cut through the air, doing little to ease my panic as I lay recovering. That window had done a number on me, and I couldn't figure out how. There was so much about my condition that needed exploring. I kept returning to the same thought, 'the devil was in the details.' Never has a truer phrase been said that applies to many things.

It was the details of things like Wolfsbane that I needed to know, so we'd all be safeguarded from surprises. We'd overcome two already tonight, and I wasn't ready for a third. My lungs were scorched from the 'bane.' Whatever was laced throughout that house left me an energy-less wreck.

Michael mentioned a strange smell from the restraints that had him weakened, and we'd smelt the berries when we first arrived. So what could be ingrained in wood and screw over a shapeshifter?

Ellena more than likely had the answers in her towers of books, but she wasn't on hand. Her smarts hooked me as much as her personality and beauty. So level-headed and afraid of nothing, yet seemed to know a little of everything. Between her and Mr Nicholls, we relied on them to find tangible evidence from the fingertip and hair samples. Not to mention a solution to stabilise the rapidly decomposing bodies. No pressure there, then.

I knew deep down she had it all in hand and needed a win since the bag idea didn't get off the starting line. Our trust in them focusing on those details meant we could play 'Save the Shapeshifter.' Now, a bedraggled Michael and a fight-less me were on tenterhooks, hoping Andrew was doing all the stampeding. If not, we were about to be in more trouble. Neither fit to tear a paper bag nor wrestle with 'the stooges.'

Michael revved a little to keep our beast purring at the ready. It was in gear with the passenger window open in case Andrew fancied a stuntman-style jump through it on the move. Whether he'd squeeze his bulky frame all the way was another story. The stomps were close. I held my breath as a rush of adrenaline came storming through on the breeze. The door flew open, and Michael lurched against the door pillar, squeezing himself as far away as possible. I bolted upright, neatly hitting my head on the roof lining.

"Peddle to the metal, Mickey boy."

Andrew slumped into his seat, a panting mess, his door thumping after him. Michael floored it, rocking me around in the seat. I pulled myself up enough to look through my window. I expected to see two, maybe three, hooded goons in suits. Nothing. Tall trees, the farm sign, and darkness greeted my gaze. I slithered away to the middle of my seat, stumped for answers and relieved.

The case had uncovered another dimension of trouble to deal with and a new player to the game. Maybe even an old one. And that scared me a little. If they were restarting anything like they did to me as a child, then a world of pain awaited us. Assuming 'they' were the same. Or ever stopped. Something about that black liquid that oozed from Sally's eye, and those hoods seemed to tie together with their knowledge of Wolfsbane and me.

I looked at Michael through his mirror, feeling a little paranoid. My eyes fixed on the edges of his, hoping I wouldn't see leaky black fluid. They had an hour on us before I was found at the warehouse, then the time it took to get to the farm. Michael would've been out cold a while before the shock treatment. So, I guessed the dots in my brain were trying to connect, 'what did they do to Michael?' and 'How long before we noticed?'

He seemed normal, or at least as normal as ever. I had to weigh up everything that had happened and anticipate what could come if we could get ahead of the chaos. That meant not taking anything for granted, starting with Michael's health and accounting for anything he'd experienced that he could remember.

"Everything ok, skip?"

"For now, lad, but that was blooming weird," Andrew spun in his seat with a worried look I'd rarely seen. Doing little to settle my doubts.

"Did you pick up on anything else?"

"Well, lad, if they were desperate to keep the old dog here. They had a funny way of showing it,"

"What do you mean?"

"I hardly had to sprint, if you know what I mean? They feigned the effort; they now know we have the relic back. I don't hear screeching tires, do you?"

He was right; I heard nothing. All the noise had been Andrew's efforts, and me getting wrapped up in my struggles. They drew guns, but no shots were fired, and it wouldn't have taken a genius to put two and two together.

Meanwhile, Michael still had his foot down. The sound of our engine screaming for dear life vibrated through the bonnet. He wanted to put as much distance between them and us as possible or was in a daze, dwelling on something.

"The whole thing stinks, Georgie," Michael finally spoke up. I filtered through the fear in his voice, even though he tried to hide it.

"I agree, for people that wanted me to make it all disappear. They seemed to be doing everything arse upwards. Now Michael, how was it?"

"How was what?"

"BEING PROBED BY ALIENS?"

"By what now?"

"Probed by aliens. Didn't you figure that part out?"

"Piss off,"

"Seriously, why do you think we were desperate to get you back? That taste you have at the back of your throat?"

"Yeah?"

"What do you think that is? Think what probing happened there." I watched Michael's face drop. I tried to wind him up and put him at ease before the hard questions.

"Fuck off,"

"I saw how you were walking; it must've been bad." I couldn't hold back the laughter any longer; Michael looked like he was about to cry.

"Not funny, you bastard, had me going for a minute there,"

"I know. It was too easy, so what do you remember?"

"I... I was out. Could feel the first few minutes being bundled into their car, then it goes blank for a while,"

"Then what?"

"I came to after a series of bends and being thrown around. Not fully, just enough for voices. What was stranger was none of them used names, just colours instead,"

Using code names with the hoods made me think they wanted to keep their identity safe from outsiders, guests, and each other. Quite smart, really. Then nobody could get each other in trouble. It raised another point: trust or a lack of it. There didn't appear to be any.

"Did you hear anything?"

"Only that plan had changed, with an opportunity too good to miss. Something along the lines of lighting the match and watching it all burn,"

I dropped back into my chair, deep in thought and facing the real prospect with jokes aside. Something very real could've happened to Michael. Why torture him in the first place? They didn't ask him anything that Michael could recall. Not that he knew anything. That man's head could be emptier than a whorehouse on Sundays at the best of times. What would he have to give them?

The house may have been used with other intentions, but something else piqued their interest, and my bet is Michael. Maybe his blood. We didn't know who had mine yet or if it would rear its head. Taking Michael's could spice up the stakes if they were in the habit of creating serial killing clouds of black smoke. I could still feel the intrusiveness of having my organs squeezed, not to mention the siphoning of bodies.

"Did you feel any needles or anything?" I said, trying not to worry Michael any more than his heart was already beating.

"What's this, aliens injecting me with LSD?"

"I'm serious, Michael. We need to know if they did anything to you?"

"He's right, Mickey. They had the time, and we have no idea how dangerous these people are," Andrew joined in to help emphasise our fears.

"Christ, you two. Like the bloody Samaritans. No, nothing happened. Nothing that I'm aware of. Now, can we get home? I'm so done with this night."

Michael's words echoed how everyone was feeling. Andrew had slumped against the pillar to close his eyes for a few. I could feel my energy levels slowly returning, but not quite right. My head perched on the headrest with the perfect view of Michael's face. I wasn't taking any chances until he proved, without a doubt, that he was fine.

I kept picturing black goo streaming from his eyes. Michael's recapture felt too easy, and the other shoe hadn't dropped yet. My sixth sense was telling me a sting in the tail was coming. The rest of the journey was spent in silence. I felt the throttle easing, meaning so was Michael.

My eyes were fighting to stay open, and I was losing. Road lights had become a blur until we finally slowed to a stop outside the station. Our timing couldn't be more perfect. Ellena was talking to Mr Nicholls in the yard—a welcomed sight after an awful night.

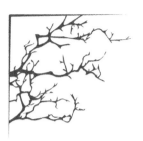

20

FILLED WITH PAIN

The night was pitch black, the full moon casting an eerie glow over everything. A chilling breeze swept through the air, causing the temperature to plummet. The whistling wind teased the tiny hairs on my neck, and my throat, dry from suppressing a swallow, ached since the warehouse incident.

The persistent smell clung to me, an enigma I couldn't shake. Downplaying it to others, I didn't want to worry them. Inhaling the essence ingrained in the house intensified the effects, lingering longer. I needed to unravel the secrets within the frail bundle of old timber.

A seemingly fragile place had the resilience of bricks and mortar. So, I returned. The grass crunched beneath my feet, liberating. The crackling frost melted against my warm soles, sending goosebumps across my skin. I passed the goon squad, and the parked Range Rover.

On a mission, I headed left before darting north. Eyes locked on the window, a blueberry glow hypnotised. The scent permeated the air. My claws slid forward, and my body reacted to danger. I wasn't scared, just attuned. A distant scream echoed from the other side of the window. Someone in trouble. The heat signature was off the scale, the hottest point of the house.

The screams grew louder, indicating pain. I had to save them, had to remove the window. Claws are already out, and I jammed them in the gap. The glow intensified as tingles raced through my tips. Glass creaked as I pulled, widening the gap. Heat blazed through with a tortured scream. A woman, her heartbeat pounding in my ears too fast.

Heat turned to flames flickering through the crevice. Embers bounced dangerously close to my face. I had to act before it was too late. The scream felt like nails dragging across my skin. Tears pooled in the corner of my eye. I felt their pain, their agony, pulling with every fibre until it finally gave way.

Thrown back onto the crisp grass, the window landed, unleashing a whirl-wind of flames.

A gap appeared, and I could see through. The woman was Ellena, flames surrounding her. Strapped to a metal rack alive with electricity, she screamed for help. Weak and helpless, the gas from the window drained me. Eyes closed, I tried to dig deep. A ping opened, and Ellena was no longer on the rack.

No, she was climbing out the window, not alone. Flames continued as she came through, staying on all fours. Her screams grated down my spine. I couldn't move. I felt paralysed with fear. Ellena was a torched mess, but the bigger surprise was Michael. Part-shifted, a yellow glow outlined him, an electric fox. A tail was visible, his eyes brighter than ever, both heading to-ward me, and I had nowhere to go. Powerless and scared, Ellena felt different, even through her screams.

'Look what you've done, Georgie,' Ellena screeched, piercing my eardrums.

'Yeah, Georgie. Look what it costs to be part of your inner circle. Look what you've done to us. Look what you've done to us. You have ruined us. You have ruined us. You have ruined us.'

BOTH CRIED IN UNISON, moving closer. The heat and electricity con-sumed everything, closer and closer. It's too close. Both are over me, and my skin begins to burn. It's agony. Closer and closer until they're smothering me...

'7 AM ON 2ND NOVEMBER,'

'Aaarrrrrggghhhh,' I woke in a pool of sweat and blood. Sat upright, the clock read 7 am, the sky still shadowed. White bedsheets clung to clammy skin, more blood than usual mixed with dirt and leaves. The grit was between my toes and all over the soles. Was the dream real? Did it happen? I could still feel the crisp, frosty grass; its lingering melting against my skin felt too present. My head pounded with the aftereffects of a hangover from hell.

I'd barely slept a few hours, but the gas effect lingered in my lungs. I could taste it, and my lack of energy surprised me. Not recovering well scared me. What was ingrained in that wood? I had to find out. Did I subconsciously return? Surely, I wouldn't have, but the dream felt vivid.

The image of a burning Ellena and an electrified part-shifted werefox Michael haunted me. A battle raged within me, a warning or a glimpse of the future? My head spun, scenarios swirling, focusing on the possibility the rack wasn't for torture but to ignite something in Michael: an evolution, a dangerous insight into what awaited.

Another kidnapping for him. How long until it's one too many? We needed him, but my fears lingered. Checking on him, scraping off dried debris, would be my next move after a shower. Books from the library held potential answers. I needed Ellena's knowledge, but we hadn't talked. Deathly tired, I wanted to ease her worries. I planned to tell her about us, honest and open.

Another thing I liked about her. She doesn't pry, even if her instinct is to do the opposite. Instead, she waits. It had been a whirlwind few days, and Michael, alone with his thoughts, worried me. My piss-taking might've added to his overnight analysis. It was harmless, meant to ease tension, but it could've done the opposite. What if he decided to return to Brentwood for that farm and answers? Whatever happened in that missing hour needed answers.

Procrastination ended; I flung off the covers, ready for a shower. A message, 'revenge,' scrawled in blood and dirt, puzzled me. Why would I write it in my sleep? The dream and message tangled my thoughts. Looking at my face in the steamed-up mirror in the bathroom, I saw it again—a message, brief but in the steam. My brain was cooked, about to shake it off, when the house phone rang.

'Who could be calling me this early, other than work?' I thought, grabbing the receiver, praying it wasn't another dead body.

"Hello?"

"Thank God you answered, matey."

"What's wrong, Michael?"

"It was awful. I had a dream... A bad dream," I pulled the handset away, feeling the sickly swirl again. My experiences isolated Michael's differences.

"The farm?"

"How did you guess?" Surprise was heavy in Michael's voice.

"I...I... Erm... Were you in a room and broke out a window?"

"Stop it right now, Georgie. I'm not liking what you're saying."

"Ellena was there, too. Strapped to a rack and getting electrocuted. You were different."

"I was glowing, and everything was on fire. I did it."

"We had the same dream. I heard screaming and broke the window again. You both came at me screaming."

"We were blaming you... That's not what we think, you know that, right?" "I know, but why are we having the same dream?" A thought crept into my mind, but I held back.

"Even worse, mate, I woke to a message written in blood-"

"Revenge."

"Exactly. You too? This can't be a lucky coincidence; there has to be something far more supernaturally spooky than that. The shit is too weird." "Hear me out. What if when that black cloud messed with our insides, and we could hear their pain, there's a subconscious imprint on us? Like their mission or motive and where we went were connected. The dream to scare us and the word to tie it together?"

"What about the blood and dirt?" No answer, just fear of hurting someone. An 'alpha-beta' connection?

"I would say go back, matey, but a part of me is saying to stay the fuck away."

"We must. The only way to be sure."

"I'm. Bringing precautions though, matey," Michael said, excitement in his voice. Should I be worried? Probably. Yet, his confidence after last night was comforting. I felt the same as always, full of trepidation. Who goes back to the scene of torture? Unless they're suicidal werewolves—detectives, too. Completely wrong, but we needed answers. Why the same nightmare?

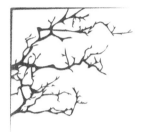

21

DAYLIGHT

Brentwood looked more picturesque in the daylight. Winding country roads from the night before now offered scenic views of hills stretching as far as the eye could see, unencumbered by streetlights. The landscape was composed mostly of farms spaced far back from the roads on vast expanses of green open spaces. Scattered outbuildings provided hiding spots, making it easy for someone to escape nefarious activities—a potential murderer's paradise. We agreed to meet half a mile away to discuss our plan or make progress towards one.

As I approached, Michael was pacing back and forth, a tray of coffee in his hands. Stepping into the early morning breeze, I inhaled the refreshing scent of clean air, unspoiled by city fumes. It was invigorating, like a blanket of cut grass wrapped around me. I silently thanked my luck that Michael hadn't yet polluted the air with his cigarettes.

When I first contemplated stopping, the sense of safety inside my car almost prompted me to make a U-turn—no sign of danger—no bloodstains, no cryptic tapes. The car felt like a sanctuary, shielding me from the madness that permeated my life.

It felt like one big supernatural wild goose chase. Sally Turnage's background story might hold the missing pieces to connect the dots. Her father had been odd and controlling, and towards the end, he became skittish and suspicious. What if her father had served as the go-between? What if he had used his daughter and her friends as sacrificial lambs, luring them with the pretext of a party? They would all be drugged, with the masks inducing hallucinations until they were picked off one by one. The other terrible things that happened could have served as a smokescreen for their secret intentions.

They were experimented on and manipulated, resulting in sudden deaths, a missing person presumed dead, and even suicide. Something said by that enigmatic cloud resonated with me, "Maybe living isn't on the menu, but you could be." What if the "dead" girls weren't dead anymore? What if they sought revenge on everyone who had toyed with them? Perhaps that was the real reason behind our shared dream. We needed to find the posh house where it all took place.

"Hey, old man, are you okay?" I called out to Michael as I approached.

"We've got coffee, so yeah," he replied, holding a much-needed cup.

"I think I have a way that might give us a lead. But it would require Locke to help with a warrant," I informed him.

"Ooh, looks like the hamster has been running on its wheel. Do tell," Michael said with a smile, passing me the coffee.

"I suggest looking into Mr Turnage's financials, searching for large transfers and their origins. I believe he sold out his daughter and her friends," I explained, receiving a nod of approval from Michael. As much as we face supernatural phenomena, we remember we are detectives first. We had to approach things by the book until circumstances forced us to deviate.

"That being said, what precautions did you take?" I asked Michael.

Michael paused, his hamster spinning now. A little smirk had me thinking the precautions weren't necessarily by the book. As well-seasoned as Michael is, I still can't get used to how he likes to colour outside the lines. He looked at me, then at his car's boot, and then at me again before taking a cautious view of the road. The boot lid popped open with a quick click of his key fob.

I was speechless. Michael had a mobile armoury mixed with other boxes containing stuff I couldn't identify besides a strange smell. He flipped the lid off one box to reveal army-green gas masks with a wide-fronted viewing space. The mere glimpse of them had me feeling claustrophobic. The idea of something so cumbersome pressed close to my face and messing with my breathing wasn't appealing. Yet, putting up with headgear like that would be a small price to pay to save myself from inhaling that mysterious purple-blue gas.

"What in God's name?"

"Matey, let's call it lessons learned. I saw what that did to you and didn't feel much better. My dream was bothering me, so I made a call to another friend who owed me a favour. Many favours."

"Another friend? You're right, though. We do not know what that stuff was. Wolfsbane is one thing, but the other felt stronger."

Getting a closer look, I noticed nebulisers, and an idea came to mind. Nebulisers are used to inhale medication to clear the airways or treat infections. What if we could reverse-engineer the gases we'd come into contact with and create a way to treat the symptoms quickly? Perhaps Ellena could add it to her to-do list.

"Yeah, I've been thinking, matey. If this is our lives now, dealing with the dark crap people don't see, then we need measures to keep us from pushing up daisies other than sharp claws and fangs. Not to mention, protect the ones with us who aren't blessed to need a manicure."

Michael and I seemed more on the same wavelength by the day. Whether it was an 'Alpha to Beta' thing, I didn't know, but it could strengthen us. My only surprise was Michael hadn't rolled out the skipper, too. We chugged back our coffees. Mine left a sting on the way, but it was soon done, and we were ready to go when I picked up on a distinct smell. Two, but one slightly masked the other. And it brought my nightmares flooding back, including the one from last night. Fire. The other was death.

The smell was getting stronger by the second, and the cloudy blue sky was painted charcoal, grey, and black. Adding insult to injury, the burning appeared to be coming from the direction of the farm. Only I couldn't pinpoint the source of the death stink or whether it was the same as the other that tormented us in the lorry yesterday, or the bodies of the goon squad.

"Hey, do you smell that, right?" I said, grabbing Michael's attention.

"I am now. My senses have been up the creek since last night."

"Did you inhale much gas other than the wolfsbane?"

"Not really."

Michael threw me. My throat and lungs weren't in top form, but my sense of smell hadn't been affected. It seemed better than usual. So what had interfered with Michael's? We strolled toward the white fence line, a good distance from the entrance. Through breaks in the bushes, I could already see the flashing blue and red lights of fire engines. Judging by the smoke, the fire was almost out.

I was picking up too many heartbeats to simply stroll to the front door. If our suspicions were right, the house had been torched. We didn't know how that would help with what's ingrained in the wood.

"Michael, we're gonna have to approach from here," I said, pointing to the fence that would take us through a flurry of trees before coming up near the left wing of the house, far away from the chaos. I'd be kidding myself if I didn't acknowledge that the situation had taken a drastic turn and felt off.

The 'off' brought me back to last night's nightmare and how Michael set the place ablaze. I could see Michael was dwelling on that point, too.

Michael followed my lead like an obedient puppy. We crouched, keeping our heads just tipping above the bush line. There were two engines, an ambulance, police units, and a coroner's vehicle, all grouped near the front. The black Range Rover had been torched, too. Either somebody had cleaned up, or Michael and I had been here during the night.

"Oh my God."

"What's wrong, matey?"

I left Michael hanging because I was trying to count. I tried to make sense of the numbers while hoping it wasn't a hallucination. Even if it meant they were back with a bang. They kept moving and staying cautiously low, making it hard. There were at least one hundred ghosts, maybe more. Whatever had taken place in this location must have trapped them, too.

A charred black frame stood where the house once did, and in the face, there was no point in carrying on. However, the loose ends were bothering me. If the structure was what I thought, the basement could still be intact, at least enough to see what we could glean from the mess. I had to know we hadn't caused this. We were sleeping and not sleeping.

At worst, I hoped we had just entered a state of flux between shifts nearing the full moon and had sleepwalked. It could account for the muddy footprints, but not the bloodstains. We had to be cautious because a purple-blue tinge lingered on the edge of the black smoke in the sky.

"Just keep low. We need to search for another entrance to the basement," I said.

"There are bloody ghosts, aren't there?" said Michael, wrinkling his forehead. I could hear his heart rate increasing. Ghosts were the one thing Michael truly didn't like. I wasn't a fan either, but we had to press on.

"Yeah, one or two," I replied, withholding the full truth to avoid worrying him further.

We moved slowly and quietly, scanning the area with my enhanced senses, looking for heat signatures in case it was just a normal person trying to cover something up. Our initial path was dead, but we stayed off the radar. The more I observed, the more it seemed unlikely that we had caused all this. We must have picked up a connection that distorted our fears.

The north section of the house was also destroyed. Among the dirt, I could still see a ripped-off window with no space left for it to fit. I kept one eye focused ahead and the other on Michael. The smell of death grew stronger, mingling with the mix of scents. It was the same smell as in the lorry last night.

"It's here," I said, trying to narrow down the location.

"I sense it too, but I don't know. My thoughts have shifted back to us being connected since the confrontation. And how could we gain something from them? They found this location through us. If true, this job could become even harder to solve."

Fifty feet to the left of the building, I could see an outline on the ground—a large square, a set of storm doors surrounded by bushes. It held small traces of heat, but thankfully not the berry-coloured lining. The closer we got, the stronger the aura of death and fear. It emanated mostly from around the doors.

We cautiously approached, scanning the surroundings and ensuring it was safe. A feeling of foreboding weighed heavily. It bothered me that not only had everything been burned down, and Michael had been kidnapped, but also that this place had gone unnoticed. Yes, Brentwood seemed quite rural, but flying under the radar seemed to be a pattern.

I flung the doors open, causing Michael and me to jump backwards. A revolting stench hit us, making me gag. We had unleashed a torrent of stomach-churning death. Michael threw me a mask, and my worst fears were about to come true. Strapping it onto my face felt like a layer of polythene. Still, it successfully blocked the smell and made breathing easier.

A ladder led downward into a dimly lit space. We didn't have torches, but our eyes adjusted to the red hues. The ladder looked old and fragile, and the floor was tainted with dried blood that had resisted cleaning. As we descended, the first section of the wall came into view. I could see faded diagrams and technical notes that only Ellena would understand. If I was seeing it correctly, they looked like examples of experiments.

Just as both Michael and I landed on the floor, a wave of terror washed over me. Déjà vu. The feeling of that horrifying basement from my childhood. I felt my breath cut short, my mask steaming up, and the red surroundings intensifying. Sensing my panic, Michael grabbed my arm.

"Are you okay?"

"I can't breathe," I said.

"It's the basement. Just picture Ellena and focus on how she grounds you," he advised.

He was right. I closed my eyes, picturing Ellena's calming presence, and remembered how she made it acceptable to be different, to be okay with being a beast. The panic subsided, but the sense of shifting remained. My instincts were on high alert. As we stepped forward, a roaring wind barrelled towards us, swirling around and through us before exiting the opening. It was a black cloud of death. They had been here.

Another pattern was emerging. We were always late for the party, only finding the bodies. For once, it would be a welcome change to beat 'death' to the punch. Whatever those girls had become or were transformed into, they had destroyed everything in their path. And all because we had already been here, they knew where to find us.

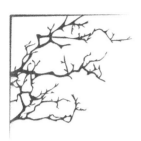

22

GRIMY TUNNEL

Fear clung to me like a shadow in a grimy tunnel instead of a spooky basement. The slimy grey concrete surrounded us, emitting a faint dampness that testified to the effort invested in its construction, its mysterious length stretching into the unknown.

With each step, the stench intensified, and my apprehension grew. Regret nibbled at me for suggesting this detour. However, amidst the gloom, a silver lining: a nightmarish dream had steered us right, leaving the house above in ruins. My attention returned to the dripping walls, wondering about their stability, unsure if they'd collapse at any moment.

Scattered old newspaper articles and book pages discussed worldwide creature sightings, from the Yeti to the Loch Ness Monster. It seemed they sought the stranger; the more enigmatic, the better.

Continuing might not have been the wisest use of our time. Still, curiosity egged us on, even if it meant losing radio contact. Turning a corner, we confronted the horror behind the stench. Metal mesh gates enclosed cages and towering pens. To the right, at least seven pens were filled with old bodily fluids and faeces. More pens ahead still held people, but sadly, they were all dead. One or two had been burned beyond recognition, invoking memories of last night's dream—Ellena's skin peeling through the flames, Michael suffering as well.

Another row of seven pens extended into a wide-open space. All the bodies had been dead for some time, decomposing and left to rot. They were possibly failed experiments, but what were the people here trying to create? Michael was speechless, and I didn't bring up the topic, but he could have easily been one of them. I noticed the older man shedding a tear, even through the mask.

None of the pens had names or labels, so we remained clueless about who or what they held. But up ahead was a different story. The open space resembled a mix between a hospital operating theatre and a library, the floor marred by the residue of the death cloud. Two more bodies lay in the room, both still wearing hoods. They would have been my next focus until I noticed a dim yellow glow illuminating the back wall.

Without thinking, I instinctively stepped back as old images flooded my mind. Michael hadn't noticed it yet; instead, he looked at me. My focus became a blend of curiosity and a darker fear I hadn't experienced since the childhood flashback to the chains. And at that moment, that's exactly what I heard—the sound of chains.

One haunting clang after another, sending chills rippling through my body. My sense of intrigue triumphed over the fear, and I grasped Michael's arm, guiding him across the stone floor as I marched forward.

The light was painted across a large board filled with information, particularly a five-foot square image of the 'Devil's Circle' emblem. However, it wasn't the familiar version we were accustomed to seeing; instead, it depicted an ancient-looking stone tablet.

The tablet appeared sandstone in colour and bore a carved depiction of a serpent in a circle with a forked tail piercing through its head. Whether the image's size accurately represented the real-life tablet was uncertain.

The first article that caught our attention was dated nearly a hundred years back: "1879 - Coal miners in Norfolk uncovered an ancient relic thought to have been buried in the mines for centuries. Symbolically, it's believed to be linked to witchcraft and the devil in the 14th and 15th centuries."

"Michael, are you getting all this?"

"Why the hell do you think I'm making notes? This is fucking." Michael's disbelief resonated with mine. Crazy was the easiest way to describe it.

So, the people deeply involved in the recent and possibly long-standing sinister activities worship an ancient relic and commit crimes in its name. Other articles discussed increased spooky sightings and other strange phenomena in the same area from that year until the tablet's disappearance in 1929.

"We are truly dealing with a bunch of deluded fuckers, aren't we?" I exclaimed.

"Yeah, but the same can be said about Stonehenge and druids, not to mention all the other creepy crap around the world," Michael replied.

"True, but you'd have to be drunk off your tits to put chunks of rock like that in a field. I reckon they were prone to sampling too much of their..." Michael burst out laughing, and I couldn't help but chuckle.

A part of me knew that if these people possessed the stone and could accomplish even a fraction of what it claimed, we could be in serious trouble with the help of their experiments. I wouldn't have believed the idea of claws and fangs a while ago.

Meanwhile, Michael continued making notes while I grappled with the next steps. We had two options: either hand over the information about the tunnels to the locals or let them decide whether to make it public or quietly walk away as we entered. Suppose they discovered the tunnels, then good for them. If they didn't, perhaps it could be for the best.

Realistically, it was most likely the latter scenario. The world wasn't ready for half the things happening lately. Fuelling the fire with conspiracy theories and abundant supernatural phenomena could easily lead to chaos. Even with our masks on, the smell of death overwhelmed our senses, especially near the two bodies on the floor.

The bodies appeared relatively fresh in time but had been subjected to intense heat. Any normal person could tell, but I sensed they had been cooked from the inside out. It didn't stop me from wanting to remove their hoods, but I quickly retracted the thought when I glimpsed their hands.

The flesh was raw, bubbling, and cracked. I could only imagine their faces were the same; my constitution wasn't prepared to witness that. As my head was crouched at table height, I noticed a loose note hanging from a book, comprising scribbles mentioning DNA sequencing from blood and merging blockchains within a sequence. It was a bit too scientific for my comprehension, but it piqued my curiosity and reinforced my suspicion of experimentation.

Michael was absorbed in his research, diligently working through various books and papers. If time were on our side, there would be a wealth of information to glean from.

"Oh crap," Michael suddenly exclaimed from over my left shoulder. I turned to see him tugging on some books on a shelf, resulting in a loud click.

"What have you done now?" I asked, feeling a surge of static electricity prickling my skin and causing my hair to stand on end.

I could hear a whooshing noise that reminded me of the approaching black cloud. Only this time, it seemed to concentrate on the perimeter of the ceiling where it met the wall. It slowly built momentum, and I noticed vents on the wall. The grills opened.

"Gas," I stated, a hint of panic creeping into my voice.

The first wisps of gas drifted through, the same purple-blue colour we had encountered at the window, and soon, a cloud gathered. We were trapped in a death trap, and I heard a loud bang in the distance—the sound of the tunnel doors slamming shut.

"We have to get out, matey," I said urgently.

"I was thinking the same thing, but the doors just closed," Michael replied, his voice brimming with concern.

The wave of gas grew stronger, permeating even through our masks. It felt like shards of glass scraping down my throat. Michael clutched a handful of papers, and we were about to run for it when I spotted a small map. It displayed a combination of blue and yellow dots scattered across the United Kingdom. I didn't have time to examine it, as the case had already been filled with dots. What harm could a few more dots do?

With the wave of gas intensifying, I realised we had to act quickly. Our masks may have offered some protection, but it wasn't enough. We needed to escape. Michael and I sprinted toward the doors, leaving a trail of death in our wake—a pattern that showed no sign of changing soon. I didn't hesitate. Springing off my right foot, I threw myself against the doors, hoping to force them open.

But they remained stubbornly shut. However, a small crack appeared, allowing glimpses of the menacing cloud to seep through. Michael followed suit, delivering his forceful blow, but the doors held strong. They were nothing more than plain old oak, or so I thought.

My knuckles told a different story. They appeared severely bruised, and the veins pulsated with a disturbing black hue. Each throb weakened me further. It would take both of us to break free.

"Michael, we both need to do it. Check your knuckles. The doors were tough to open, but being here has made us weaker somehow," I explained as panic welled inside me. Then I noticed the support beams scattered throughout the room. They were made of the same wood.

We both took a few steps back, realisation dawning upon us. The gas continued to spread and drift toward us. We exchanged a quick nod, and then we ran. Charging forward, we crashed against the doors simultaneously, breaking through to the open air beyond.

My hands throbbed with pain, heavily bruised from the impact, and the veins remained an unnatural black. We were safe, for now. But the list of dots that needed connecting had grown even longer.

At least we had gained some valuable information. Exhausted, Michael and I slumped in the grass. I couldn't help but notice the familiar feel of the grass beneath me, reminding me of last night. It was still early morning, and we had already escaped another nightmare.

No one was in sight, but there was still a lot of activity near the front of the property that we wanted to steer clear of. Ripping off our masks, I grabbed Michael's arm and pulled him to his feet. As our hands brushed against each other, a spark passed between us. It was no ordinary static electricity—flashes of yellow confirmed it.

My mind drifted back to the dream, and I saw a fox-like shape formed by the yellow lines surrounding Michael. He must have seen the concern on my face, but whether he noticed the strange occurrence or ignored it, I didn't know.

"Are you okay, Georgie?" Michael asked, genuine concern etched on his face.

"Er, yeah. We need to stay low and quiet, keep on making progress and try to get in touch with Locke," I replied, attempting to keep my voice steady and my worry hidden. There was more on my mind than what we had just witnessed. Putting the dots together presented us with yet another problem that could prove immense.

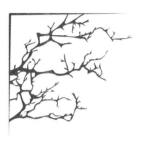

23

KIDNAPPED

"So, let me get this straight. In your infinite wisdom, you two thought it would be a great idea to return to where Michael was found after being kidnapped. All based on a crazy shared dream,"

"Yes, guvnor,"

"Did you not think hundreds of people could be there this time? Or remember how lucky you were the first time. For Christ's sake, Georgie, the wolfsbane dam nearly wiped you out,"

I couldn't argue with Locke's point. In hindsight, we were rash with a heightened sense of self. That nightmare really messed with us, and the fact we had the same one made it all the more important. Especially as I can't shake the worry something happened to Michael. That static rumbled off him the same as I saw.

"Sir, it was so much more than that—too many unanswered questions. Like what the hell is, things like wolfsbane and certain woods seem to make us weaker. I don't know enough to keep everyone safe and find the bad guys,"

"There will be plenty of time for that. And I recommend looping in Ellena. She is a whizz and has more skills than meets the eye. One of the reasons I wanted her on this unit was when I thought you might be different. For now, you need to make some headway,"

'Knock knock,'

"Come in."

'Sir, a Mr Etherington called for your detectives. Apparently, he's had a change of heart,'

Alice's dad was adamant he didn't want anything to do with us, and his life had spiralled into drinking after losing his job as head of the council. So what's changed his mind? Gauging his daughter's reaction and testing her chemo signals to see if she could have anything to do with the murderous black cloud could be key. Or if Mr Etherington knew anything.

We had to balance this side of this case: the real world with real consequences and heartbreak. I looked up at ADI Locke; his heart had been beating fast throughout our conversation, and the sweat pebbles told me he was struggling to hold back but knew we didn't have the time.

He sat in his big chair, a position of power, yet he knew how powerless he was compared to us, so he was holding back to keep control. They say knowledge is power; some may say the real power, and Locke had that in abundance. Exactly how he knew what he did could be a bigger bombshell than us being werewolves.

Locke Intimated he hand-picked Ellena; was that the same for the real Wainright? It would've been nice if we had the chance to find out, but I'm now even more intrigued by Ellena's other skills. As I let thoughts of her drift through my mind for a second, the chaotic world around me fell silent. We had to move on before Mr Etherington changed his mind again. For some strange reason, I suddenly couldn't. I sat frozen in my seat as if I'd gone numb from Kanaima poisoning. I stared blankly at Locke, getting a curious expression in return. Then it happened. A short spark of an image. It's more like a mini-movie clip or memory.

It's a hallway in a house with light brown wooden floors and a dark brown carpet runner through the middle. The hallway led to a flight of black steps ahead and a doorway to the left. There's blood. I could smell the strong iron scent of blood and saw an arterial spray rain bowing across the wall. The clip was brief and unrecognisable from anywhere we'd been before.

I snapped out of it to two sets of eyes burning into my skull. Michael craned forward to rock his head in my eyeline while Locke opened his mouth with no words coming.

"Are you ok, Georgie?"

"Er.... No, not really. You know that dream we had the same. I just saw another scenario. A clip of a hallway in a house with blood sprayed over the wall,"

"Did you recognise it?" Locke broke his silence.

"No, we hadn't been there before. Or at least I hadn't,"

I checked back to Locke's face. It wasn't as open-mouthed, but enough to tell me he saw something different with me. A change of situation that has not been encountered yet.

"Georgie, your eyes changed. They turned black with a red ring around the edge as if your pupils widened. Not happened before?"

I looked away for a second, pausing to think. There had been so many occasions where something different had happened. But never eyes described that way.

"No, never."

Neither said anything for a moment. I felt like one of those 'freaks' that 'P. T. Barnham' had in his circus. More concerning was the dream that turned out to be a real fire, so it had a real meaning behind it. Now, here's this scene of blood spraying a house. Coincidences have never worked out well for us. Mr Etherington wants to speak, after all. Suddenly, I see what could only be surmised as the intro to another murder. Possibly a frenzied one. Something that has happened so far didn't track to the others in this case.

Then I remembered the state he'd been in the last time we met. He'd clearly been hitting the bottle hard. What if... No, he wouldn't... Would he? Surely he wouldn't and then call us to speak, or was it to confess? The blood I saw didn't have the same calm besides the fact that the previous ones hardly left evidence. Let alone interior decorating.

I sat and hoped it wouldn't be the case that a parent of a surviving child hadn't lost the will. He hadn't reached a point where he could only bend so much before breaking. More to the point, the change in my eyes was another 'new' for me. Was this going to be the theme now, something new every day?

"Well, let's hope it's a false alarm. But just in case, I suggest you 'blue light' it to Mr Etherington's house,"

Was Locke reading my mind? It felt that way. At least in the grand scheme of things, we shared the same worries, and he took my weird prelude vision seriously enough. A niggling worry popped into my head. What if somehow it was a misdirection? Made to see something the killer or killers wanted us to. Or residual effects from the wolfsbane and the substance engrained in the wood. That same worry made me second-guess my instincts, the sixth sense that had served me well.

'46 NEVILLE ST. SOUTH Kensington - Alice Etherington,'

We stood outside listening; the front door was shut, and nothing obvious raised alarm bells nearby. No passers-by. A few heartbeats along the terrace, and I was trying to narrow down what houses they were coming from. One glaring difference from the last time we were here was the smell of death. Not the black cloud, at least.

We neared the front door, and that unease that seemed to give me a cuddle was alive and kicking. There was one beating with the hunger for adrenaline. Only one... I immediately searched for excuses like the daughter could be out with anyone else living there. Or it was the daughter and the father, in a drunken haze, had forgotten he'd called for us and went for a walk.

Michael was the old dog of the two of us, with a million years of experience. His face looked like he'd been beaten with a trout. That told me he didn't like the situation.

Another story was whether my little party trick with the eyes had played on his mind too much. I knocked. Doing the polite thing, hoping for an anticlimax, and the worst-case scenario was a drunk father with sins to unload. The first wrap of my knuckle vibrated with slight movement. I didn't need to think twice, Michael, either. His eyes went bright yellow. My claws didn't slither this time. They flicked. No pain, no noticeable blood.

Was this another instance of my evolution? I've repeatedly stood by the saying 'the devil is in the details', and it's been said to me more recently. But it's so true. And the details were beginning to stack for me. It wasn't like I was back in school, and another spot had appeared, or I'd noticeably grown an inch taller. Which came in strange growth spurts, I might add. I had been a gangly 16-year-old, then a borderline almost by 18, before eventually settling to a more respectable rate. Michael had more than likely been the tortoise of growth. Slow and limited. No, this was a scale of strange; none of us knew what to expect.

For a second, I thought it cool to have claws on demand and perhaps no more stinging or waking to 'bloody' bed sheets. With this morning, hopefully, my last. With them out, I felt different, too. To describe isn't easy because it's not like I had a benchmark or family that could tell me what it was like to have been a pure-born werewolf. Yet, the little things had steadily been happening, and I gradually felt stronger. Spike after spike of adrenaline tore through my veins. A second wrap on the door caused it to nudge open a little.

Enough to tell us the place was insecure and saved us from having to smash the door open. The unknown situation on the other side unnerved me, and Michael wasn't much better. I carefully breezed the door open a few inches to gauge any smells on the other side. I nearly called out to announce us, which is by the book. We're taught to do that. No sooner had there been a gap to allow a rush of stale air from inside. My foot stepped backwards. Michael looked at me as if to say, 'What the hell?' but that moment told me my premonition or whatever I would call it—had come true. I smelt blood.

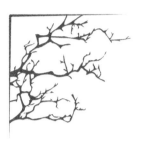

24

EMOTIONAL WRECK

A window on the other side must have been open because the relentless stink of blood kept coming. Michael bounced beside me, and I had to hold the eager puppy at bay. Beyond each whoosh, I heard metal rattling, shaking hands, and frantic breathing. It carried the stiffness of a man. Mr Etherington had done something bad. He was waiting to surrender or confess his sins. Or... A scenario we didn't want to happen.

Nobody would—a standoff between a bloke, two sheets to the wind, and two shapeshifters. The whole thing didn't make sense. I knew we could breeze in quickly and disable Mr Etherington before he did anything. But if he was as emotional as I was picking up on, whatever had happened was fuelled with pain. His daughter may have come home that night. Perhaps it had only been physical.

I shushed Michael before slowly taking a leap of faith, easing myself across the threshold. My foot creaked on the light brown wooden floors, and I stepped out of my body. I was there, yet not—a surreal cloudy detachment from my consciousness. Every detail was the same as I'd already seen before. The rainbow of blood mirrored the horror, making how I could see this before it had happened even more damning and confusing.

We were being walked like dogs on a leash, taken from one place to the next. Never be in time to make the save; only go pick up the pieces. The door near the stairs was open. Further spatters of blood painted the floor on the way in. I could hear the flexing of metal. A blade was being toyed with. My ears twitched at the sound of metal picking against the fabric.

Conflict, anger, pain, and confusion wrestled with each other in one big whirlwind of emotional chaos. There was something else, though, something different. An aroma that I couldn't place to go with the few that had appeared recently. Making me think back to Locke. Considering we'd dived into a hornet's nest, he'd been fairly okay. Yeah, he gave the obligatory bollock-ing, but that was just a flex of the 'pips' on his shoulder.

Now we were on the cusp of another storm. And it was brewing a few feet away. I didn't know why, but I suddenly had a feeling that Mr Ethering-ton or whoever wasn't human. At least not fully. If that was the case, we may have missed another detail entirely.

"Georgie, you know I'm not one to bail on a fight. But I'm sensing some-thing really not good about here," Michael whispered, perching his back against the wall before the doorway.

I felt bad for these families. I really did. If what Sally said was true and so far, it appeared to be heading that way. They had been destroyed the moment they got into that limousine. My hunch had been that despite their already modest wealth. The parents had been blinded by powerful people throwing their cash around.

"Well, pull up your big boy pants. And brace yourself because the vibe I'm getting from him is unpredictable, and something other than human is around." Michael did exactly that, stepping beside me. His foot was heavy, causing the boards to creak so much for stealth.

"I... I... can hear you. I called you. I c... can't cope,"

It was the voice of Mr Etherington, at least of the one we spoke to yester-day. He stammered, but not through drink. We were in the doorway facing a room of gloom, and blood flowed across the floor. I was getting riled up, and Michael was, too. Tastebuds had woken, and there was another problem to contend with. The vibe Michael was giving off wreaked of savagery.

Michael gave me a look of 'sorry, I can't help it' as his claws danced in the stale, blood-riddled air. A person looked Sally's age, Alice was dead. Black goo oozed from her eyes, and her skin appeared yellowing, as if the cells were breaking down rapidly along with any organs. Her throat had been cut from ear to ear, gaping open to reveal her jugular's pink and white glistening re-mains.

Mr Etherington was a pasty, pale wreck. Sweat poured down his forehead with a puddle already soaked through to the halfway mark of his white ribbed vest. His eyes bulged and ached with the weight of pain and, if we're reading the situation right, secrets.

"Hey, Mr Etherington. You called us, and we'd like to talk to you, but it would be far more comfortable without that big knife, don't you think?" Michael spoke first, trying to take his eyes and mind off the blood.

I scanned the room, looking for the details to diffuse the situation. Anything that could give me a clue as to what drove Etherington to slice his daughter's throat open. On the mantlepiece was a silver-framed picture of Alice and what appeared to be Etherington and his wife. That was the chink in the armour I was looking for. Yet, it had also become another worry. Where was she? I couldn't see anything that pointed to remembrance. Looking around, there were plenty more pictures like that one. All happy and together.

My ears strained to listen outside, checking for anyone coming home. Nothing but silence and death. A jumbled whirl. Isolated in one particular spot across the road. They had to be following or watching from afar. I hadn't picked up on anything when we arrived. But they were here now and full of hatred, only not for us. A problem all the same. The details were mounting, and we had to find a solution fast. One that didn't involve further bloodshed.

"Mr Etherington, is Mrs Etherington due home?" I said, cutting my attention back to the dulled grey knife dripping with blood.

Etherington's face changed. He snapped alert. His heart jumped to racing speed—a sudden look of remembering. I watched the corners of his mouth curl downwards. Mr Etherington had done something else, and it was bad.

"She... she... Got hurt, I had to end it,"

"End what?" Michael said, tilting his head. He caught another smell. Alice's corpse and the blood across the floor threw me off. There was more upstairs. And we'd got another answer.

"I had to end what we had started. She wasn't my daughter. Not anymore,"

"What did you start? Who's 'we?' put the knife down and tell us," I felt more dots could lineup, but I didn't want to push. Mr Etherington was a bomb waiting to go off. Only a matter of who was going to be the spark. Us or the 'death' outside. Michael and I were like coiled springs, weighing up the odds. I'd been calculating the distance between his hand holding the knife and us.

We were quick, but the tip hovered dangerously close to his exposed wrist. Or he could turn it on us. We would've healed, but having already been shot before, I wasn't thrilled at the prospect of being gutted.

"You know the saying. If something sounds too good to be true. It is. We were in debt up to our eyeballs. Invested in a sure thing, only to find out it was nothing more than a shell. We didn't see the sleight of hand,"

"How does that figure into this?" Michael snapped, glancing at Alice.

"Because an attaché approached me from alleged influential people. They promised to clear out debts and then some. With a catch," There's always a catch. Mr Etherington wasn't the first to fall foul of it and wouldn't be the last.

"What happened with being of the council? Any records? What was the catch?"

"A series of anonymous transfers. I lost the job because I attacked the guy who recommended the shell company. The catch was that I'd allow my daughter to be a part of a top-secret research organisation looking into anything from the common cold to cancer,"

"Didn't sound too bad, but did your daughter want to?" "She was keen as mustard, but it niggled me, and I told them no. Only I'd taken two weeks to think about it. By the time I'd responded, I'd received details for an offshore account with regular transfers being made. More money than I would earn in a lifetime,"

"Would've been simple: say no and tell them to close the bank. Who did Alice work for?"

"That's just it. No one. As far as I was aware, no details for a job came up, and the money kept coming. We were left in peace, and my wife enjoyed what the money could bring. So what the hell? Then the party invite came."

There was the link, a couple of dots with lines drawn. Mr Etherington was paid under the guise of a job for his daughter. I would guess that the shell company was involved, too. It is designed to make him lose money and need help. The job may not have surfaced, but that didn't mean his daughter hadn't taken part in some tests.

"So, why did you kill your daughter?"

"That thing on the floor was no longer my daughter. Whatever went on at that party, Alice was never the same. None of the girls were. One died, one went missing, and another killed herself. Let's face it: they all died that night. Made into something else, Alice's body had been decaying ever since. Her eyes changed like a spider's, and her arms and legs would sprout wiry black stems."

The toxin and decomposing of the bodies, cocooning the organs, were all spider-like. Mr Etherington discovered firsthand what happened—at least the fallout. Sally had mentioned the mask's smell and the drink's taste. The bigger question we needed an answer to was which ones were a success.

"Why did you kill her, though?"

Michael wasn't giving up; the details were strange, but it was a valid question.

"I thought you, of all people, would understand. I had been in the bathroom upstairs, came out to see Dianne talking to Alice, and suddenly Alice freaked out. She began changing, and those things came out of her arms. A quick swoosh and Alice ripped through Dianne's throat. I panicked and ran."

Throughout his recall, Mr Etherington's heart rate didn't deviate, nor did the elevation in his speech pitch or speed. He appeared to be telling the truth, but what the hell had these poor girls become?

"And you so had a machete in hand? And what do you mean, of all people?" I said, taking another look for open drawers or cupboards he could've reached for.

"It was after the party. That's when I realised what the money was for—our silence. Weird things kept happening, like the front door being broken open. Our car was stolen three times, and credit cards were frozen and unfrozen sporadically—dead animals on the doorstep. Then I turned to drink but kept the machete under the sofa in case of another break-in. When I reached it, Alice was downstairs, and her face was unrecognisable."-

- "She kept going at me with those stems, and I had to stop. The world slowed down, you know, one of those surreal emotional moments. The thing coming at me was no longer my daughter. She'd killed the love of my life. I saw her as nothing but a parasite using the body of my dead daughter. So I reacted, flung the knife out and before I knew it, Alice was on the floor with her throat cut and looking normal."

Tears pooled around Mr Etherington's eyes. His signals were not changed, and it sounded like he had to make a tough choice. One that, if I were ever in that position and had to take my child's life, I don't think I could. I re-scanned Alice's body. Her arms looked like pincushions with a painting of blood on her hands. The bar moved again when we thought we'd got a handle on things.

We hit an impasse. The acrid stench of death still lingered outside, whether for Mr. Etherington killing Alice or something else entirely. We'd heard his truth, yet a nagging feeling persisted that there was more to the story. Mr Turnage had been just as uncooperative. While examining Alice, I detected a sudden surge of adrenaline from Etherington. The blade shifted. Michael twitched, and my hackles rose.

"You of all people, you said. What does that mean?" The sound of the sharp blade on the fabric unnerved me.

"Detective George Reynolds is the man who is more than meets the eye. More than the world knows. But some people do. Powerful people would stop at nothing to keep bathing in the dirty secrets that helped build their power. There's so much more to all of this than you know. More than what happened last year, what's happened here already today and what's yet to happen. These streets are no longer black and white, and if these bastards get their way, what happened to my daughter? To you. Would become the norm."

"What is it you think I am?"

"My life may be over; don't take me for a fool. Funny fact is that money can be useful sometimes—the devil, you know, and all that. Money helps find and hide secrets, so when the time is right, and the person is right, they will know how to use the secrets, especially if they retrace steps through what's not yet cold. Maybe even to someone who has held onto some words for a rainy day."

My ears perked up. Etherington had become cryptic and reminiscent of old foes. My feeling that he knew had just come true, and it gave me chills. The image of that smug Melanie came to mind.

"Your life won't be over as long as you put down the knife. We can record this properly and explain, so we have a leg to stand on."

"No chance, Mr Reynolds. My life is already accounted for. Knowing you were on your way, I downed enough poison to kill a herd of horses. Living without my family is not worth it, but I needed you to know and see for yourself. And urge you to see through the lies and politics. Because they go hand in hand."

For a moment, I was at a loss for words. Mr Etherington had taken his life to be with his family, but he had taken measures to seek the truth. He wanted us to seek it. I could hear his blood-curdling in his veins. I'd misread the eyes and sweat accompanied by adrenaline spikes. The effects of the poison took a grip, and now his blood had boiled.

Michael and I were helpless as blood oozed from his eyes. Pink froth curdled through his lips as Mr Etherington's veins bulged and throbbed. A shaky hand reached into his pocket to retrieve a small piece of paper and a key. He reached out to me as his body writhed and flopped with blood oozing. I heard the spine-chilling pops and sloshes. His blood smelled of arsenic as it flowed freely.

"F...f...f...follow th...th...the monnnney. Key f...f...from re-traced...st...st...steps."

I clutched the note and key in time as one final, violent, writhing blood spurted through the air, and Etherington slumped in a heap. The machete fell to the floor. Its bloodied glimmer caught a slight reflection—my red eyes.

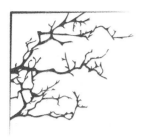

25

BEATEN DOWN

I sat toying with the ordinary key—silver and slightly smaller than a house lock key, resembling a locker key, but not quite. We left another crime for the locals to manage. At the same time, all three bodies were taken to Mr Nicholls, with Ellena preparing to give them the once-over.

We dragged ourselves around the gloomy house with little standing out. Mr Etherington took his life after losing his world. I could sympathise a little, but what drove him was far scarier. Now more settled, Michael busied himself drinking through the coffee jug while reviewing his pocketbook notes.

A curious detail puzzled me—the small piece of paper with the key was blank. I played the whole scenario over in my head, wondering if we could've done things differently. Faced with an unknown risk, anyone else without our heightened skill set wouldn't have known about the blood or a possible knife, making it all riskier for them.

Etherington gave the impression this case was far bigger than we could've imagined. So far, the details would back that up. The body of an M.P. was stolen back, and he had the 'devil's circle' branding. We were subdued by persons unknown using wolfsbane, knowing what I was, and Michael became a bonus. The mess at that house was a mysterious change in direction. We didn't know what had been ingrained in the wood yet. They all wore hoods, like at the party.

Those poor girls didn't stand a chance. So far, Etherington and Turnage's parents seemed to be in on the action. I was checking through my notes when I found myself writing, 'Death is a masquerade,' which would have been true if we had looked at the situation back then. The VHS tape was to get our attention after the first victims hadn't. So, yeah, that phrase was fitting. The real masquerade. But how much did Etherington know or find out?

'Detective George Reynolds, the man who is more than meets the eye. More than the world knows. But some people do. Powerful people would stop at nothing to keep bathing in the dirty secrets that helped build their power. There's so much more to all of this than you know. More than what happened last year, what's already happened today, and what's yet to happen. These streets are no longer black and white, and if these bastards get their way, what happened to my daughter? To you. Would become the norm.'

'My life may be over; don't take me for a fool. Funny fact is that money can be useful sometimes—the devil, you know, and all that. Money helps find and hide secrets, so they know how to bring those secrets into the light when the time is right, and the right person comes along, especially if they retrace steps through what's not yet cold. Maybe even to someone who had held on-to some words for a rainy day.'

'Follow the money. Key from retraced steps.'

I'd recorded the last of what Etherington said. He knew what I was too, meaning he'd had to find out from someone, but still, why a blank note, and where was that house that hosted the party? I stared intently at the details so much that I drifted into a foggy haze. The world faded from my ears. Everything became so peaceful I didn't want it to stop, much like the strangeness of the 'out-of-body' feeling at the house.

That was until a faint 'Georgie, Georgie -are you there, Georgie' began worming through my eardrum. The voice was soft and sweet. Even muffled, it felt soothing. My attention was being pulled back to the real world. The haze snapped away, my eyes cleared, and I thought I was staring at an angel.

"Ellena? Sorry, must've drifted,"

"I'm not surprised. It's been full-on. Are you okay? You've hardly caught your breath, and your body's been put through the wringer," said Ellena, curling a delicate smile at me.

She wore a figure-sculpting white blouse, a short black fitted skirt, and boots. A mix of beautiful but battle-ready with heels on boots that I wouldn't like to take a stamping from. Ellena certainly brightened the day. Until I saw the pile of papers in her hands.

"I'm okay. Sorry, we haven't had the chance to catch up yet. I really want to,"

"It's okay. Thanks to your heroics, there'll be plenty of time for us to get to know each other better." I hung off her every word. If I didn't know better, I would've thought she was a 'siren' or supernatural temptress. I was well and truly under her spell; only one other person had had that effect on me—Helen.

"I would like that,"

"Me too,"

"Oh, Locke mentioned earlier that there was more to your skills than we knew. And you were brought here with a purpose," Ellena smiled, eyes darting to think. Not an 'oh shit, I'm trapped,' but how to dumb it down for me.

"Yeah, he said he'd given the heads up. My expertise is varied—history, science, biology, chemistry, and a keen interest in supernatural things. When I was younger, I saw a ghost in a haunted hotel. Since then, I've been hooked, believing there's more to it all, especially since the planes of existence aren't as rigid as we think. People choose not to see it."

"So that's why you weren't freaked out by me?" her interests explained a lot, but she still didn't see Locke's purpose.

"You could say that. With you and Michael, it's different. It's like having superpowers, if that makes sense," We laughed, imagining Michael with a red cape trying to fly.

"He said you could help with gases we've been coming across."

"The wolfsbane and mountain ash?"

"Mountain, what now?"

"What that house was made of, where you went. Where Michael was taken, it's mountain ash. Rowan trees were burnt, and ash was made into the wood lining. Creates a supernatural barrier inside and out."

"It weakened the hell out of me, but I could rip a window off and smash some doors open. But my body felt bruised and battered," I said, checking my knuckles, picturing the bruises from punching the basement doors.

"I gather you have demon blood mixed with werewolf and human. You can withstand a lot more and break through barriers. But it takes a toll until your body heals."

She knew her stuff, and I was grateful. The bigger question: how could we combat wolfsbane if it happened again?

"Michael has masks and nebulisers in his car, which gave me an idea. Is there a way to reverse-engineer wolfsbane effects? A spray to wipe away what we inhale."

"Not sure, but maybe a gum or cookie? If it's the same colour, you eat it, neutralising the effects. But with an open wound, you'll have to sweat it out before it reaches your heart."

"Wow, how?"

"I'm sure we could think of a few ways to get your temperature up," Ellena whispered, cheeky as she perched on the table's edge, swinging her leg over the other, showing ample thigh. My heart jumped, and I felt heat oozing from my collarline. I'd briefly forgotten just how dangerous Ms Ellena Walker was.

"I don't doubt that for a second. More fun when it's a joint effort." Ellena smiled before breezing close to my ear.

"Oh, really. I'll let Michael know to make himself available for you," she pulled away, making me laugh and getting Michael's attention. He glared at us, bewildered, making us feel like naughty schoolchildren. Oh, Ellena had me on strings, and she knew it.

"Speaking of which, I take it those papers are to do with us?"

"Crap, yes. Well, let's just say I'm due major brownie points. I managed to inflate and create a mould from that tip. Enough to make a fingerprint," I was in awe and on tenterhooks as Michael breezed over.

"Ladies, what am I missing out on?" he said, glimpsing Ellena's thighs, composing himself.

"Well, that print, you won't believe it. Francis Collyer,"

Michael and I stared at each other in disbelief for a few reasons. Francis was the other name on a penalty notice. Francis died of an overdose at the party. The dead can't receive fines, and more importantly, how did a dead girl's fingertip end up on a murder victim?

"Wow, I owe you one,"

"Well, after my next trick. Let's call it dinner,"

"Oh, what's the trick?"

"Subtracting DNA and chemical composition from the tip. It's no coincidence an M.P. is dead, the inspector drained with the others, and the toxin cocooned and destroyed organs. Spiders."

I looked puzzled, then remembered the notes in the tunnels. Experiments with DNA combinations. But on happy-go-lucky girls?

"You've got to be kidding me. I hate spiders, snakes, scorpions, you name it. I'll be creeped out," Michael shivered, screwing up his face. I'm not a fan, but how can a human drain and mummify organs before they turn to gas and destroy the body?

"Yep, my hunch is a hybrid 'super black widow' toxin. Several can do that. Amplify it, make it human-size—a killing machine. With Mr Nicholls's help, I've been reverse-engineering the DNA sequence."

"If so, can you make it into a suppressed gas?" I said, thinking we could spray the black cloud if it got close. Even if it risked my life again.

"Absolutely, an Epi-pen type, just in case."

That was the plan. Dots joined, thanks to Ellena. How did Francis come back from the dead?

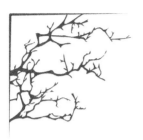

26

CANDLE AT BOTH ENDS

We were finally on the verge of some much-needed rest. All I could think about was another family decimated by death. Locke had noticed the toll burning the candle at both ends had taken. I could still feel remnants of the wolfsbane in my chest. Being told it was mountain ash used as a barrier for the supernatural felt like one detail too many for the day. The paper bothered me. It had to mean something, but it was... blank. A little like what we've been coming up with lately.

Yet, the paste's texture differed from what I'd felt before, older with a cream tinge and a little stronger than the average. Were the key and paper linked? The former reminded me of a vintage cupboard keyhole or a grandfather clock. It fitted something old, that much I felt sure about. Etherington made it sound like he'd used that dirty money to buy secrets. To think the saying used to be 'money makes the world go around', sadly, the reality we've come to know is 'secrets are equally powerful'.

'Any detectives from the murder task force receiving?' I heard a radio scream out in the hallway. "This is ADI Locke. Go ahead,"

'There's a call that needs your attention. Do you have anyone?' My heart sank. So close, yet so far. "Early turn is about to changeover."

'An anonymous caller reported that there's a dead body in Trafalgar Square. D.S. Dalton and DC Reynolds would be interested as it's connected to what they're looking into. Stand by; there's been another call... A limousine has been reported outside Nelson's Column covered in blood,'

"God, they're about to go off shift. Any other details?"

'The first caller sounded emphatic with their names. As for the other call, it's being updated now. Wait... There's a message,'

'They reap what they sow' all in blood.'

"Show us assigned and have local units set up cordons around the square. The local authority must divert all traffic away. Can you send it up the chain to command for a blanket blackout of the press? If it's linked, we need to keep it closed."

'Cordons are in motion, and the council is being called as we.' My fingers were poised on my key in the locker lock, having just closed it. I saw Michael's head drop as he re-opened his. No rest, for the wicked sprang to mind. A limousine, just like Sally mentioned on the night of the masquerade. Our serial-killing 'black widow' come death cloud had just set a huge target on some powerful people, and we were being lured in.

"Sorry, boys, they're playing our song again. I know you both have been through the wars and run ragged. I promise to get you a few days' break after this one to recharge your batteries," Locke breezed toward with a solemn look on his tired face. The last of those words sounded heavenly. We may not have been in the unit long. Still, the two cases in quick succession have been heavy going. They have taken their toll on all of us mentally and physically. Especially playing puppy sitter to Michael. Some food, sleep, recuperation, and, with luck being on our side, dinner with Ellena.

"It's ok, boss, duty calls," said Michel, trudging over and tapping out the last cigarette from his box. He screwed up the empty packet, nonchalantly throwing it over his left shoulder into a bin basket ten feet behind him. It landed no sooner than I heard frantic running echoing through the hallway toward us. Ellena. "Great, you're still." the scent of her floral perfume whipped through the air first. Toying with my senses as the breeze swirled across the short hairs on my cheeks. Her soft voice brightened my mood of having to stay on.

"What's the matter, Ellena? The boys were about to head to another crime scene. Late turn are due in, so need to stay on," said Locke with a smile, trying to spare another of our tired team the extra work.

"I know, I heard. I have plenty to do here, but I finished the first of my projects. So I come bearing gifts," said Ellena, handing me a small black box. It felt quite light. Whatever was inside wasn't much, but it hadn't been long enough to create anything to counteract the wolfsbane. The box and I faced two small black metal tabs. No bigger than a fifty-pence piece, but square with a tiny red bulb and a small button. I liked Michael for inspiration after seeing the contents of his car boot. He looked equally clueless, which surprised me. I'd figured he'd seen most things by now.

"Erm, thank you, but what are they?" I said, catching the big cheesy grin on her face. Ellena had done something good and was pleased with herself. "Emitters. Thin enough to fit in your warrant card wallets. They are crudely made prototypes, but they work in an infinite range. After last night, I didn't want to take any chances. If anything happens or one of you is taken. Press this, and it beeps in my workshop and the ADI's office. It's also high frequency, so if one of you loses the other, you can find each other again. It might sting your ears a little, but it's worth it." Ellena surprised Michael and me, but Locke stood, arms folded, looking smug. He had that 'I told you so,' expression. This must have been one skill he'd alluded to.

"Told you she'd be vital to us. As Ellena said, last night was a scare we could do without happening again. If it does, we have a way to locate you." "How? I get that one of us can hear it, but how would you see?" "The same way trackers work; it will ping to my machine a longitude and a latitude grid reference for us to map. A directional beacon display in our cars will point in the right direction." Brains and beauty, what a combination. Another moment, I let the world fade away, and all I saw was the pureness of her face and pale complexion. Her blonde hair draped to the right, and the black frames of her glasses sat neatly, catching the reflection of the fluorescent light above heads. Ellena made the gadgets in an afternoon while working hard on DNA, tracing who the fingertip belonged to, and assisting Mr Nicholls with the endless supply of dead bodies.

"How on earth can you do all of this?" "Oh, there are so many more surprises to come if you want to find out. You best come back in one." "Ahem... hey, guys. I need to come back in one piece, too, right? I like surprises," Michael butted in with his typical timing, smiling and feeling like a spare wheel.

'NELSON'S COLUMN, TRAFALGAR Square,'

The sun had faded from another tragic day. Strips of purple coated the sky, and what would usually be a very busy circus of tourists was now under siege by a police cordon, tape flapping between black lampposts. My first thoughts on the view were that it probably wouldn't have caused a stir without the designer paintwork. The positioning wasn't normal, but it would soon be forgotten.

An otherwise posh-looking limousine brazenly parked in front of 'Nelson's statue', covered in blood that fast became overwhelming, setting my taste buds ablaze. It being human. Michael struggled for control too, not so much his eyes now, but I noticed the claws on his right hand slowly slide forward, spraying the air with his crimson fluids. They stung as they came. I noticed that much as he attempted to shake it off.

With nobody nearby, I tried mine again to see if they were like last time or if it had been a strange one-off. Painless and quick. They shot to attention with no blood, which relieved me while wondering what would come next in my staggered evolution. A part of me wished it had all happened the other night. Get it over and done with, so I knew where I stood. It seemed god or some different opposite, like the devil or whoever was writing my path, had other designs for me.

The limo had the obligatory blacked-out windows for those who like to be sneaky bastards, so we couldn't tell if anyone was inside. The way the call came out over the radio hadn't sat right with me. It sounded to be from the killer asking for us. How else would anyone know? If somebody had been inside, they would've mentioned more detail other than there was a dead body. Inquisitive people would notice the details, and certain things would stand out, even in shock. We hadn't heard enough.

The human blood had alarm bells ringing, and my hackles danced in the sundowning's brisk air. I couldn't grasp it, but felt far more confident this time. Michael's body language was also wide and open, oozing self-belief. It had to be what Ellena had made for us. A safety net if one of us got kidnapped again or lost. The writing was across the side that the public would've seen. The surrounding area was full of shops and lit advertising boards for brands like Pepsi and Panasonic, flashing away. 'Reap what they sow' was thickly smeared and chaotic with an excited hatred that had me thinking the killer or killers had enjoyed what they were doing. If that were the case, the murders might not stop once they had revenge.

The nearer we came, the stronger my sixth sense grew, matching the aphrodisiac of the blood. The concrete jungle around us was surreal, and I figured the cordons would work well, bottlenecking the square. This was a ghost town. Command came through for us by stopping the press. It was just Michael and me approaching an otherwise luxury limousine. Making it easier to get away with any slip-ups from Michael and his eyes. The last thing I wanted was for the other solitary aspect left from our dream to come true. Lightning and fire, with Michael causing another to burn to death. In the dream, it was Ellena. This time, it could be me.

My ears were working hard to filter through the cold and rhythmic chattering. From what appeared to be thousands of pigeons descending on the square to watch the show and take a stranglehold on Trafalgar Square, with plenty of scraps at their mercy. In reality, maybe a few hundred. Enough to cause chaos with my attempts to filter past their heartbeats.

I could pick up on nothing from the taunting chariot of death. A few flies buzzed around the blood, and by the cracks in the door line, it was dry but fresh enough to attract insects. Blue bottles were trying to get in on the action. There was definitely a dead body inside. My sense of smell couldn't reveal anything, particularly because of another scent masking it. It was mixed, throwing everything off, which became a red flag.

Another cursory look to Michael, reading his chemo signals, making sure he was ok and not wavering under the anticipation of another dead body. I daren't try to count how many so far. If we were to include the flurry before we got involved, then it had to be easily double figures. That was without the girls themselves. Yet, I also felt other moments were still weighing heavily on his mind, but he wanted to act like they weren't. Michael gets a twitch or a spasm around the top eyelid of his right eye when he's stressed or worried. It's the little things that mean the most. The little things will hurt or, worse, get us dead. There were a multitude of details about the car that fed my doubts and fears by the second.

The sprays of mud and horse manure around the wheel arches crammed in the tyre tread and papered up the wings. Told me it had been on farmland or somewhere off-road and regular enough to make layers and dry out. The boot, rear window and other surface areas that weren't coated in blood had pebbles of rainwater. The weather in this part of London had been dry for the last forty-eight hours. All of that told me it had been at least twenty miles or more outside of London, rural like that farm, but I didn't recall the smell of manure, so somewhere similar. Then I noticed, barely visible through the rear tint, was a sticker, 'Epping Luxury Autos,' a little bleached from the sun, but I could see enough.

Two feet away, the vibe I picked up was strong, with a lot of blood and something else. It was too risky to let Michael look or go too close. Besides, it was my turn to take a hit for the team. If he kept guard, we'd be ok with no surprise guests. At least none stayed visible.

"Hey Michael, you ok watching out?" "Sure, why is that?" "Call it a gut feeling. Definitely not wind. Seriously though, there's something off with all of this, and it could be a set-up," "Ha, funny fucker. No, I get what you mean. Summoned here to a lonesome limousine like the story. Not to mention it smells funky, so yeah, have at it, matey,"

I pulled the door open, releasing a wave of pent-up putrid. With it came that other strange scent I hadn't been sure about. With the door wide, my feet were inches from the car's body, and I was about to step inside when a pool of red steadily flowed forward, raining down on the pavement. The door had been holding back the tide. Michael whipped his head away, quickly shielding his weathered face as the wind brushed his neatly sculpted greying hair. I caught the hint of yellow in his eyes as he turned. It was strong and had me drooling, but we had to push on. Yet, another reason to have kept Michael at bay.

Pulling on my gloves, I skirted around the blood to slide onto the first empty black leather seats. No sooner had I been at an angle to see the inside in its entirety, an overwhelming wish that I hadn't slapped me across the face. It was horrific, with blood sprayed throughout. Also unusual, as it meant the killer had changed their modus operandi unless that was the point. Confusion. That wasn't all, though. Photographs and newspaper clippings were papered all around, varying in content and having no particular pattern. Sadly, the grand prize was another two statistics to add to our list. Both were in charcoal grey suits composed of black hoods. I had a feeling they wouldn't be anyone we'd expect.

I was busy looking at the dead seated together with arms around each other, huddled, when something warm and wet dripped onto the top of my latex hand. Its blood coming from the roof lining. It was a message.

Blood continued to drip from the letter 'S', it read. 'You should've listened and stayed away.' A rush of anxiety and prevention tore through me and left me dreading what would come.

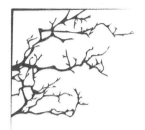

27

EERIE SILENCE

IN COMPLETE DARKNESS, rescue and police cars cluttered the scene; heads huddled into a mass. That's what the photograph revealed. A young man cradling a bundle wrapped in a blanket or sheet. It hit me – it was me.

The child was rescued from that inferno by a young police officer who became my mentor, guardian angel, and friend. Also, my 'Beta.' A photo plucked from my tragic past, scattered among many, captures different life stages, including moments from the previous case and crime scenes. As I delved deeper, my eyes darted across the seats toward two bodies; hooded heads slumped against a closed privacy screen.

Not just me; Michael and ADI Locke, too. A particular shot of Locke in a shadowy Baker Street alley, receiving something from a guy, though too dark to discern. Recently, mirroring his attire from last week. How the killers got these shots puzzled me. The girls weren't watching us; these were snap-shots from lives under surveillance. A bizarre pattern emerged.

My photos spanned childhood until I met Mr Nicholls in the coroner's office. Michael's after the 'Kanaima' case and him at the hospital with Ellena. Locke's from our first week on this unit. Call me cynical, but this surveillance hinted at unknown entities monitoring the supernatural – making Locke something, too.

I've sensed he's different but couldn't pinpoint how. The timings suggest-ed a connection unless I missed a detail. The bloody message was a chilling statement – we hadn't heeded the warning. The pictures sickened me, invading personal lives and unearthing haunting memories. Queasiness crawled up my throat, pooling around my gums, a change from the usual bloodlust.

Turning to the dead, their hands displayed decay similar to previous victims but were less severe. Yellow-gold wedding bands hinted at two more shattered families, akin to the Etheringtons. I hesitated before lifting the hood on the nearest body. Sitting made it hard to judge size, but the frame was narrow, reminiscent of someone recent but elusive.

Queasiness intensified as the hood lifted. A chin emerged, skin taut over angled bone. Familiar facial hair and cheekbones, and, to my shock, the face revealed Mr Turnage, Sally's father. I moved to the other body, longer and wider. An evidence bag quickly sealed both and was concealed in my pocket for busy moments.

Facial decay matched the VHS tape guideline, which is around thirty minutes—primary wounds, a two-inch slice through the suit jacket into the chest wall, puncturing the heart. Mr Turnage had wrist slices and chest punctures, possibly frenzied. Blood streaks down his legs, possibly his, inside the car. Tiny forked puncture holes adorned their necks.

These felt personal. Near them, poking and prodding, I sensed something – pain, a vibe that unsettled me. Determined, I searched for the 'devil's circle' symbol. Flapping the jacket breast revealed an I.D. card on a lanyard. The other shoe dropped – another M.P., escalating the importance. 'Department for Science, Innovation and Technology' read his title. Mr Daniel Dowden.

"Michael, it's crazy in here," I spoke as if he stood beside me, knowing his curiosity.

"Why, what's going on? Is it as bloody as it smells?" Michael's tone, almost cheerful, avoiding the dirty work.

"And then some. Everywhere, with a message: 'You should've listened and stayed away.' Oh, we have fans, too." I paused. "Loads of pictures. Mine from the fire rescue to recently. Yours after I bit you, and a snap of ADI doing an exchange in a dark Baker Street alley."

"Because of the supernatural stuff? But Locke isn't, or is he?"

"I've been thinking. I reckon he's something. The question is if he knows it or isn't sure and thinks working with us might help him find out."

"Could be. But all of that is strange."

"Well, here comes the other shoe. Dead M.P., Daniel Dowden, and Mr Turnage."

"Holy shit. Not sure who I'm more surprised about. That wasn't a show that dropped. That was 'mafia-style' cement boots hitting the Thames floor." Michael's darker life left me questioning again.

"Well, the hits keep coming. Both decay around thirty minutes, but these seem secondary to other wounds. They wore hoods, like at that house, laced with something." A slight blurring in my haze, a dizzying sensation, but I shook it off, feeling uneasy.

"Right. Seen enough? Understand the grandstanding?" Michael raised a valid point I'd overlooked, the bigger 'dot' of all this. Why the grand revelation? It would be poignant in a limousine, a nod to the past. But the Parliament's carnage should be common knowledge, not covered up for it to work. It left me puzzled about the endgame.

Michael hummed outside, pondering like me. The chaos felt like a taunt, the killers showing us what they found. Studying the blood and photos, it hit me. The killer wanted us to target the people doing surveillance, conducting experiments on helpless girls. Mr Etherington's last words hinted at knowledge, possibly paid for. If the information was that accessible, the killer might have stolen it to assert they're the lesser evil. How did the M.P. fit in? If masked at the party, no one would know each other unless someone had a guest list.

Thoughts circled in my head. Then clarity struck. The killer had a physical guest list, explaining the pictures and our sudden inclusion. We were in their crosshairs because we refused to back down.

"Michael, smell around the car,"

"What for?"

"Anything other than blood. They have a guest list to kill and anyone getting in their way. It's a trap. I'm not touching anything, so use your other eyes and search."

"Get out then, be safe,"

"What about the bodies?"

"We drag them out quickly," Michael suggested, aware of the fragility.

"They're fragile, though,"

"Matey, I will look, but if push comes to shove, we drag them out and worry about the mess afterwards."

Michael circled the car, and I scanned the inside, searching for traps. That lingering smell persisted. A substance from burnt trees formed a supernatural barrier.

Nothing stood out. Closing my eyes, I focused on Michael's footsteps. Listening for nuances, I leapt to sniff deeply, catching a peculiar scent. Like plasticine, what schools used.

"Michael, can you smell plasticine?"

"Not yet. Why?"

"Getting a weird scent. Could be from elsewhere, I guess."

Coincidence was troubling. A fresh smell when we sought subtlety. Now, a substance from burnt trees forms a supernatural barrier.

"Michael, does the front open?"

"Hang on, I'll check," he rushed to the driver's side.

The handle clicked, but it wouldn't open. He tried again, but the same resistance. The door flew shut.

"Not funny, Michael."

"What?"

"You shut the door to shit me up, bloody bastard. You win."

"Matey, I'm still by the driver's door looking to see if I could jam my Leatherman in the lock—old school car break-in. Listen," he tapped on the window, but my fear spiked. He didn't shut the door.

Avoiding blood, I tried the handle. It wouldn't budge. A gap appeared, but it bounced back with a haze of bright purple.

"Michael, it's mountain ash. Move away, or it will weaken you."

"No way, not leaving you."

Another click. Panic gripped me—a form of mountain ash. The door handle activated a release, completing the barrier upon closing.

"Michael, it's mountain ash. Move away, or it will weaken you."

"No way, not leaving you."

'Click.' A loud click echoed before ticking started from the bodies. A sense of wolfsbane Déjà vu hit me. The warehouse body flashed in my memory.

"I hear it too," Michael shouted.

"Get your radio away, now."

"I'm not going," he pressed the EMR button, and his radio screamed. I turned mine down.

'This is D.S. Dalton. We may have a bomb situation in the limousine at Trafalgar Square. Detective Reynolds is trapped,' Michael transmitted. Once the alarm was pressed, we had seconds to communicate. Hearing the word 'bomb' made the ticking more real.

I moved toward the door. It bounced back with a purple haze—a mountain ash barrier. Panic gripped me.

"Michael, please go," I begged. Taking him with me was pointless. A million thoughts rushed through my head. Ellena included.

We hadn't had that dinner. My actual family didn't know I existed, and now, neither side would get the chance. Michael's staying was senseless. It came from a good place, but I couldn't let him die.

I ripped Mr Turnage's shirt open, revealing a 15-inch slice from the sternum. The ticking came from inside. Two enormous blocks of Semtex rigged with a wired fuse and detonator. A flashing red light acted as a hypnotic beacon. I only had thirty seconds.

I stepped back in disbelief. Grabbed my radio, tears rolling down my cheeks, and looked at the photo of 'child me' being pulled from that fire.

'This is Detective Reynolds. The doors are sealed. Cancel all units. It has been a pleasure, and thank you,' I slid the radio away. Twenty seconds remained. My radio squealed.

'George George. The present now,' Ellena's voice rattled through the foggy muffle as the world drifted away. I whipped the emitter from my wallet. As I moved it, a clip felt moveable. A quick flip of the catch, and it came loose. A small blue, jelly-like tablet with a scent like wolfsbane.

"Michael, please go. I have barely ten seconds."

"I can't leave you. It's not right."

"You must. Now leave."

"No," I had to make him, to spare him. I let instinct take over.

"Michael, go," I ordered, an echoed roar of words rattling the car's frame. His feet scampered.

'Eat it, Georgie. '

I heard through the radio. I thought, why the hell not? And chucked it down my neck. It tasted sweet and strange. It tingled inside my mouth before a temporary numbness spread through my throat. My veins were on fire as adrenaline tore through my body.

'10...9...8...7...6...5...4...3...2...1,' 'Boom'

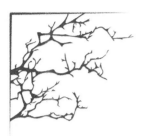

28

FALLOUT

Thick black smoke tore through the dimming red sky, a scrapyard of metal debris painting the concrete canvas as flames roared and swirled angrily. Stray, charred photographs were whipped into a frenzy and sent on their merry way.

A crowd gathered amidst blood, guts, and stray limbs that came to rest among the dust. Some still burned with fleshy tips, dancing with yellow embers.

"Georgie, wake up. Come on. No time to be sleeping on the job, you lazy bastard."

A torched roughness, unique as grit and smoke, toyed with the cavern of space alive with adrenaline moments ago. Battered, bruised, and flat out, with a metal door shielding from the floor, I reluctantly pulled open my heavy eyes, wondering, How the heck did I pull that off?

The feel of the inside door leather mixed with torched metal gave little relief to my body's aches. Every breath was riddled with relief. I curled my thumb inside my palm, wanting to make sure it was real that I was... alive.

A controlled flick saw to that, letting a claw slide forward to bury itself deep in the crevice of my skin. A short, shrill pain shot through my hand, and blood dropped to the door. The heat was to my back, and I could hear every crackle and pop. I was a little scrambled, trying to recall the last few moments.

The aches aside, I felt strange, the similar after-effects I had from the wolfsbane and mountain ash. I remembered chomping down on a tablet concealed in the emitter Ellena gave us. Oh crap, Ellena. I'd heard her voice telling me to 'eat it now' and the sweat-numbing taste.

"Piss off, old man. I don't know what's worse. Being blown up or electrocuted," I fired off at the feet of Michael as I dragged myself from the heap.

"On a scale of 1-10 and looking at the smouldering intestines over there. I'll take the electrotherapy," Michael retorted with cocky relief before gripping my arm to steady me upright.

"Well, I'm still waiting for my balls to drop back from my lower intestines. So it's not all sunshine and rainbows."

"I figured you'd been waiting for the last thirty years for that," said Michael. He had a spring in his step; all it took was me being nearly blown to bits.

"You realise we're back to square one, right?" At least that's how I was feeling, surveying the wreckage while piecing back together my memories.

I had been by the door trying to force it open when Ellena told me to eat. The timer ticked down, and I felt a surge of adrenaline with the realisation the mountain ash wasn't blocking me as much, and there had been far more of a gap from every push. Just as the explosion ripped through, a final push helped me tear the door off, and we were thrown clear. Whatever Ellena had created did the trick and weakened the effects of the 'bane of our lives' so far—a genius.

My memories were slowly syncing up with the pre-rattled state. The killers had to have been working through a guest list. I still had the seized masks in my pocket. But having any kind of list meant the murders could be far from over. Mr Turnage was the second parent of one girl to 'meet their maker,' albeit one had been their hand.

"Since when was any of this going to be easy?" said Michael as we strolled the wreck. Michael kept trying to get a paramedic my way, but I had none of it. The last thing I wanted was to be carted off to the hospital as a concussion precaution. Besides, I could feel any knocks, cuts, and bumps healing.

"Soco, are you receiving Detective Reynolds?"

"Oh, my God. Go ahead, Georgie. Are you okay?"

It felt so surreal, a feeling that I've acknowledged far too often of late. That's what it was. Hearing Ellena's voice again was heart-warming, bringing another tear to my eye. Only this time, it was one of joy.

"Well, it looks like I will come back in one piece. So thank — "I couldn't announce the real reason I had for my safety over the radio. At least I gave her some peace of mind, and dinner was still on the agenda.

"Thank God, and will update you when you're both back."

We kept walking in circles, but nothing fruitful was standing out. Every few feet were corpse parts and entrails. If I were to guess, the smaller sections were from Turnage, as his chest cavity had been housing the bomb. We were ready to call it and leave the area for local clean-up and bagging.

When I noticed a flap of skin caught on some metal, it was a section from their backs, but the imprint drew my attention. Or should I say branding? The symbol for the 'devil's circle,' at least one had been a member. It seemed wide so that it could be Mr Daniel Dowden. Another dodgy M.P., We couldn't rule out Mr Turnage from having the same. Only his would be like trying to piece together a jigsaw. Looking at those pieces and thinking over Turnage prompted a little spark that could be put into the next move.

"Michael, that makes two parents. I think we need to find the other parents of the girls. Maybe we'll get lucky and catch the killer before it happens."

"How about some rest first, eh? Besides, you still have that key to figure out."

I'd nearly forgotten those details, especially the blank paper. I pulled it from my pocket with an irrational hope that something would magically appear, like the real person's address behind all this. I must've been staring too long in my bewilderment because I suddenly had Michael looking at me, puzzled.

"So you figured out what diary that goes to yet?" Michael said confidently, which made me question whether I should've seen the same thing he was. Instead, I was now questioning how he concluded a diary. This prompted me to imagine him going home each night and writing his deepest thoughts and feelings before he went to bed. Making me snort a chuckle. That puzzled look became a glare.

"I hadn't realised it went to a diary. This paper confuses me."

"Show me," Michael said, taking the paper and key.

"It's a page from something quite old. My guess is the same book. The question is, where?"

"Wait, what if it's for eyes that see differently? He knew what I was," I said, checking the coast was clear before shining red. Sure enough...

'Look for the beginning to an ending,' cryptic.

Dim, atmospheric lighting wrapped in a warmth that made a person forget about the day. Especially me. At least for an hour or two, anyway. We could have kept going all night and still not got near figuring out the bigger picture. Or say enough prayers that I had survived.

The warmth of the shower bellowed down on my bare skin and felt heavenly as I gradually slipped into something more like myself. I should've been going home to sleep and recharging my fried battery. Something else was more appealing, or should I say, someone else.

No sooner had I returned to the station with the cryptic clue rattling around my head than Ellena made a beeline for me. All but hung off my neck after sprinting through the corridor. I didn't know if it was a relieved outburst at a friend or more. She smelled wonderful and made the world piss off for a few seconds—no 'shop' talk. I booked the masks for Ellena's attention in the morning, but kept the key and paper.

Instead, I received my marching orders from Ellena. Figuring it best, she cashed in on that dinner date before anything else happened to me. In fact, Ellena took the initiative and booked a table. After Locke had finished giving me the line manager talk and checking I was alright, a big cheesy smirk spread across his face before enlightening me.

"She's been worried sick, you know. Then you put the message out, and she nearly collapsed. The entire office went quiet. Most closed their eyes, and tears fell. Ellena was beside herself. She has it bad for you, in case you hadn't noticed," Locke said, lowering his voice so nobody else heard.

"I've noticed. Honestly, she has got under my skin, too," I said, looking at Locke. All I could see was the picture of him conducting a dark alley transaction with a face barely visible and half a foot shorter than he was, which had me looking at him. I focused as hard as I could without making it obvious that I thought something was up. That I thought he could be something supernatural.

The brown of his eyes rippled with the texture and pattern of a sawndown tree. Yet, I was bothered. Whether it was the after-effects of Ellena's concoction or that my condition was still evolving, everything felt dialled up in such a confined space. Perhaps the adrenaline from a near-death experience. There seemed to be an auspicious layer over his retinas—a lens, but not for eyesight.

That photo had only fed my suspicions. No, it seemed Locke was hiding the true colour of his eyes. His pupils aside. With the smoke finally cleared from my airways, Locke gave off a scent I hadn't noticed before or hadn't been attuned to. Death and blood that's been masked by strong aftershave.

The powerful people who had me on their list now had Michael and Locke. One was still adjusting to whatever he would become. The other had red flags glaring but was on our side until he was not.

With that touching moment lingering in my thoughts, I got whisked away by Ellena to a 'Miller and Carter' steak house.

I basked in the musky amber glow emanating from the ceramic light, which lovingly caressed our table. A candle, momentarily the centre of attention, danced with delight until the genuine star of the evening sauntered back.

Her hair glistened under the ceiling light, shimmering her perfectly pale skin. Ellena was the epitome of beauty, intelligence, and down-to-earth charm—qualities any man would give his right arm for. I considered myself fortunate to have her attention and to express gratitude for the additional strength she provided to break free. Ellena was intoxicating, making me feel at ease with myself. That I was the only part human didn't matter.

In her eyes, the demon, the wolf, and the human were all components of the same mystical package. Ellena was the last person I wanted to hear from when my world was dark. Fortunately, light emerged from that darkness, bringing us to a dinner table. Ellena wore a radiant smile that warmed me from the inside out. It was just unfortunate that death awaited us in the real world.

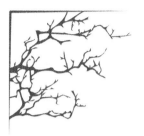

29

LOVE BLOSSOMS

ELLENA HAD TAKEN CHARGE of everything. Given the recent chaos, I saw it as her way of looking out for me. Though the bruises had faded, the aftershocks still rattled my head. Maybe a check-up wouldn't have hurt, but rapid self-healing had perks.

Our waiter, a slick-haired man in his late thirties, couldn't keep his eyes off Ellena. He strutted over with a bottle of 'malbec' and glasses the size of fish bowls, leering at her. I felt a pang of jealousy, a rare emotion for me. The guy was pushing my last nerve. Dinner with Ellena was already a stretch, and I didn't appreciate the open admiration.

"Sir, Madam, your food will be over shortly," he announced, and his squeaky voice made me grin. Ellena sensed it, brushing her leg against mine to grab my attention. "I know, right? I wondered if his balls had dropped or been castrated," she said, breaking my restraint. We both burst into laughter.

"God, he looked so smug. I heard him," Ellena continued, unfazed. It was one of the things I liked about her: her straightforwardness. I could see why the guy was staring. Her chest fought against the confines of her blouse, but that was just one of her impressive attributes.

"You look beautiful, especially after the thirty-minute struggle to drag myself from the shower," I told her. Ellena blushed, and her rosy cheeks added to her charm.

"Well, I wanted to lighten your dark and dangerous day. The grief I felt when I feared the worst. But to hear from you again and know you survived. That's when I really knew."

"Knew what?"

"That you, Detective George Reynolds, have me trapped under your spell? It's crazy, yes, possibly reckless, but you're like a drug I never want to kick. Werewolf and all."

"Reckless? Definitely. Almost a lamb to the slaughter. Your voice was the last I wanted to hear when I thought it was the end. When I survived, you were the first I wanted to let know. So, if I'm your drug. You are a hypnotising lamb that I welcome into my clutches. Not to eat, but to explore and enjoy you."

"This lamb likes the idea of wandering into your big, strong clutches, as I say, claws and all. I'm a reckless, hopelessly stupid old romantic of a lamb that sees nothing but good in you. A willingness to put all others above himself to save them. This feisty little lamb wants to help you do that."

"Be careful what you wish for, my hopeless little lamb. I bite off more than I can handle."

"Well, that means there's more for everyone else."

"Speaking of which, what was that wonder tablet?"

"Ooh, that old thing, yellow wolfsbane mixed with high amounts of adrenaline and cocaine."

"What? Eh?"

"Yellow wolfsbane ingested counteracts any inhaled wolfsbane and mountain ash. Cocaine breaks open your neurotransmitters and dopamine uptake while widening blood vessels. The adrenaline scorches earth in its wake, boosting your supernatural strength." Another level of astoundment. How she would think of doing that was beyond me, reaffirming my thoughts on Ellena being a beautiful genius.

My keen sense of smell came alive, and drool circled my gums. I heard the brown two-way door swing. It dragged forward the strong, enticing smell of steak, chips, and salad. A lot of steaks. Ellena knew me well already. The dribbles of 'medium-rare' pudding they ate had stirred the beast in me. The thought of ripping through the meat and blood to taste it was almost an aphrodisiac.

The same waiter came prancing along with his prissy smile, making eye contact with Ellena before he'd even reached the table. He was playing a dangerous game. The steak had the wolf side of me feeling a little territorial, even if that wasn't usually me. My fingers wrapped around the table. Elena grabbed a hold soothingly. I looked down to see my class was out. Ellena's smooth touch cupped my fingers, and I suddenly felt lighter. She whispered...

"It's ok, Georgie. He's a twat. We both know he doesn't stand a chance on any."

I sunk back in my chair and smiled. The claws slid away in time as the players came down—two big pieces of rump steak.

"I figured you would need to replenish your energy. The amount of wolfsbane you've inhaled lately has weakened you. You don't sleep, so the best way is food. And I can tell three-quarters of you are here, but something is bothering you." Ellena was far keener at picking up on signals than I gave credit for.

"Oh God, I've been looking forward to this and some time with you. But a niggle is bothering me about this key and paper." I pulled what Etherington had given me onto the table. The steam drifted up my nose as I sipped a mouthful of wine.

"Show me."

Ellena twiddled with the key, scrunching up her cute little nose, creasing the centre of her forehead. While the other hand kept rubbing the paper between thumb and forefinger. Ellena hovered the paper over the heat of the candle.

'Look for the beginning to an ending,' appeared.

"From Mr Etherington?"

"Yeah, he said he knows about me and the money he was paid to keep quiet, like the use of his daughter. He used to buy secrets. Was at pains to give me this,"

"The paper is old, almost leathery, at least a hundred years, maybe more. But that key, Georgie. That thing is maybe three or four times that. So, whatever it goes to,"

"-is as old as Michael?" I cut in, joking but out of surprise. "More or less, yeah. Seriously though, that's a bloody old book or" Ellena handed it back to me. We now had more questions than answers to go with the hundreds already.

We began eating, but our minds had become preoccupied. Ellena smiled throughout. And she was very much like me—a thinker. Neither would rest until we knew.

"Right, mister. Let's finish this lot off and go for a little walk. I'm curious, just like you. A meal is fine. How about we have some real fun and go on a treasure."

"You never cease to amaze me. So full of surprises, it's amazing," it was true. I meant every word. It was at this moment that a sad thought popped into my head. 'Where's the other shoe?' it had to be dropping, eventually. This was too perfect an end to the day. Ellena was perfect, especially for me. My luck hadn't been great until now.

"You say the devil is in the details. Those little things matter to you. If that's the case, then they do for me. Certain red flags wouldn't have flown under the radar if more of us had done that." Ellena smiled as she had done throughout.

"You mean Melanie?"

"Exactly. If I'd seen the stuff you look for, Melanie wouldn't have done so much damage,"

"But you found out. You put the pieces together when all around you were scratching their heads for answers, me included. You saw through the bullshit. It was you who saved that case. And deep down, it's because of you I say 'the details matter,' if you hadn't, there's no telling how high the death count would've been," I had a feeling Ellena would carry some guilt where none was due. It was on all of us, and we've learnt from that.

I kept catching the leers at her from the 'ball-less' waiter. My head was on cloud nine. No matter what anyone did or said, Ellena was hooked on me and vice versa. She was happy to walk in the dark on a scavenger hunt to satisfy my morbid curiosity. It was absolutely crazy. And I loved it.

We carved our way through the delicious food. The steak was to die for. Every slice of dripping half-cooked piece of beef fuelled the wolf. I could feel the red of my eyes trying to glow with happiness. The only step greater than this would tear through a cow myself.

The moment may have seemed fleeting, but it had been the first real fraction of time to feel normal, and I couldn't have wished for finer company.

Deep down, we both knew another day dawned soon enough, and horrifying chaos wouldn't be far enough.

The last mouthful of wine rolled down our throats, and the 'bill' was soon coming. As we stood, I took a deep breath and savoured the ambience of normal life. It could be a while since 'It' and 'I' are reacquainted soon enough.

The sound of 'I wanna dance with somebody' blaring through the speakers capped it off. I'd got lost in an amber daydream when I felt warm, thin fingers slide between mine. Ellena cupped my hand. My daydream got broken, and the first thought I had. 'Was this really happening?'

"So, where did you want to try?"

"Look for the beginning to get an ending. How he spoke seemed to point to the Kanaima. Even speaking to someone keeping secrets for a rainy day,"

"So, let's go back to where we met for the first time. A pleasant night walk along the canal, just me and you, sounds romantic. Together, we can make the worst situation. Good," Ellena was right on all counts, not least the walk idea. I could only hope we found whatever the key belonged to.

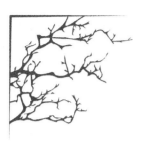

30

ROMANCE IN THE AIR?

Old Ford Bridge - 11.30 pm 2nd November 1987

Under the midnight blue sky, a slimy black surface lay before us as we stood on the bridge, gazing out. The half-moon rippled through the murkiness, bringing us back to the starting point of the 'Kanaima' case. In the week since, a lot had transpired, yet this time felt different. No nerves, no confused bloodlust, just a steady hand, cupped in one belonging to a beautiful woman.

Ellena tucked her chin against her warm coat, resting her head on my arm. The scent of coconut drifting from her hair added to the feeling of security. Silently, we retraced the route I had taken before, each step feeling like heaven. No need for words; our content breathing and heartbeats spoke a thousand words.

The winter air cut through our coats, but it didn't matter. We shared body warmth, our breath painting the air with white clouds. The cosy smell of burnt wood captured the mood perfectly. Frosty grass and gravel crunching underfoot didn't put me on edge this time.

I didn't panic into the shadowed trees beyond the fence line. My eyes focused on the heartwarming sight of Ellena's paleness glowing at night, surrounded by her rosy blush and flowing gold.

"So, little lamb. Still happy to brave the cold with me on this senseless jaunt?" I said, savouring every second of my glance in her direction.

"Depends if this little lamb makes reckless and stupid seem endearing," Ellena said with a teasing smile.

"Everything you do and everything you are, I find endearing," I replied. As we neared the mooring with the bridge a few hundred feet ahead, I could still smell the remnants of dried blood.

"Well, mister, I find the big bad wolf equally endearing," Ellena swivelled in front of me, looking up. Her arms cupped mine, and her face tilted to meet mine. I was hypnotised by the blue swimming pools capturing the moon.

"This big bad wolf has fallen for its prey," I said, diving headfirst and disarmed.

"What a hopelessly stupid old romantic lamb," Ellena said, placing a warm hand to cup my stumbled cheek.

"What a hopelessly sick and twisted werewolf," I replied, feeling her perfect skin beneath the grooves of my fingertips.

"You are my drug to wash away the chaos and horror that this world now offers us," I continued.

"And you are my light to tear through the shadows and become my anchor in my darkest hours," I added, feeling and smelling her warm, sweet breath against my chin. My body had come alive with nerves, excited ones I hadn't felt since Helen.

"So, you masochistic wolf, you going to kiss me or what?" I said, pulling her in tight. The warmth of her lips against mine sent sparks flying through my body. We kissed deeply, and I heard her heart full throttle. Even under her coat, the tiny blonde hairs on her arms came alive excitedly.

Ellena was intoxicating, and I didn't want to let go. Her fingers dug deep into my sleeves, and Ellena didn't want to leave either. All the waiting and tension had built to this moment. My recklessness had met her recklessness head-on, and sparks flew.

Wrapped up in the moment, the world faded away, along with the never-ending danger and litter of dead bodies. We felt like normal people, momentarily wishing to be trapped like this. Until the snapping of twigs in the distance broke us apart. Ellena heard it too, her heartbeat against my chest, throttled like a racing car.

Ellena cupped my hand again, and our attention shifted back in front of us. The scent of firm heels, slick black shoes, and thick streams of 'Marlboro' tobacco announced Michael's arrival from the shadows under the bridge.

"Still creeping in the dark, old man?" I asked.

"Sorry, Georgie, I came here and hadn't realised you were here too. Didn't mean to interrupt," Michael said, stepping ominously into view, his coat pulled tight against the cold and smoking.

"Disturbing what?" Ellena and I laughed, and Michael chuckled—clouds of tobacco.

We had all come to the same beginning for the ending. The question was, what were we looking for? Ellena and Michael mentioned the key leading to a diary, possibly a few hundred years old. I couldn't see how that would help put an end to this.

Shadows of the chaos from the crime scene were all that could be seen. I'd been lucky so far with the ghosts, but that was partly because the bodies didn't linger—a trade-off I'd happily have made. A ghost haunting me and the body not decomposing so fast would mean there had been enough time to gather further evidence. It was the perfect moment to try using my other eyes again, as nobody else was around, and we could let the wolf out.

Michael headed to the other side, leaving Ellena and me to our investigation. Under the bridge, I could see the moment we first met Ellena and Melanie, walking over to take over the body as I slid the scroll away. Nothing else stood out.

Step after step, I traced where I first found that old dust. Michael shook his head across the way; he hadn't found anything either. It felt like a wasted journey, but what else could 'Look to the beginning for an ending' mean?

"Georgie, do you remember when I gave my first speech to the guvnor?" Ellena asked.

"Yeah, you said, 'I got this,' and we thought you showed great character," I replied.

"Yeah, I was talking about this being the secondary scene and the primary being—"

"—two hundred feet down the way to a mooring. And the first scene," I finished her thought.

"Exactly, Georgie. That was where it really—" she started.

"—started," I interjected.

"See, my little genius," she teased.

"Ooh 'my,' I like the sound of that. This little lamb has a few tricks up her sleeve to keep you on your toes," Ellena said, smiling.

"We walked past the mooring on the way and saw nothing obvious. Then again, nothing has been obvious since we started on this unit, and the mooring makes sense. I don't see how it could hide a diary that would be at least A4 or 5," I said.

"Well, you lead, I follow," I added, cupping Ellena's hand. If we couldn't make the most of such moments, when would we? It felt weird, but I had to cherish these moments of happiness.

I couldn't shake the feeling I had at the restaurant—the sense that the other shoe was about to drop. It had to happen soon. Michael followed the line to the warehousing. I could barely see him without my werewolf eyes, as there was no lighting. Last time, at least one had been on. Ellena had her arm scooped around mine as we crouched closer. My knees creaked and wobbled, and I didn't enjoy being so precariously close.

Little by little, I edged forward while Ellena kept still, holding me from slipping in. The black and white mooring looked normal. Again, I saw what happened that night—the way I picked up the frayed edge with traces of blood. But now, nothing seemed obvious, and I was about to stand up.

I couldn't say what it was immediately, with most of the surroundings painted red. But there was a glimmer or a ripple under the moonlight, the most conceivable. Then, the angles changed. The same glimmer ran deep within the width of the canal water, up to a mooring on either side. My eyes switched back for a second, and nothing could be seen. Changed back, and it looked thin enough to be wire or fishing line.

I pinged the nearest section with my claw. It bounced like a guitar string but was much stronger. The tensile strength of the metal appeared clear. We should've walked away, but we all knew better and had to try. The night wasn't getting any younger, and we all needed rest for the journey ahead. Besides, the suspense was killing me. Ellena held tight. I gripped the end and began pulling.

For anyone looking in, we would've seemed crazy, a mime pulling thin air. The surface had a protective coating that helped reflect any surface to blend in. Etherington had taken a big risk. Michael just stood and watched as more and more lines came up.

Were we really doing this? Searching the black of a canal for something that could be a fool's errand. I turned to Ellena for reassurance. I didn't know why, but I had that sudden compulsion for her input. She squeezed my arm gently and gave a nod of approval. So, I carried on.

I must've been pulling for a minute. The dregs of water on the line soaked my hands as they progressed. Until finally, the actual weight was felt. Eventually, it broke to the surface—a holdall wrapped in a clear, vacuum-sealed bag tied to the line. After another minute, we had it amongst the crisp, icy white and green grass on the backside. We scoured for a way to open it, which seemed elusive. Ellena's heart raced, just like mine. Michael stayed on the other side, looking around, seemingly expecting the other shoe to drop.

"Georgie, just tear through it," Ellena said, loitering close to my shoulder. Every inhale of hers made even unpleasant jobs like this seem easy.

"I was trying to be delicate," I said, smirking back. One swish and my claws easily tore through it, releasing the pent-up staleness. It wasn't the stink of death or rancid blood; it was old. Whatever was in the holdall seemed to match Ellena's theory—made of leather mixed with other materials.

No time like the present. The bag came open next, revealing what felt like a large book wrapped in a smooth material. My fingers were poised and were about to lift it when my neck buzzed with trepidation. I saw Michael curl his shoulders. My claws grew big, and I suddenly shifted. For a moment, I'd forgotten Ellena was with me. I panicked, shielding my face while one ear sought the danger.

Ellena didn't falter. Her warm, gentle hand caressed my face, stroking through the fur and trailing a finger over the pointed tops of my ears. Her hands cupped my face, gently tilting me to face her. It was the warehouse all over again. Only this time, she didn't breeze to my lobe. No, her lips drifted to within an inch of mine. Her warm breath teased my face.

"I said, wolf and all," Ellena said, before locking her lips on mine. A different spark flew through me again before we parted. Ellena paused and gave a separate, shorter kiss on one of my fangs. In those few seconds, she truly accepted me, possibly more than I'd accepted myself.

My hackles rumbled again, snapping me back to the moment. This time, they felt aggressively defensive. There was danger around us. My eyes scanned for heat signatures or the slightest movement that wasn't a squirrel or a fox.

"You feeling this, Michael?" I whispered, still crouched but gripping the bag with Ellena's hand.

"Yes, matey. My senses are trying to locate it, but it keeps moving position, a slight scent too."

I knew what he meant. Whatever the danger was, it kept changing direction to throw us off. I gripped Ellena tightly, pulling her close and trying not to dig my claws into her hand.

'Whoosh, whoosh, whoosh,' three low claps whipped through the air. I dived across the gravel, dragging Ellena with me, before looking around to pinpoint where the shots were coming from and if Michael was alright.

"Holy fuck, that was close. Somebody is shooting at," Michael shouted as each 'whoosh' crashed into the brick wall behind him.

"Keep low. I can't tell where,"

"Matey, there's a sharp snap trails off. Only a silencer does that."

"Fuck, had Etherington set us up, you think?"

"Doubt it, matey, but somebody wants the contents of that bag, and we're target practice,"

'Whoosh, whoosh, whoosh,' three more claps rocked out. This time towards Ellena and me. One clipped the metal railing above our heads. Ellena twitched with fright. I gripped her head and used my body to shield her. Panic and adrenaline dripped from her pores.

"Ellena, stay low and close." My eyes bounced left and right, expecting to see something. Anything to tell me where they were coming from. With my eyes closed briefly, my ears and nose soaked up everything nearby.

"Peppermint and Calvin Klein,"

"What's that, Georgie?" Ellena whispered.

"I can smell Peppermint and Calvin Klein aftershave,"

'Whoosh, whoosh, whoosh,' whipped out again. First, toward Michael, crashing into the wall again. The second cracked against the railings just past my face. Then, the third whipped through the daunting dark of night. Cracking a sound wave in its wake.

'Aaaarrregggghhhh,' rattled through the air, riddled with pain. My heart sank, and the other shoe had finally dropped.

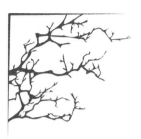

31

NOTHING GOOD LASTS

'Boom, boom, boom, boom, boom,'
Only the relentless pounding could be heard in the deafening echo, drowning out everything but my panicked breaths. A wall of white cloud filled the space in front of my face, my legs soaked in frosty grass, my frightened body heat melting what lay beneath.

A scream, loud and riddled with pain, pierced the air. Adrenaline flooded my system, making it hard to discern whether it came from Ellena or Michael. Frozen in place, I questioned whether I had screamed without realising it. Fear held a tight grip on my limbs, including the wolf.

A low murmur reached my ears—Ellena. It was the motivation my body needed to finally move. The numbing slowly wore off, revealing that I had used my body as a shield, crushing Ellena's beautiful, yet diminutive, figure.

Unbelievably, the icy wind whipped through, bringing me back to the present. 'Blood' blasted from east to west, and I knew who had been hit without checking. Better safe than sorry.

"Ellena, you okay?"

"Yeah, you?"

"I think so, but I'm not sure Michael is."

'Michael?' I whispered, but got no response. We were ducked into the shadows, gaining a little cover, but I couldn't rule out the gunman using night vision. I pulled Ellena toward me, keeping her head low.

I had to keep Ellena safe and get to Michael. Even at night, I had enough bearings to gauge our surroundings. The spiked black fence beside us was five feet tall, and I could easily hoist Ellena over and inside, where she could hide in the darkness. Still, she'd be exposed for a few seconds by lifting her. The canal's width was at least twenty feet, and I had no room to sprint and jump across.

To the north of us was the gunman, without us knowing the range he had on his firearm or skill set. To the south, we'd be heading back to where we came from. Some marksmen could make a shot up to a mile, and the path to the old Ford Bridge was nowhere near that. My ears listened for Michael. He barely had a heartbeat and wasn't healing.

My heightened senses checked for 'Calvin Klein,' hoping they'd disappeared. Sadly, it wasn't to be. Yet, within the melee of aromas, I picked up on more, and it scared the hell out of me. Not only sulphur from the bullets, but wolfsbane again, and stronger.

The complications kept coming, and that wolfsbane-laced bullet was slowly killing the surrounding 'tissue' and spreading. It had seeped into the first few veins nearest to the wound. Michael could be in serious trouble if we didn't get a move on. I didn't know to what extent, but he wasn't moving.

"Ellena, what happens if wolfsbane gets in the bloodstream?"

"Fuck, have you been shot after all? Where?"

"No, not me."

"If it gets in the blood, it could spread to the heart quickly."

"Michael got hit. He's not good. I can smell dying flesh."

Ellena's face displayed shock and panic. While I wondered if Ellena was now having doubts. Whether she could endure trouble like this, I wanted to ask a question, but first, we had to survive. All our options, or lack thereof, swam around my brain. Then it hit me. How the scream bounced, and how hard it was to tell who it was. The bullets echoed. I could still replay the change of pitch.

I whipped off my coat and threw it over Ellena, figuring I could make her lie low in the dark with a black coat to help. She could blend in. Using the warehouse's boxed space, I could project and echo my howl to throw the gunman off while I crept closer to the bridge.

A rifle would be useless at such a short range. If I moved quickly enough, I'd be up the slope within feet of whoever had been brave enough to try picking us off. The why could come out in the wash, over whiskey or coffee, maybe both?

"Ellena, keep as close to the ground as you can with this over you. If you hear howling, don't be alarmed. I'm going to throw them off if I can."

I'd pinned my plan on the notion there was only one shooter. I was picking up on other heartbeats, but I couldn't focus. My attention was split without being in two places at once. I looked across the way. Michael lay lifeless. Time ebbed. I dug down deep and brought forward the bowels of hell.

'Rooooooaaaaaarrtrrttrtttt,'

It was loud, much more than I'd expected. Metal rooftops vibrated, and foundations shook as shutters rattled in their runners. My roar rocked out from where I needed it to. No doubt it would've had the gunman shaking a little, too. This was where I needed Michael to keep still, so another bullet didn't get sent his way.

My ears pointed ahead, a slight rattle before I caught a glint of light from a scope. It seemed more angled to the east. My footing was sturdy amongst the grass, with the ground quite firm. Keeping in the shadows, I moved stealthily, avoiding the dim yellow of limited street lamps. My claws were full and ready to go, with everything painted shades of red and grey. Then, out of the blue, came a response to my diversion. Another roar boomed out—something I hadn't expected.

Again, from the east, only further away. I knew it wasn't me, a delayed echo or some other nonsense notion that sprang to mind.

My gut reckoned it could be the skipper. Andy. As much as he would've been helpful, he'd already stepped back into the fold more than he would've liked. Perhaps by roaring back, he played along. Could he sense our trouble? There's a lot I still didn't know about being a werewolf and communicating nonverbally was one of them. That rattle I heard earlier lasted longer. Another round chambered, and that glimmer was still directed towards the warehousing.

I bounced the last few feet to the slope. It was now or never. Their aftershave was stronger, and for the first time, I got a sense of fear that wasn't ours. My hackles rumbled again, only this time, far harder. Another dimension to the danger had surfaced, but I couldn't tell where. I was about to land in a trap, or the bad guys had a backup plan. Whatever the scenario, nothing good was about to come.

I crouched by the concrete siding and green railings, trying to keep my cloudy breathing to a minimum, so I didn't give myself away. A darkened figure stood at the centre of the bridge with a long black rifle, silencer equipped, perched on the wall. The rattling happened again, and they were panting. The roars had them spooked, but their deep swallows of saliva had me thinking they didn't want to be here, doing this.

Their aim remained the same, and I was relieved that Ellena was safe for the time being and another shot hadn't yet been fired in either direction. It. I had a panic sweat building. Ten feet separated the shooter, with Michael's life hanging by a precarious thread and me.

'Fuck it,' I kicked off from the slope top to sprint at the shooter, reaching within halfway in a flash when another loud crack ripped through the air. I saw the light from a council tower block almost one mile away—a flash before returning the space to darkness. My ears homed in on the piercing whistle rocking through the air.

My next step landed on the pavement within three feet, only to be thumped back on my heels by a sudden flame and a geyser of blood jettisoning toward me. That quick flame ignited immediately before a sea of blue, red, and yellow ripped over the gunman's body, followed by banshee screams of pain.

This was more than a fire. The shooter was being torched, scorched, and obliterated by a level of fire I hadn't witnessed. I counted three seconds, and they were fully engulfed. The rifle dropped into the water. The splash broke the hypnosis of my stare in disbelief—the backup plan. However, the flame gave me an idea.

I grabbed a fallen branch and soaked the end in the flame before sprinting to Michael's side, trying to keep it lit. I shouldn't have worried. Whatever the precursor to the flame was, it couldn't be easily extinguished.

Michael was prone across the floor. Black, veiny, tree-like tracking grew up on the side of his face. Tantalising blood dripped to the floor from his slightly arched back. The bullet had gone straight through. Michael's breathing laboured. Ellena peered out to see me on the other side.

'Georgie, his emitter. Use that gun. Stick it on the wound and burn it,' Ellena whispered, getting to her feet and wrapping herself in my coat to stay warm.

"Cuh... cuh... cuh... trouser pocket," I grabbed it.

"Hey... Told you before, dinner first, Cuh Cuh," Michael just about had the strength to smile and crack a joke. I only hoped it wasn't his last. The back came off quickly, and the gun was soon buried in the wound. It felt squishy. Then again, I'd already chopped into his flesh. What's a bullet wound between friends? I squeamishly pressed the gun, listening to the sizzle of burnt blood and flesh. A cloud of purple sprayed the air.

Michael jolted a few inches off the floor two seconds later, making me jump out of my skin. Eyes wide and bright yellow. His torso curved and writhed. He looked in pain, gasping, but the black tracks were disappearing before my eyes.

Footsteps scampered in the distance, and Ellena was running toward us. I continued to press the flame as Michael wailed. We had survived another clusterfuck of a mess. Ellena had the bag, and whoever those people were, they wanted us quietened and the bag's contents back. I thought the shooter was nothing more than a lapdog, too nervous and unaware of what they were taking on. The other was a professional on standby to clean up, whether a success. Now, we had to figure out the next steps. Hopefully, sleep will be on the menu at some point.

Michael sat upright as the last of the purple cloud dissipated. His eyes dimmed a little, and the blood stopped. The physical wound was healing, but we'd all felt further mental scarring. Eventually, there would be more scars than the normality for the person who carried them. Ellena wrapped herself around my shoulders, kissing my cheek warmly. Her scent soothed the internal struggle I was having. Just the ending I needed and could get used to. Now, what the hell was so special about an old diary? How dangerous were these doors we were knocking on?

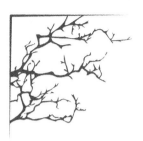

32

The rules of this game were elusive, and the boundaries for the disturbing occurrences in the shadows had spilt into everyday life. Eerie darkness enveloped us, and the air carried the scent of burning wood smoulders.

Fatigue clung to me, and the stream of troubles seemed endless. We could have slipped away unnoticed, but the guilt of leaving the mess for a random passerby was too much to bear. So, we did the right thing and called for help. Flashing blue lights danced across the puddles, casting an eerie glow over the cobblestones of the bridge, mingling with burnt debris. LFB (London Fire Brigade) had put an end to the torment of the tortured corpse. Traditional hosed water proved futile against the relentless brilliant blue, and we watched as paramedics tended to Michael.

The smell lingered, tormenting my senses, and in those spare moments, I grasped the enemy's intent for a swift cleanup. The projectile or bullet they used was no ordinary ammunition, with a mix of combustible metals and acidic undertones. The body was stripped bare in minutes, and LFB had to resort to spraying powder to control it.

Michael protested while pinned to the bed. We had to pretend he caught a ricochet instead of a direct hit to meet Locke's requirements. Wolfsbane, slowing his healing, proved fortunate. Just before the ambulance arrived, I added a quick jab with a claw to cause some surface blood, which is necessary for the story.

Surviving was one thing, explaining it another, especially considering Michael's condition. Ellena, seemingly psychic, concocted a solution. More alarmingly, the supernatural secret we harboured was no longer hidden, and wolfsbane became the weapon of choice against us.

Ellena protected the bag, and my arm remained locked to prevent escape. The case details consumed my mind, and I couldn't savour the moment with

Ellena just yet. Mr Etherington had left us a clue, but uncertainty loomed – had he been watched hiding the bag, or did we have a tail all along?

Distractions, perhaps Ellena's beauty and the chance to open up, clouded my senses. Michael arrived separately, undistracted, yet he didn't pick up on the danger either. How did the shooter manage to be armed with wolfsbane-laced bullets?

Cording off the bridge, I felt on edge, rattled. A body had burst into flames mere feet away, and the shooter's blood still clung to my shirt. The traumatic sight required an explanation to the first officer, and my acting endured the test. My primary concern was Michael's welfare, revisiting an old crime scene while he was pinned and Ellena had hidden. I crept to the bridge top.

They were eliminated before I could reach them. If only the officer and others knew the truth. Danger lurked under their noses, unbeknownst to them. Ellena and Michael remained steady, with Ellena surprising me the most.

Anticipating that Ellena would turn to me and express that it was too much, she surprised me by scooping my arm as she did during the pleasant walk and nestling her head on my shoulder. Warm and soothing, something missing in my life for some time.

Yet, I couldn't settle. Big dots were missing. Hooded people in Essex, experiments, kidnappings, a death trail. Girls with aspirations, a deadly party, government cover-ups, and a wave of supernatural murders. Parents are involved in the 'blood-drained' mess, receiving money and trading secrets. The 'black widows' killing MPs, a trap nearly having me blown up, and branding from the 'devil's circle.'

Now, Michael had been shot amid the chaos. Thoughts filled my mind while a chilly wind battered our faces, noses stuffed with the stink of burnt flesh. Burning was too mild; voices likened it to charcoal or burnt tree bark.

Incinerated flesh and clothing left gooey slime where feet once stood – a sight I wanted to leave. Michael escaped, and Ellena practically snored on my shoulder. The bag caught my attention. The longer we sat with it, the more I noticed its uniqueness. Old, dirty, and something more, a weird vibe drawing me in.

"Bloody hell, Georgie, them wolfsbane bullets are no joke. The next one is yours," Michael said, strolling toward us with a familiar swagger, waking El-lena.

"Hang on, old man. In case you've forgotten, I nearly got blown up," I said, forcing a tired smile.

"Yeah, but I've had my throat ripped out," he quipped back before reaching for his trusty cigarettes.

"Don't remind me; I had to bite you, or had you forgotten?"

"Now, how about you two bloomin call it evens and keep it down, eh?" My head jolted left at a familiar voice — Andy. I was still unsure whether to call him Skip.

"Well, look what the wolf has dragged in," Michael called, cigarette mid-air.

"I take it the roar worked?"

"Yeah, but how did you know what to do?"

"Well, it wasn't full of pain and not quite anger. Plus, it echoed, and I could pinpoint where you were. So I roared back, hoping it helped until I could get here."

"Well, it worked, but there's trouble brewing, and I fear we won't see who it comes from."

"Aye, well. About that. There's been another body. Good old Lockey boy is down the road in a car."

"Why hasn't the radio rocked out?"

"Because it was left on his blooming doorstep."

"Why is he here?"

"A little shaken up and needed space and air. He called me just as I was leaving. So I told him where you were and that you needed help, although it seems you handled things. He posted two officers outside and came to get me."

"I don't get this. Why so direct? Now, why his home?" I said, getting confused by the minute. Was Locke dirtier than we thought?

"Well, there's a note with this one. The killer can't get you to back off. So they try intimidating your boss and hope he backs you off."

Still, it wasn't sinking in, and I ran on empty—another body. The day had been littered with them. We nearly joined the list while somebody else had been weaving a different agenda in the background. Had the killer realised we were harder to kill than imagined and wanted to focus on the real bad guys in their eyes? What I found strange was that we were being shot at.

Whoever the killer had on their list would've wanted us to end the chaos before they became too exposed, not try to kill us themselves unless there had been another play we'd missed altogether. Someone that moved in them circles but not quite with them. Someone who knew about all this and us had been searching for the bag's contents.

They discovered that Etherington had bought it and what he may have planned to do. They kept a distance for us not to pick up on them and tried to take us out once we had the bag. Albeit badly, I might add.

"Do we need to see the body if it's much like the rest? It could be photographed and sent to Mr Nicholls?" I snapped, tugging at my hair, feeling the strain of everything thrown at us. I was really in need of a holiday.

"Well, ordinarily, with everything that's happened, no, lad. But this body is a Mr Edward Cornell, the father of Selene Cornell, the missing and presumed dead girl."

"But Andy, seriously matey, can't it wait? This old dog needs his beauty sleep," Michael said, blasting the side of my face with his cigarette smoke, perching himself on the creaking arm of the bench we'd commandeered as a base camp.

"Well, lad, I'm no expert and hadn't the pleasure of seeing it, but Locke seems to think it's a push in the direction where the killer wants you to look and the note all but says that. Particular words stood out, lad. 'Use your skills for the greater good, not what is easy—last chance to see beyond the smoke and mirrors. Or next time, we'll obliterate your insides instead of toying with them.' That's the gist anyway, lad. There's more, but that bloomin seemed poignant."

My hand jumped to my stomach, a knee-jerk reaction as a residual memory popped into my head, thinking back to the lorry and the black cloud squeezing my organs. The way Michael gasped for life as his face turned bright red. How could I push back? Michael felt it, too. His free hand pressed over his heart while taking a moment to gaze across the black waters.

I didn't need to be a mind reader to wonder what was going through his greying head. His wrinkled eyeline focused on where he'd been lying. His eyes drooped with slight flickers of yellow. Every inhale caught a tinge of his drying blood on the pavement, returning my attention to his stained shirt.

"Can the body be taken to my lab, then? Less distance to go. We need to discuss a few things out of prying eyes and ears. Then some much-needed sleep before we go again." Ellena barely raised her head, but enough to join in the conversation.

"I can see that, lass. I'll get Locke to see sense and dust off the single malt on his desk. There was something else I needed to bring to our little supernatural circle. That might answer some old questions." Andy's heart sped up when he mentioned the last part. Only I wasn't sure if it was excitement or fear. I hadn't known him to fear anything. If we're a betting man, it was an exciting revelation.

"Right, base it is, then. My car is at the other bridge, so we'll head back that way," I said. Andy nodded while Michael stared blankly at the melted black mess on the pavement.

"Andy, is it ok if I jump in with you, matey?"

"Sure."

"Hey, Michael, walk with us. I need to pick your fossilised brains about something," Ellena said, hugging my arm tight. I wasn't sure what her plan was, but I suspected she'd picked up on something or had information she'd held back because she wasn't sure.

"Yeah, come on you, old git. I need your perspective at the mooring as we passed," I said, trying to read what Ellena was doing while making Michael feel less like a spare wheel.

"Just get to the office and stick the kettle on."

A quick nod, and we left the scene with no one noticing. Michael pulled his coat in and did his buttons before raising his collar to shield himself from the chill. Ellena reached out her spare arm to hook through Michael's and pulled him to her side. One on either arm, but Ellena tilted her head to my shoulder again. I got the impression at that moment that she'd realised how low Michael looked.

A sullen face, another exhausting winter night. I looked at the moon, remembering tomorrow night was the full moon and the super-moon a week away. We were all in for a rough ride with the wolf in 24 hours, and if we ended up squaring off against one of the bad guys. We will be at our most powerful, but also volatile.

The walk down the slope felt odd. A lite while I bounded up it to chase down a gunman. Now, this was more of a walk of shame. Neither spoke for a few seconds. I just enjoyed Ellena's scent for a while. She soothed me, and how she embraced my 'shift' felt centring.

"Right, boys. When we return, give the body a once-over for anything I wouldn't see. Then stock up on some presents I've made for you. If this is going how I think it is, you'll need all the help you can get, especially tomorrow."

"You remembered the full moon."

"Of course. Trust me, Georgie, I'm in this for the long haul, and you better make sure your butt stays safe, you understand?"

"Hey, girly, what about my butt?"

"Well, it's a little fat. Oh... Of course, you too, old man. Who else would we have to make fun of?"

"Bloody hell, now it's two against one. I can see why you match well with the shit magnet."

"What's that, my endearing personality?" I said, cracking a smile that didn't need to be forced.

The problem was, throughout that, Ellena's heart changed, followed by a sudden gulp. She changed what she was about to say at the last minute. And I felt it was about Locke, which intrigued me by what Andy had in store for us. Other than the dead Mr Edward Cornell.

By my reckoning, that made the fathers of Sally, Alice, and Selene all dead. Francis was back from the dead. Leaving the parents of Maria, Francis, Susan, and Grace as potential targets. Not to mention the guest list.

"Oh, guys... Erm... I think Locke is a druid," finally the courage of her conviction. The comment hung in the air with all the shock of 'surprise pregnant,' leaving Michael and me speechless.

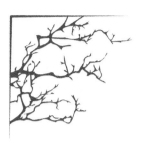

33

BUBBLING

The boiling water surrounded me with searing heat, pushing clouds of steam. All I could do was stare and wonder when our luck would turn. As the bubbling reminded me of burnt blood, I felt sick to my stomach, tired of always being the target or the cleanup crew. The smell of cheap coffee granules did little to inspire energy. The cavalry came, Andy walking in carrying a single malt, Michael placing a bag on the table, and Ellena jotting notes.

Each face I looked at seemed a little beaten. Andy, reading the situation, noticed the bloodied hole in Michael's shirt and the spray on mine. We should've been changing, but neither of us felt like it. Whiskey might not be the solution, but it could soften the blow of defeat.

The light cream, cigarette-scorched walls hardly excited us for our 'supernatural detective operations.' Let's face it, that's what we are now. The normal belonged to everyone else while we played with monsters that could reach within our torsos, squeezing our organs inches from our last breath.

That Locke could be a 'druid' didn't seem real. Ellena dropped the bombshell thought and left it hanging with our confused faces. All I could imagine was somebody old and Stonehenge. It just didn't compute in my tired brain.

"Come on, Georgie, my stomach feels like my throat has been cut," Michael said, trying to psych himself up a little.

"Well, it was kind of ripped through," I quipped as I poured. The black liquid had my reflection, and for a split second, my eyes flashed red. I hadn't even tried, nor were they controlled. I was irritated and letting it show.

"Got you there, Mickey boy. So, Ellena, isn't it? Please look after our Georgie. He's due a win and has a heart of gold. The only downside is he's a flipping shit magnet," Andy said, chuckling yet sincere.

"Don't worry; with all of us helping, anything is possible," Ellena said, looking up from her folder with a beaming smile. She'd been writing feverishly since she sat on a mission, whereas I couldn't think of anything worse. Each of us took turns staring at the elephant in the room.

The way things had gone, it would more than likely be anticlimactic. I was pacing while the rest sat, whether it was restless anxiety or the tiredness that would take hold if I did. All I was doing was delaying. A conversation needed to be had, and the bag needed emptying. All before the body arrived.

I dragged a chair lazily, grating on the floor, making everyone look. Andy got to pouring the whiskey while Michael lit a cigarette. All we were missing was a pack of playing cards, and we'd have ourselves a game of poker.

"Right, you lot. I haven't been about much for many reasons, but after Mickey got kidnapped and found, I wanted to find out more while I was off the radar. One mission was to lay to rest my niggles over your—"

"And?" I said impatiently.

"Well, there's a lot more than meets the eye. He goes to a closed-down electronics store in Forest Gate regularly. I broke in when he left once, and to my surprise, it was full of herbs and books and a lot of weird crap I didn't understand. These weren't old or the kind that goes in food or as a tea bag."-
"Moon and sun charts, solar systems. The works. Then I saw a symbol on some old books. I mean old, like older than Mickey. It had swirly lines in four quarters, knots on a rope type, designed as curving triangles. The writing inside wasn't English or any dialect I'd encountered on my travels."-

- "But I recognised that symbol and wracked my brain, trying to think where. Then I realised. It was tattooed on Locke's back. I'd caught a glimpse when he changed his shirt and thought it was interesting. But when it matched the books, I had to dig more, and according to research, it identified a druid. Particularly 'protector' ironic, eh?"

Andy's theory matched what Ellena had said; only she didn't explain further, even sounding slightly scared. The look on Andy's face as he sipped the whiskey coffee told me he was serious and his heart didn't skip a beat. Not that he wouldn't have known I'd listen, but I didn't see a need for him to lie. Ellena nodded in agreement and showed me her folder. She'd drawn the symbol Andy spoke of before flashing it to Andy, who nodded.

Why would Locke have all the herbs, and what was he doing with them? Could that have been what he was buying in the photo of him in the alleyway? After hearing that revelation, I also needed to share what I knew. Or, more exactly, what I didn't know but had seen. Whether the two correlated, God knows, but the group finally had to hear it. This was the only way to get on the same page.

"Well, I may not know or understand what that means, but when I got called for the quick turnaround for this case while you two went to the hospital. I sat in Locke's office, trying to stay awake. So I got nosey. You know, from the wolf's point of view. Anyway, the floor by his chair had a large dried and recently cleaned up puddle of blood,"

I said, gauging their reaction to see who seemed the most surprised. Michael looked startled. Ellena wasn't far off either; their hearts jumped in unison. Yet, Andy didn't seem fazed. I wanted to push him on it. With my edgy mood, I wanted a little battle to wake me up, and testing how much Andy knew seemed obvious. Then, the rational part of my brain told me not to rock the boat because he was barely back, and I didn't need to push him out again. So subtlety it was.

True to his words, Andy gave nothing away between sips of his drink. Looking around us, we were limited in numbers compared to what we knew existed, and we hadn't even scratched the surface. I thought, how much longer could we do the cloak and dagger around everyone else without raising questions? We needed somewhere private for talks like the one we were having. Or the present that still awaited us in the bag.

"So, boys, are we going to see what all the fuss is about?" Ellena grabbed centre stage, prodding my arm before smiling at me.

"About time, too. If I took a bullet for this crap, it better be worth it," Michael said, smirking. He had his sense of humour back, but his statement had an element of truth. Whatever Etherington hid and had people after had to be worth killing for.

Michael slid it across to me, passing the parcel time, minus the music, with only anticipation throbbing in my temple and a low radio to set the tone. My hands hovered over the dirty blue bag. That same vibe was given off. My eyes darted around the table as I dived in. Everyone shifted forward in their seats; pupils fixed on every movement I made. The tips of my fingers brushed the surface of the wrapping, and I got a little static, almost a mini-surge of power or adrenaline.

The way I felt when I ate Ellena's gum she'd made. The group was on ten-terhooks, and I had to consider winding them up by going slow. Sadly, my patience wasn't at its greatest. I wanted it done before we had to delve into another dead body. A little question crossed my mind: to ask Michael if the number of deaths he'd seen in his career was worse before or after we crossed paths and then worked together.

I don't know why. Perhaps the idea of that corpse arriving soon made me think I'd already seen a lot in such a short time. For some, it could be too much.

Andy would've seen a lot as a marine. He'd allowed nightmares and hauntings. I guess, as any soldier would have to live with. I had a bundle wrapped in a black velvet cloth in my hands. Half the thickness of a shoe box and A4 plus a little more. A lot like a telephone directory. The vibe was crazy. It felt like a part of me, but not.

The eyes bulged, and for reasons unknown, both Michael's and Andy's glowed. We'd been having trouble getting Michael to learn control, but Andy had it down to a fine art. Perhaps they were getting the same vibe as I was—I thought, hoping nobody would walk in. Then again, it was a little after midnight, and any rational human would be home in bed. Unless working nights.

Unlike us, who escaped and got dragged back in by our curiosity. Locke would've summoned us, anyway. At least we had freedom for a little while at the restaurant. Heavy is the head that wears the crown of a trouble seeker. A little politer term I played over in my head as I toyed with the weight in my hands. Better than being called a shit magnet.

The first layer flipped open, releasing a breeze of history, a little waft that had me smelling the antiques of it. While also urging caution over potential fragility. We got to see the spine first—dark red leather, but not as ordinary as that description painted in my head. The leather was raw, and the essence I picked up on felt alive. A marbled blood red. Literally blood. Unmistakable anywhere.

What's more, I felt it was human with a little difference. Michael and Andy seemed to think so, too. Michael's nose twitched, and the claws had already grown. We had already felt special and hadn't even exposed it yet. My senses had been stirred, but I was doing everything possible to remain in control. Deep down, it was for Ellena's benefit to show I could control that side of myself. To at least be human around her. A seed of doubt was rooted in the back of my mind. With all the research and how intrigued by it she'd been. Was it the wolf she liked more?

Was I going to regret letting someone in? Was I going to be made the fool by finally dropping my guard? I didn't want to have these doubts, but that moment on the canal and the caring touches throughout felt too good to be true. Ellena couldn't smell what we could, the vibe I got from it, but she slipped her arm under mine as if she'd read my apprehension.

The other side flopped open, releasing another wave of that stink. Yet this time, I allowed it to slip on because what was in front of me looked far more exquisite, frightening, and alluring, rolling into one. Blood rippled throughout the cover, wrinkled skin. The longer I stared, the more it seemed skin. It was human blood for sure, but tainted. The ancient-looking book was familiar, almost as if it were a part of me. I knew that couldn't be the case. It didn't explain the feeling.

The frightening part was its exquisite craftsmanship, the detail. Its edging was lined with slithers of bone, and so was the title. The alluring part, 'Bestiary,' the world's first encyclopaedia on things supernatural - was created by Professor Arthur Freundricksen in 1679. Those words hypnotised me before my brain recalled why Mr Etherington left this for us. Why he'd got his hands on it in the first place, let alone how something so dangerous in the wrong hands could be gained. I saw where the key went.

A large clasp made of normal bone and... fangs. My stomach turned at least once while the excited kid in me wanted more. The notion that I was in this, well, what I was, anyway, didn't even register. A leather strand looped into a small pocket at the top of the spine. It connected to a rather large and slightly unnerving fang. Whatever had that in their mouth once must've been huge and frightening. My fingertips brushed the surface. It was. We were one. That's the easiest feeling I could come to. A synergistic tingle that teasingly trickled through tips to tendons, tempering tension.

"There's a letter, Georgie," Michael said, hoisting an arm forward with claws out to point toward the top of the book.

There was a stiffness to his tone, edgy. This book was doing things to us we hadn't expected. Sure enough, a cream envelope part over the edge of the thick fan of pages. I teased our trepidation while toiling with the genuine fear that we'd just been given something that would not only broaden our knowledge. The number of enemies plotting chaos in the shadows had become unquantifiable.

34

PRESENTS

Velvet cream paper pinched between thumb and forefinger, tugging the envelope free. The contents felt thick with a little weight to them. Something slid inside and felt loose, like another key—the devil's dilemma. I was torn by what to open first. We needed one of these to give us a chance to catch the killer, a detail to make up for the man-made mistakes that had brought so much bloodshed.

In Mr Etherington's last moments, I got the impression he had wanted to help fix what had been done. His part in it, at least. I couldn't even dare to imagine what he had to do, killing his daughter. He said that, in his eyes, Alice was no longer his daughter. None of the girls were the same after that party. Perhaps the book had an entry on the 'Black Widow' and whether it or they'd had any weaknesses. With the envelope in my hands, a look at the clock had me conscious time wasn't on our side.

The corpse was being recovered slowly to prevent the risk of accelerating decay. For now, I was leaning towards not showing Locke the book. Perhaps we should have some secrets if he was what Andy and Ellena thought until Locke came clean. He knew what we were, but not all information flowed both ways.

A claw flicked free, and I tore through one side of the envelope. A folded A4 paper and a small silver key with a stubby body. A lot smaller than the one for the book or my locker. A padlock, perhaps. Ellena had a broad smile with a fast heart. Michael's eyes were narrowed, watching every movement of my hands. Andy, though, remained calm.

'To Detective George Reynolds,'

'We wouldn't have met properly when writing this. The other day on my doorstep wasn't my finest hour. There haven't been many finest hours lately. Not since the shell of my daughter returned that night. Maybe even a little before that. For this to land in your hands, I'd likely be dead. Poetic justice, considering I made a deal with the devil.'-

'I was naïve and got blindsided. I'm not the only one to fall into that trap. I found out Alice and her friends were targeted as a group. The people behind it all picked at each set of parents' weaknesses so we couldn't fight if anything went wrong, which it did. I resisted at first and tried to return the money. All that did was make me lose my job. So I hid in the bottle. To everyone looking in, I'd become a drunk. Instead, I used that as a front to dig a little. Found this book through a dark network of collectors in Romania.'-

'I had to attend a secret bidding war at a distillery on the outskirts of a village called Cosminele. No sooner had I won than I was on the first flight out. It had so much attention, and I wanted it for answers to what my daughter and her friends were becoming—an encyclopaedia of anything that went bump in the night and had been discovered through the centuries. Only to get to the auction. It had been stolen from a sadistic group of scientists going one step further through evolution and making monsters themselves. They were crossing bridges of the supernatural.'-

'Professor Arthur Freundricksen didn't just create this book. It's led to believe he may have amassed ten different volumes over the years. All jammed with information on creatures you'd never imagine in a million years. Or the people mixed with them. Detective Reynolds, this is just the tip of the iceberg. I know what you were born into and what you were made into. Unfortunately for you, I'm not the only one. Powerful people out there seem hell-bent on creating bizarre and dangerous creatures. To what end, I don't know. Only when somebody has the power is it never enough.'-

- 'Think about it. Parliament threw a huge party and used it to experiment on impressionable girls. Who's saying how many others got affected? The point is parliament, the fucking government, for Christ's sake. What if they could infiltrate No 10 Downing Street or Buckingham Palace? Think of their world summits and the other countries and dictators involved.'-

- 'These people could make creatures on demand to win wars or assassinate upon request. There's so much bad in the world already. Now, there are the shadows. I followed your last case against that demon. You may be different, but you're good and can go toe to toe with the bad guys. You can't do that with next to any information.'-

- 'This book should give you an idea of what's out there. The key is to a safe deposit box held by J.P. Morgan. In that box are a set of keys and the deeds to an old warehouse down by the embankment. It has a loading bay with a basement for ample storage. There were secret tunnels under London from this place, but I didn't get to look.'-

- 'I have no one left to atone for the sins of the father, but you could be good enough to help keep people safe. To do that, I thought you'd need a safe place where questions wouldn't be asked. A place where nobody would look for dangerous books like this one. It may not make up for the bad I've done, but their dirty money finally has a purpose.'

'Good luck, Detective Reynolds.'

There had been much more to Mr Etherington than we had realised. Admitting his mistakes was one thing, but he'd tried to correct them. Or at least battle future abominations created by people happy to hide the shadows and feed their thirst for power.

If this book was one of ten volumes, where were the other nine and how many supernatural beings were there? When we thought we had a grip on what we knew, the bar moved again. This book was created in 1679, three hundred and eight years ago. In all of that time, the world had been oblivious. Etherington used his money in the hope we'd make the most of the space to investigate this stuff out of the public without the fear of books like this falling back into the wrong hands.

A look at the others shared my surprise. We were in the tea room handling something well out of the remit of ordinary police officers. Yet Etherington had great foresight. None of us knew how dangerous life could get from now on.

"So, the man kills himself after killing his daughter, who supposedly killed the mother. Do we believe that, Georgie?" Michael said, dropping back in his chair, forehead wrinkles clapping together as he thought. That was a good question. Did I believe what he'd said at the scene and in the letter?

"Michael, I read him the whole time: his heartbeat, the seconds between gulps, pupil dilation, the works. Even the chemo signals from his sweat. Pain and sorrow mainly, but when he spoke of the money and allowing his daughter to join that sham of a program. Regret," I said, and as I heard my words out loud, I bought into it even more.

The man messed up and wanted to do some good from all death.

"I've heard of those black-market auctions, lad, and they're no joke. Sketchy as hell just to get in the same room. So, if he's done this as a dying declaration. Then who will look for a gift horse in the blooming mouth? Maybe even a blessing in disguise going forward, lad. But tonight, there's nought we should be doing. Other than a quick butchers inside that book. Give the body a once-over before some much-needed rest," Andy said, his eyes darted to the book.

He was right, though. I stowed the key and letter away before pulling the book closer. It gave the same rumble of static energy. With the other key ready, and hung an inch from the clasp. I got hit by a sudden bout of nerves. My hand was visibly shaking. Not once had I experienced that before. It had to be the aura it was giving off that slowly caused some doubts to fester.

I took a deep breath, and I took the plunge. Old dust jumped free from the lock. Bone, blood, and dirt were all I smelt. The fangs clicked open. Even an ominous act felt a little menacing. A chorus of drums pounded heavily around me as excitement and fear mounted equally.

My fingers dragged a clump of pages together, vaguely remembering where the envelope had divided. In case there had been some significance. I possibly even hoped it had. With the pages fanned open, I got wafted by a rush of blood. The pages themselves looked old, as expected, but still had a slightly leathery skin look. A dirty marbled cream. Yet, it was the writing that got me. That's where I'd smelt the blood from. Most definitely human. But it's not normal.

The text was old script style on one page, yet the writing was different on the next, where pages had been divided. Italic and slightly fresher. Wide eyes were fixed on the contents. They were looking at the pictures. I hadn't taken them on board yet. This was a horror story, 'Raven the Revenge Reaper,'

A demon reaper of souls for the power to seek revenge. That's part raven, part human. It originated in Norway, targeting the weak and wronged in search of souls to keep their power thriving. Pure enjoyment from murder and chaos. It will plague dreams.

Pure enjoyment from murder and chaos. It will plague dreams.

Then, in everyday life, until a willing victim gives in, the demon will become a guardian, offering immortality until revenge has been taken in exchange for their soul. The only catch is the soul is drained immediately using the raven's talons, leaving behind a mindless zombie. Known weaknesses. Its claws or bullets are laced with neurotoxic snake venom.

My stomach flipped. The diagram was truly horrifying. Even on paper, its eyes felt like piercing my brain. With imposing wings and large talons, it stood on a mountain of skulls—a creature we didn't want to come across soon. There was more writing, but my attention soon shifted to the other page. Another drawing, much like its writing, is recent.

Like the deadly spider, they called it the widow, a monster manufactured for maximum destruction. It spliced human and demon DNA blockchains with the most dangerous 'widow' family of spiders known to man. They were blending their venom and amplifying beyond any known anti-toxin. Classification of this creature has been deemed uncontrollable and should be destroyed. They're too connected to a shared trauma from the human side and seek revenge. The subjects died but were bought back through demon DNA synthesis and could bond as one. Separately, they can subdue and syphon all fluids from their victims within minutes.

The corpses are mummified while turning their organs into cocoons, producing a toxic gas version of their venom that erupts and decays the rest of the body until nothing remains—highly dangerous and highly volatile — approach with caution. When subjects are joined, they become a black cloud that can penetrate at a cellular level and destroy their victims from within. Weaknesses are unknown so far, only that they're bound by supernatural law. Especially shapeshifters. Learn the laws, and you learn how to defeat the 'widow'. Initial tests showed freezing temperatures slow the monster down and cause the cloud to thicken enough to restrict phasing through physical matter.

Demon DNA and blood. How did they have that? Who else had they toyed with using it? My mind raced. My blood hadn't resurfaced yet and had demons in it. Did these people have mine and use it to experiment on vulnerable people like those girls? That's all I could think of, and it felt like a kick in the balls. I imagined Andy and Michael thinking the same. There was no way of knowing, nor could we track it down. It caused panic that those bastards may have synthesised it to grow its volume, and their experiments may be endless.

That was all we needed with the standard supernatural, like the Kanaima. I was lost in a morbid daydream, staring at the 'blood' writing—each thin curve and stroke. The aroma played with my nostrils. My mouth watered a little, which was to be expected, and my fingers wrapped against the table-top. Changing pitch as my claws pushed forward. I'd sunk into a pool of self-pity for a moment, imagining I could've been partly responsible, even if it had been the only way to save Andy's life. I toyed, drifting a claw above the lettering. No real weakness to speak of, so how did the book help us?

'The laws of the supernatural and shapeshifters,' we didn't know what they were. All of it was new to us. Unless it wasn't. I thought back to earlier and to anything that had happened with this case and the last. 'Devil in the details,' indeed. That warehouse with the dead bloke in the chair. That woman's corpse on the table could've been related to me. 'Wolfsbane' had to be one of the laws, along with mountain ash.

If they weakened us and knocked us out, would it do the 'widow,' Michael still the bundle he nabbed from the death tunnels about that symbol that could be a powerful ancient relic? We just don't have the time, with one disaster after another.

My claw dropped in frustration as my free hand forced another sip of tepid whiskey-laden coffee past my lips. No matter how many mouthfuls we took, it wasn't washing away the bitterness of not knowing what the hell we were doing. With every hour that passed, I felt the bend.

Little by little, I creaked under the strain. All eyes were on me for answers and guidance through a world I'd known for two minutes. How much more bending would I need to do before I snapped?

The tip of my index claw planted on the word 'widow', and the smell of blood turned damp. A wave of it consumed the surrounding air. It tugged at every hair littered through my nasal passage. Dirty old dampness mixed with death and lots of it. It was my turn for chemo signals to go haywire. I reeked of panic, wondering where the stench had come from. Had the body arrived? My head bounced to Ellena, who spoke but couldn't hear. Then, Michael and Andy all took their turn doing the same.

"Michael, you smell that?" I asked, but still nothing. "Andy?" Nothing. I felt my heart quicken, and then the room decayed. It faded from the tea-room. Slimy water seeped from the cracks, and tobacco cream became dirty grey stone. Our table became a silver gurney holding a long body bag. I looked up in time to see the room widen. Several other gurneys scattered throughout with the tense sound of beeping flicking my ear drums. I was sitting in the middle of another dirty, haunting basement. How?

35

TORTURE

Three men in white coats and black hoods, much like those in the limousine, stood in front of racks sparkling with electricity. I could discern at least one outline of a person—a young woman bound by wrists and ankles. The musky-acrid stink of death wafted from every direction. Black liquid ran through clear tubes into the right side of the woman, similar to what had leaked from Sally's eye, while what looked like blood was being pumped and drained from the left.

My head spun with confusion and fear. One minute, I had the bestiary in the tearoom; the next, I watched scientists in hoods experiment on at least one woman. My finger tapped the description, and then it all changed. Similar to what happened in Locke's office. It had happened again. The murder scene in Etherington's house had already occurred, and I was given a glimpse.

We'd thought it was a one-off. Now, I'm not so sure. It was dark, with more papers plastered across the walls of a large open space. The men walked around, oblivious to my presence, and the woman squealed with pain. I tried to look at her face, but it was blurred. Long dark hair and a slim frame, but that was it. What was the purpose of these visions? Remnants of events. Or was this an evolution of my abilities?

Once was random, and the second could be a coincidence. But I didn't believe in coincidences. So, I looked for details that could be clues or fragments of information. These visions had to be for a reason. Etherington might have called us if we hadn't gone when we did. We wouldn't have the book. So, what was I supposed to learn from this one? Other than that, I could feel the girl's pain, which was excruciating. The longer I looked, the more I realised I witnessed the process that made the widow, or at least part of it. And she was one girl from the party. The hair made me think of Selene.

I counted the body bags and six others. Had they all died that night, as Etherington believed?

Sally had told us a story, a jumbled mess of memories, and a tale woven by those who ruined their lives, maybe even some farfetched reprogramming. Not that I knew if that was possible. Nothing could be ruled out with everything that's been witnessed so far. A draft ushered through, bringing another smell: horse manure. Lots of it. I'd seen it caked around the wheel arches of the limousine, many layers and crammed within the tire grooves—another coincidence to stack on the pile.

There had to be more. I was rapidly concluding that this basement connected to the house that held the 'masquerade party,' the first clue being the manure. I tried using Werewolf's eyes, but wouldn't change. Nor would my claws come. Limitations I hoped were limited to whatever this was. My sense of smell worked fine, but that's all. A detail that seemed a little confusing, but I had to play the cards I'd been dealt.

I spun on the spot. The grey stone beneath my feet changed. Pebbles, fancy-looking, smooth, and assorted colours, much like a driveway. A posh driveway. Sally had described as much. Then came the walls, the section behind the racks, and scientists crumbled to reveal bright white pillars on either side of some steps. The picture before my eyes formed more of what Sally spoke of on that fateful night.

The scientists turned in unison. Their white coats morphed into smart black coats and bow ties. Their masks remained, and trays of champagne flutes were thrust forward. The smell of manure changed. There were four numbers on one pillar, but again, they were blurry. The rest of the grey wall had become a large, extravagant housefront. Exactly as we'd been told. My brain was making connections through this vision. How it was happening confused the hell out of me, but the little details lined up.

I just needed one little 'dot' to paint a picture of where it all began. The wind whipped around me, and the gurneys became tall fur trees bordering a limousine to my left. Another smell breezed past liquorice. It had come from the drinks. They were laced that night, and the masks contained hallucinogenic at the very least. It all looked as described and reeked of money and power. Yet nothing else to give me that 'dot,'

Until I caught the reflection in the limousine's rear window.

The darkening purple sky cast a shine across the black. It captured the driveway entrance; I looked over my shoulder, but it was still a grey wall. In the window, it had the entrance and a street sign across the road. Only the words were back to front.

'eunevA tunlaW.'

We had a street name, and suddenly, everything slowly crumbled away again as the tobacco cream walls reappeared along with the table and the bestiary. I was back in my seat, viewing the table, and I quickly scrambled for a pen and paper. My audience was back. I grabbed Ellena's folder and pen in a rush to write the words as I saw them.

Only when I'd noted the last letter did any remaining liquorice, acrid death, and fur tree aroma fade from my nose. I'd realised the strange expressions gawping at me. All three were wide-eyed and full of panic. My claws were on display, resting on the table beside the pen. My heart thumped as I tried to gather my breath and senses.

"What the blooming hell, lad?" Andy said. I spun my head and took a deep breath.

"What?" I said, as if everything was normal.

"Your bloody eyes, mate. Completely ghost-grey, you were in a trance for the last ten minutes. Just like in Locke's office," Michael said, quickly pouring everyone a double.

"It happened again. I touched that page, and I was suddenly in a basement. Only it was the one where the girls were experimented on. I felt their fucking pain,"

I stopped, reliving that moment as I thought of Alice lying dead on her lounge floor. A shell of the girl she'd once been. With absolute agony, causing tears to trickle down my cheeks. Ellena saw and pulled herself close to my shoulder. The smell of her hair warmed me inside.

"Then it became the driveway of a posh house. The same Sally spoke about. Their drinks were spiked, and the girls never stood a chance. There was a limousine, and the window reflected the driveway entrance. I couldn't see it normally. Only in the reflection, along with a street sign,"

Michael pulled the paper toward him. His heart remained steady, but the wrinkles on his forehead told me he was thinking. Grabbing the pen, Michael rewrote my writing before dropping backwards, eyebrows raised.

"Walnut Avenue? I have to say, mate, I'm equally impressed and spooked," Michael said, finally cracking a smile. I imagined what everyone was thinking. That I was going crazy or that we now had another needle to find in a haystack. We'd already done far more with less. Yet it could well be the 'dot' we needed.

"Right, so we have Walnut Avenue to find and what supernatural laws the 'Widow' has to adhere to," Ellena said, grabbing her book back to make notes.

"There were tall fur trees, and the limousine that blew up said 'Epping Luxury Autos' as for the laws. Start with what's affected us so far and imagine how it could debilitate the monster in the cloud."

Ellena gave a confident tilt of her head, raising her eyebrows in surprise and a sweet smile just for me. Meanwhile, a van was pulling into the yard. The body had arrived, and our work had only begun. But, boy, was I exhausted.

MY MIND WAS STUCK ON how powerless I felt when I couldn't project claws or use werewolf's eyes in the vision. It's not like I'd had the abilities all that long, but to suddenly not have them. I felt vulnerable. Almost as if a limb had been removed. I think the term is actually 'phantom limb syndrome,' where the body tries to use the missing arm or leg even if it's long since gone.

A lack of claws or colour-changing eyes seemed trivial, but I've had them since I steadily got a grip on what I am. We were in the dark depths of the chilly station basement. Sanitary stainless-steel furniture and beige-tiled floors that sloped to a drain. I gathered that the basement was initially used for the coroner and as a temporary morgue until they finally got their own space. Locke thought it would be best for Ellena to re-open it, considering the varied species of dead bodies we could see.

Mr Nicholls, on the receiving end of the normal ones so far, had been lucky. He may have even had a few over the years and not realised. Possibly more victims of the supernatural than he could wrap his head around. Ellena's space was perfect and could be more so if we got the green light for that embankment warehouse. A dying wish declaration and all that. It's said many hands make light work, but many werewolves?

We stood around the table, looking at the body bag. While Ellena had her fingers on the zip, seeming a little like 'prey,' exquisite prey indeed. Each metal crocodile tooth echoed in my drums. As the first gap appeared, out came the stink—the usual rancid, deathly decay. I could hear the flesh solidifying and cracking while the organs steadily shrank in their cocoons. The fact I could tell all of this was happening was a notion beginning to weigh me down. Made no better by my lack of energy, that vision had taken a little more out of me than I'd realised. Nothing a week off couldn't cure.

The head came into view, taut white skin decaying to an old, dead brown. Edward Cornell's hair was a curly mix of dark grey and black. His lips had deflated and pulled tight to reveal a mouth of teeth and gums that looked decidedly creepy.

This one, though, had the least amount of decay yet. Andy said a note accompanied the body and yet, being a father, aside. I wasn't seeing the sudden rise of importance that couldn't have waited until morning.

"Here, lad, I know you're wondering why now and not morning," Andy said, and it wasn't the first time I questioned whether he was reading my mind.

"What the hell? How?" I said. Our conversation, or lack of words, left Michael and Ellena scratching their heads.

"I know you by now. Besides, I would've thought the same. But this has Locke rattled. You'll see why it is so important," Andy remained calm, seemingly unfazed, considering how he described Locke.

It was nothing more than a folded piece of paper. Part of the writing showed through, and there wasn't much to read. A niggle in my mind made me think this may not be the real message.

'Hello, detectives. Time to choose a side before it's too late. As someone who knows what it's like to have free will taken away. We thought you would understand. We are all pawns in the game of secrets and lies. Yet you protect people who would also want you dead. Time to cut the head off the snake. Could it be the one that leads this country? Now Press play,'

"I take it, politics and the prime minister?"

"Reckon so lad,"

"I hate to state the obvious, but do we have an idea if the body was?" Michael interrupted, bringing up what I was thinking.

"God knows, let's assume not,"

Ellena opened the body bag completely while I put on a pair of gloves. I'd figured it would be another VHS, but judging by the size of those, there weren't too many places on him for it to be hidden. The stink was already kicking up, and I didn't fancy being around it any longer than I had to be. Amongst all of this, I was relieved this case didn't follow the last. Instead of ghosts, it's now visions I experience.

Whether it's evolution or the blood moon had me all screwed up. There was no way of knowing until life settled down a little.

I didn't need more surprises, especially if they came asking me to find peace. My sense of charity only goes so far. We knew the killers, so now it wasn't about identifying someone. This was to shape a credible narrative and end it. Yet my pain had left an impression, and I couldn't help but feel sorry for them.

Ellena worked one side, I did the other, Edward wore a suit, and we were coming up empty. Pockets, the waistband, and even random hiding spots like down the legs. Nothing. I remembered the bomb, and the sliced stomach. On came the red. I could see the hidden sweat stains, even pee spray, down his trouser leg. Back to the upper body, I breathed deeply, hoping not to catch on to what I feared.

Unfortunately, hope hadn't been our friend of late. My eyes caught a faint horizontal stain. It could've passed for another sweat crease, but the rancid was too great.

"Michael, grab us the camera," I said, ensuring we recorded wherever possible regardless of opinion or circumstance. Especially with the prospect of a proper environment to display this stuff without scrutiny. How else would we learn and adapt?

"What for?"

"His." Ellena looked at me funny, then twigged before grabbing forceps, a scalpel, and a tray.

"Oh great. Why do murderers always have to bury something in the body? It's fucking gross," Michael said, getting into position.

I ripped the shirt open, releasing a draft of dead organs and flesh. The slice was neat enough, but with the skin decaying and shrinking, the slice had pulled tighter and narrowed to the width of an envelope. They'd taken the piss a little, making it look like a letterbox.

Ellena swished the scalpel through any stiffened flesh. The crunching gristle had my neck twisting with a chill. Before she fished through with the forceps. Andy was too busy setting up the TV and VCR to be concerned about the mess. His nose twitched at the scent, though. A little flash of yellow trailed in his wake.

Out came a line of silver attached to clear plastic wrapped around a VHS. Michael got busy snapping away as Ellena laid it on the tray before cutting it free.

"Right, you lot ready for an anti-climax?" Andy said, jamming the tape in the player and waiting to press play.

"Story of my life," Michael quipped to the button click.

All we could see was Edward Cornell. In the first few frames, he's seen leaving another limo; in another, he's captured talking to dead m.p. Daniel Dowden. Then Edward Cornell is dead in his armchair, holding a sign with the writing 'No10,' slowly decaying.

'Dowden was dirty, daddy dearest was dirty. All the fathers were dirty and enjoyed the spoils of dirty money. It all starts at the top. Some get the power and want more, while others look for power and don't stop until they have it. Then, all the dirty men came together and threw a party.'-

-'High-profile criminals masquerading as good people. For us, Death is a Masquerade. They made us because they wanted a weapon. One after the other, all got drugged, made to hallucinate and mutilated before being experimented on. For some, death came straight away, and the process was quick. For others, it took time. The lights were on, but nobody was home. What they didn't expect was how our friendship bond would connect us. We became one. Now, they will all pay, and it's going to the very top, guilty or not. Unless you lead us to where it all began and delivered the main guy's head on a spike.' -

-'Now, it depends on how much you love this corrupt country and what you will do to save the big lady at the top. However, it would be best if you were on our side. The darkness goes deep, and so are the pockets. Compared to them, we are a fly in the ointment. Nothing more. What's a few dead corrupt politicians when behind the veil? There's so much more. Death is coming. Do you want to die with them?' Ominous, we stood in silence as the gravity of the situation hit us hard. All but confirming the girls became one, and all died to become this thing. If the fallout meant the corrupt creation died once more, it could be an act of mercy unless there was any secure place to hold them, hoping to reverse the process. I knew deep down it was too late, but they hadn't deserved to become this. Whatever way we looked, the ending was going to be sad.

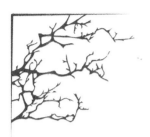

36

ANOTHER BASEMENT

The hums of my engine created hypnotic drones as we sliced through the darkness and empty streets. Street lamps blurred by, one set after another. It felt like hundreds flashing in the top corner of my eyes as I clung to the wheel for dear life.

My eyes were cranked open as wide as they could like cartoon matchsticks propping lids before clapping down blinds. We all waited while Ellena finished up. We already had one body stolen. The rest had either blown up or decayed to dust. In the basement, a huge walk-in safe, stored classified files going back over a hundred years and was highly fragile.

With next to no gaps, it's almost airtight. Ellena got to put part of her earlier plan into action. We rigged a tank of liquid nitrogen to slowly seep in and keep the temperature cold enough to hide the body for now. During her inspection, Ellena found another branding from the 'devil's circle' like M.P. Daniel Dowden and the secretary of state for business and energy. We needed to keep the location of this one secret. Andy told Locke to disseminate misinformation to the other bosses and only them.

If anyone else up high was dodgy and the coroner's office got attacked, we'd know where it came from. Michael's idea. Quite smart. It was also twofold; if anyone came to the basement for it, we'd be gunning for Locke. Unless either of us had an alter ego. Michael still had the deep cover, but has been in limbo so far, and his branding has been gone since becoming a shapeshifter.

We were edging towards the endgame, and I could feel it. The upcoming full moon was going to make life hard. We had a street name and an ultimatum. Our batteries were flat and needed charging before the fight ahead. I saw too many moving parts to control. I wasn't the sergeant, a D.S., or even an ADI, but I felt I had to look after everyone until this case was concluded.

So, I suggested that we all crash at mine, safe in numbers, and I could keep an eye on the other 'moving parts' to ensure all bases were covered. Michael was sceptical at first but eventually saw sense. No sooner had I begun driving than all three were sleeping, leaving me to my thoughts.

My head played the tape over again. A clear threat to our political structure. Not that I didn't think the system was corrupt, but death wasn't the answer. If we could get to the person responsible, at least to prevent another murder. Then look at how they connected to the girls. All we had were pieces. Other detectives were already combing through the finances and phone logs for a connection for Etherington, Turnage, Dowden, and now Edward Cornell. All we needed was a tiny link to open the floodgates. I could feel it, though. More death was coming.

We finally reached mine, and I did the usual paranoid scanning of the area. I scared the next-door neighbour's cat shitless. It was two o'clock in the morning, but that didn't matter. Not if we were being followed. I set Ellena up in the bedroom, Andy had the spare room, and I took the sofa while Michael made himself comfy in the recliner. Everyone had gone to bed. I double-checked my room before Ellena all but passed out.

I poured a whiskey and sat in darkness. A shard of moonlight sprayed through the window to the table, highlighting the wrapped bestiary. I was tempted to look some more. Then it crossed my mind: Did I need to see more images of monsters before bed? Enough was already going through my chaotic head to fill a few more volumes.

My glass swirled with brown liquid glimmering under the night light as I reflected on how things had gone. Everything was calm. That explosion hadn't faded enough from my mind to forget it. Even if that's what I pretended to the others. In reality, all I'd done was push the pain down. And I kept pushing after each incident that rocked us on our heels.

All that did was build pressure, and I had to release it. The way the car blew up, I flew with a raging fire chomping at my back, bringing back the house fire as a child. Ethan had unlocked those memories for me. Now, I had them waiting to latch onto any new trauma as a trigger. The explosion also reminded me of being burnt alive, left to die, and only getting saved at the last minute, a char-grilled mess. That same night, I changed Andy's life, too.

Last week I had to change Michael's because he was about to die. What risk was I going to bring on Ellena? She wasn't supernatural like us. Her life could be ended in the blink of an eye. That black cloud toyed with my insides, and I could fight it back. The Widow would rip through her, and that had me rattled. It felt wrong under the circumstances. Innocence made bad. Their murder rampage had to end.

I downed my drink and got myself comfortable. For hours, sleep was all I wanted. Now I had the chance. My head was restless. I kept returning to 'the devil is in the details' and what had been carved into that body in the warehouse. A true statement and the details had me awake.

I could see Michael curled into the chair. Now and then, I would catch a flash. A shimmer of static yellow. Not from his eyes but rippling around his body. That is another reason I wanted him here. To make sure nothing else happened. The other shoe was coming, and this one would be big. Some may get hurt. I could feel it. I hadn't settled into my new demon wolf's skin yet. Michael had one growing, and after learning ADI Locke has this druid side to him, I was almost at the point where I couldn't bend any further.

I lingered on the 'seconds' hand, tapping its way around the clock. My eyes slowly became heavy, and the world in my still half-unpacked lounge blurred before the matchsticks finally snapped.

'IN THE MIDDLE OF NOWHERE,' pitch black with street lamps scarce. Towering fir trees bristled in the breeze as far as my eyes could see. An impromptu hoot from an owl amidst the silence had my neck hairs jumping as a sheet of mist grew to inhale anything in its path.

The main road became a winding tarmac grey with sparkling cat's eyes dancing through the middle. That grey now turned into waves of white bounding up a steep hill that nobody would want to walk in a hurry. The sign stood proudly in the darkness across from an ungated entrance, waiting to be swallowed whole exactly as it looked in the vision.

Assorted pebbles, all pristine and smooth, even in the night's gloom, painted money. The house bulked with stature, a typical silver spoon-in-mouth type. Yet, we knew the silver spoon was laced with experimental chemicals to alter a victim's DNA. As I walked, my red eyes surveyed the driveway, and all that could be seen were the shadows of over-eager crowds from the masquerade party.

Each enticed to devour the liquorice scent with the trays of champagne thrust forward. Each with a mask in their hands laced with LSD. Haunting amber lights littered the downstairs windows on either side of the white-pillared mouth. The nearer I got, my hackles danced with trepidation. Death could be smelt—strong, overpowering rushes of putrid, slotted decay.

Large, double oak doors stood between me and another body. One was already ajar. As my hands quickly patted my pockets for more special gum, my claws sprang to life. Reactionary, making a mental note to know exactly which pocket had it, should the need arise. The door yawned, and each juddered hinge rocked around my eardrums.

Heartbeats thumped and sped up—at least two, maybe more. I tentatively stepped inside. White marble quickly became grey cobbles. My skin trembled at the feel of electricity fluctuating all around. The walls were dark. Even with the red glow, I could barely see my claws before my face. I expected a hallway up ahead, like in the story. Instead, there's dampness and squeals of pain. And blood. Lots of it. Strobes of yellow flickered through the black, breaking above my head. All I could sense was anger, pain, and fear. Some of the last was mine. Fear of the unknown and what the tormenting stench of blood was doing to my tastebuds. They were alive, causing my claws to grow longer and thicker.

The squeals kept coming, but I couldn't narrow down their origins. At first, up ahead, then behind and beside. I followed the aggressive yellow streaks and picked up another smell the nearer it seemed. Burnt flesh being scorched by electricity. The squeals were closer. I could feel the pain. I lived with each stomach-churning second of it. A dim glow arched over the back, and I could finally see where the noise came from.

A ten-foot by six-foot wide wire rack upright with electricity rifling through it, wave after wave. There's a woman strapped. She reeked of fear and sweat, wriggling with all her might, with tubes feeding black goo on the right and blood being sucked through tubes on the left, just as I saw in the vision. It was the shadow that was standing in front that scared me more. No taller than five foot eight and alive with strobes of lightning streaks warping and engulfing their entire body.

The heat and power emanating had me stepping back for a moment. 'Helpppp,' squealed, echoing, tugging at my emotions and drawing me back in. I stepped forward, heating a loud crunch beneath my feet. Thick, frosty grass enveloped my bare feet. The surrounding dark slowly brightened. Not by much, but enough to see tall trees as the wind whipped through a strong swirl of horse manure. That shadow stops fiddling and turns to face me.

Unparalleled anger is all I could feel as the shadow slowly faded into my skin—warped, animalistic skin. It's Michael, but different. He's pissed and flings an arm at the woman on the rack. Firing off strobes of electricity torching her shadowed flesh. My stomach doubled over with each pain-riddled cry.

"Told you, Georgie. You should've been on our side. Now, you'll lose it all and cost this corrupt country its leader. You will be responsible for all the death that's coming, and there's nothing you can do because you don't understand the rules of the game."

Evil Michael snarled his words that cut deep. Death was coming whether I liked it, and he was right. I didn't know the rules of the game. The remaining shadow shifted from the tortured woman as Michael fired another strobe that fried her stomach flesh. It was... 'Ellena.' I could smell her cooked flesh and flooding tears. Her pain was mine, and it was excruciating. I had to do something. I had to help.

I dashed forward, swiping my claws at Michael. The rack faded. Her tubes disappeared, and Michael's electrified aura grew. His body spun as I swiped my claws across, dropping back into a chair. The manure stink disappeared along with the trees, replaced by a stack of boxes and a coffee table.

My heart felt like it was going to explode. The table was mine. That shadow had completely gone, leaving behind cream walls. Ellena's skin slowly healed, and Michael's electricity became more vibrant. Ellena stumbled forward, crying. Her pain was consuming. Our bodies felt linked. Every skin tear, scorch mark, and laceration could be felt. Ellena dropped into me just as any sign of torture disappeared, becoming a lounge. My lounge.

My heart pounded quicker and quicker, sending a shooting pain to my temple. The dizzying, breathless struggle to organise my thoughts and get coherent made my eyes close. I heard a voice. My name was called as the breath-lessness worsened.

"Georgie. Are you ok? Georgie?" rattles to my brain. My eyes bolt open at Ellena. I'm laid out on my sofa. I could feel wetness coming from my chest. Glancing down, I saw two slashes, five claw streaks on each, and blood oozed from the wounds soaking my vest. My cheeks were warm, and I quickly re-alised Ellena was cupping my face while I searched for breath. Sweat pep-pered my skin as I sought rationality.

"Georgie? I said, are you ok?" Ellena repeated, and I finally felt able to talk.

"I...I... think so. The dream was so real. You were in danger from Michael," I said, looking at Michael, noticing the tail end of that electric strobing around his body.

"Georgie, you're bleeding," Ellena highlighted my vest front. I could feel the healing.

"Because I don't understand the rules of the game."

"What?"

"That's what Michael said while torturing you on a rack. You were burnt and drained of blood. It seemed so real. I was at the house in my vision, thinking it was to catch the bad guy. All I heard and felt was pain. Then I saw you, trapped. Michael was full of electricity. You screamed for help."

"I'm fine, silly. Look,"

Ellena knelt beside the sofa. Moonlight shone through the window, cap-turing her perfectly. She was wrapped in one of my oversized football t-shirts and joggers. Her just-woke-up appearance looked stunning. But Ellena was right; she was fine. A shame I wasn't. That dream was far more real than the visions, painfully so, and it scared me. The thought that it could come true scared me, from Ellena's torture to Michael's evolutionary switch of sides.

I couldn't shake the comment. The rules of the game. Had my subcon-scious been trying to guide me towards a key component to help us? We had to learn the rules, and fast.

"So, why does it feel so bad?"

"The same reason I've worried about you every time you've gone out looking for this stuff. It took far too long to realise that this stupid lamb needed a sick and twisted werewolf to balance out her reckless."

"Well, this sick and twisted wolf has enough reckless to match. Just look at the limousine crime scene photos."

"That's why I've been working hard on things to keep you safe. You might heal from a bullet, but what I sense is coming. Will take more. And I'm tired of watching you do all the 'bending'; you'll break eventually. I can't have that."

Ellena breezed close, and her body heat warmed me. Her heart was on fire as she hung her arms around my neck. Her piercing blue eyes hypnotised me, and her mouth was a magnet. We locked together, and I didn't want to let go. My body bristled with excitement I hadn't experienced in a long time. Electrified lust rippled as my hand brushed Ellena's arm, sending goose pimples bouncing over her body.

That lust worked both ways. I could feel her hard nipples pressed against my chest. The flimsy shirt did little to hide them. Ellena forced herself against me, making me squirm as my body reacted, giving away my awkwardness. Ellena paused the kiss to giggle before we continued. I was pressed against her stomach, and she enjoyed my uncomfortableness. We both knew we couldn't go any further, even if the desire was there and our bodies wanted to. We had unparalleled chemistry, and the tension had been building, but Ellena was better than that. We hadn't even had a proper date, and a woman like her deserved much more. In our line of work, gossip spreads quickly, and I didn't want Ellena to be seen in a bad light.

Our kiss broke, and Ellena snuggled into me. We both lay on the sofa cuddling; it felt like the most natural thing in the world. We both felt safe. For now, at least.

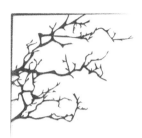

37

FINALLY, SLEEP

The best sleep I had in a long while, and I mean a very long while—five years at least. Who would've thought a sofa could be so comfortable? Perhaps it was the company. I'd drifted so deep that I hadn't noticed the lack of pressure on my chest. After that very real dream, Ellena helped me settle better than I imagined. All the trouble that plagued us disappeared from my mind for a few hours until a new day dawned.

I stirred slowly at the sound of a spoon crashing around in a cup. The smell was unmistakable, the perfect way to wake up. Coffee. A look at the clock showed it was only 7.30 am, meaning I'd only slept a few hours, but this was quality over quantity—all thanks to the goddess from the kitchen carrying two cups. Wafts of steam breezed to her face.

Even this early, she looked great. Then I saw the state of the table and the surrounding floor. I got the impression Ellena had been up a lot longer. If the pen jammed in the tossed-up hair bundle told me anything, the little lamb had been working on us, not having to be so reckless. Her eyes looked slightly bloodshot and crazed. This wasn't her first dose of caffeine. I daren't ask what had her in such a whirl, but her bulging eyes, beaming straight for me, had me thinking I would have no choice.

"Ooooh, finally. Here, take this. Don't look at the mess; it's not important. But take this and drink up. I said don't look at the mess," Ellena was bouncing like a child full of one too many 'E,' numbers. Her focus darted quickly to me, then to the floor and back again.

A moment in my dream shot back to me. I remembered a certain someone surrounded by electricity. Michael. The old git was still out cold. If I didn't know better or could hear as well, I'd say he was dead, as he appeared not to be breathing. The steady thumps reassured me otherwise. However, if one element of that horrid dream came true, he may have to end up that way. Until then, he's the geriatric member of our dysfunctional pack.

"Erm, how many of those have you had?" I said, taking a cup. Mmm, the aromatic smell of caffeine.

"Three, I think. No, make that four," Ellena said, with all the energy of an excited puppy, as long as she didn't start pissing on the floor. It was all good.

"So, what brought this excessive need for the black stuff?"

"Your bloody dream. You said the cockney prince warned you didn't understand the game's rules. That made me wonder what the hell those rules could be. It has to be important, right? Dreams often manifest an answer or clues to a nagging problem," Ellena said, smiling as she scooted onto the edge of the seat next to me as we drank.

"Christ, I'm glad that was all I dreamt, if that's the case," I said, thinking of the other crap that bugged us.

"Well, you'll be pleased to know I found some stuff. A lot based on the little bits, we surmised. Did you know there could be up to twelve types of wolfsbane, with the yellow being the deadliest? Oh, and you know that little thing people do over Christmas with standing under a certain plant?"

"Mistletoe?"

"Has many uses and is commonly used by druids. Could be cures, barriers, or even disarming of someone who isn't who they appear to be."

"What you're saying is Locke should know all of this?" That comment made me question what else our dear old ADI was holding back. He knew what we were, so why not reciprocate? What if he had all the answers and withheld the information on purpose?

"He could do. Let's say, like we all are, that he's trying to find his feet with this new dynamic that's going on. Also, that mountain ash is a great defence on the go. Get in one big space, seal the thresholds and anywhere that could be an entrance or exit, and it contains all the supernatural."

Ellena gave me an idea. If we ended up luring the 'Black Widow' to that house once, we found it and could somehow trap them. Maybe we could debilitate long enough for a permanent solution that didn't result in further deaths. Even if the individual parts were already dead, we didn't need to end them again if we didn't have to.

"First, we need to find that house and who owns it. Out of this mess, if we can arrest those girls' murderers, then they get a little justice. The other hard part will be the burden of proof."

"Well, I can find DNA on a knit if I had to. So give me the opportunity, and I'll make the connection for you." Ellena smiled confidently.

"I have a nagging fear that somebody will intervene to make us keep quiet."

Listening to Ellena's confidence, that thought crept into my head between sips. That 'shoe' will be just when we think we've won, and then it drops. There had to be a way we could stop that from happening. For a year, the country was led to believe a young girl had an accidental overdose, and two others got tickets for drunk and disorderly behaviour.

Instead of the truth. That all the girls died that night. What found their way home was nothing but ticking time bombs. That was the level of deviousness we were dealing with.

"Well, let's leave them with no choice. Sing it from the bloody rooftops if we have to," Ellena said, before taking a big gulp of coffee. Even in haste and almost spilling, she made it look attractive.

Ellena placed down her now empty cup, causing me to look at mine, three-quarters full. Before she dropped to the chaos on the floor, her hands moved with quick, uncoordinated flurries, grabbing different papers. Whether it was my sleepy haze or still a little punch with a delayed concussion from the bomb or any melee of drama that followed, I couldn't help but sit and be in awe of this woman before me.

Little Lamb stood out from a male-dominated environment. She held her own in a supernatural dominant group. And it didn't faze her—no signs of breaking from the bending. Ellena dug her heels in, rolled her sleeves, and looked for another course for us. Instead of being freaked out, I woke her in the night with my drama and the scary possibilities. Ellena helped me settle and used what I said to give hope that we could swing momentum back in our favour.

Handing me some of her notes. Aside from the scribbles, she thought that if we flooded the air with yellow wolfsbane gas, the widow could lose power as we do. I was intrigued by mistletoe. Not only did it seem strange for something so innocuous and used at Christmas to be involved in this strange

world. I wondered if we could use mistletoe somehow to force them to separate when the window was under that black cloud.

"Speaking of no choice. Has Andy stirred at all?"

"The only things that have stirred are my brain and stomach," Elena said
before having that light bulb moment.

Wide-eyed and glowing at the sudden remembrance of a detail she
couldn't wait to share. Ellena grabbed two pages of a map. I didn't need it
close to knowing what was being shown. She'd narrowed down two locations
for the address in my vision. It wasn't like we had a door number; what I'd
seen was blurred but four digits.

"So, there are only two 'Walnut Avenues' anywhere that could be coun-
tryside or farmland. Based on the smell of manure. Chingford and Epping."

My head bounced up to look directly into Ellena's eyes. She'd narrowed
the location down more than she knew. The limousine that blew up in Trafalgar Square nearly took me with it, but I remembered the sign in the rear window. 'Epping luxury Autos' is too much of a coincidence not to be true.

"It's Epping. It has to be. It's what I saw in the limo. You know what,
though, how does this all sync up?"

"What do you mean?" The trouble was, I didn't know what she meant.
Or what was I trying to get to? Maybe the coffee hadn't hit the spot yet.

But in concluding the likelihood where it suddenly felt too easy. Not that
being blown up or shot at before watching the body incinerate was easy. That
shot from the tower block could've got me, but it didn't. Had I read the situation wrong? A guardian angel? Even that didn't track.

"Hear me out. On the one hand, we have that party. It goes pear-shaped.
A dead girl, friends that became victims nobody wanted to know. One girl
made herself seem the centre of attention and 'had everyone under her spell,'
then disappeared. Nobody has seen or heard of her since. - The bodies drop
alarmingly a year later. A mix of police and politicians. Then, the parents of
the girls. All the while, this supernatural entity is making a big show of revenge. I'm having fucked up dreams. Michael got taken, and we still don't
know what's been done to him."-

- "There are people behind the corrupt people playing 'god' with dangerous consequences. - I guess what I'm saying is, who are we trying to catch and
stop? Are the victims killing out of revenge? Or the go-betweens who took

dirty money to ease their conscience from selling their children off. And who knows what or who else? Perhaps even the low-life politicians that threw the party with enough skeletons in their closets to fill a cemetery. With plenty that's been branded by the 'devil's circle' unless anybody could get that now. - Which brings me nicely to the puppeteers. How many strings are they holding? And where are they?"

Ellena tilted her head, tapping her finger on her lip, thinking. Hearing my words aloud made me wish I hadn't picked up that phone call from Locke. An urgent call straight after rinsing Michael's blood from my mouth for what felt like the one-thousandth time. The VHS was gross, and I don't think Locke understood the gravity of the shit his friend had found himself in.

"Why can't we take them all? I don't mean straight away, but forewarned is forearmed. We know what's happening now. Or at least more than we did when the first case dropped. The puppeteer will come. They will keep coming with different puppets until, one day, there's a chink in their armour. Politicians have been dodgy from the get-go, change like the weather, and have the morals of a priest. So let's work on the 'black widow' and the immediate people they're after. Then see where the chips fall."

Ellena said in her non-condescending, non-judgmental, and reassuring way that she has. A soothing smile and the way she directed through the problems like they were nothing.

"Sounds like a plan. If we can pull it off. I can't say why, what, or who. But there's a niggle that there's something or someone, another 'dot' we haven't seen coming."

It felt good to say it aloud after finally putting my finger on the itch. With all the bullshit 'dots' we'd just laid out. The missing person case was the biggest issue, not making sense, and the father seemed to have the next most energy donated to him and the recording of his whereabouts. The limo, the meeting with M.P. Dowden, then the sign with a hint at number ten Downing Street. The tape slotted into his stomach was almost symbolic, as much as it was sadistic.

'The killer stomached enough of him.'

"Could be, but I see something else in that bestiary. We all got caught up in your vision. Did you see the small text underneath? Next to the question mark?"

I did not know what she was on about. I, too, had been so wrapped in that scary shit. Ellena grabbed at the silk-wrapped bundle. It was thrust under my nose, and immediately, I felt that pull again. It had to be the blood. Sure enough, pages opened, and I saw what she meant. It was a little disconcerting and intriguing. The newfound supernatural geek in me was lapping up the weird and unknown.

'Seems to function as a hive mind. With one element able to control, assert dominance and make others bend at will. Doesn't even need to be part of the devastating cluster form.'

My heart juddered. The subtext begged the question, who could have this supernaturally powerful collective bending to their will? Picking off the guilty one by one. An agenda. A hit list. A clearing of the decks over past mistakes.

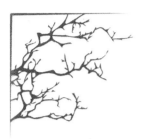

38

BEND

All the talk of rules and being made to bend. Ellena uncovered the likely house in Epping and how the 'Black Widow' might work. I sketched what I could remember from the visions, the layout from the driveway, the big door, and the windows bordered by the fir trees.

Suppose this was where we suspected, and there was no telling who or what could be inside, only that the space was vast. In that case, we'd need an element of surprise, maybe check for another basement entrance like that farm. What I couldn't reckon on – would they have the same supernatural protection as the farm?

Consider these factors, and if there's no protection, we must find a way to seal it ourselves. Also, the legal side – to stay on the right side of the law and do more than collect body bags, we needed a solid reason to enter. A vague dream wasn't going to cut it. We had to find the connection between the chaos and that house. Then I thought, what if we could determine who owned the property and if we had a link to parliament, we'd have a welfare check and a danger-to-life excuse?

Yet, it all seemed like needles in a big haystack. Unless Ellena had a trick or a book for that, she'd already done so much in such a short time, even if it was off the back of three... no, four coffees. While I laboured with my one. My drawing went off on a tangent, taking the little things like Michael's war chest in his car boot. From what Ellena made with the gum, we didn't see what else she had in store for us: the book and the dead father of the missing girl Selena Cornell to contend with.

Was there a way mountain ash, as powder ash, could make it easier to spread? Or spray the wolfsbane, as fumigators use. I ended up doodling gas tank backpacks and guns. It looked far-fetched, but maybe we could need something like that one day. I got deep into my fixation when I got crept up on. Not In a someone-pouncing-surprising way. It was that sense of danger way.

A sudden ruffle of my hackles caused me to jolt my head up to look around. The pen dropped onto the paper before Ellena turned to my worried face. I could smell it. I could smell them. That morbid aroma of death. It was close enough and strong enough to make my body react in a mind of its own again. All claws jumped out, full and thick. What was different this time was that I felt my face morph a little. I had always been too busy to tell whether it had been much before.

This time, along with the red the ridge of my nose and the shaping of my ears. A curious detail came with those changes. My sense of smell shifted a level as my airways and nasal passages widened. I could feel my ears move and twitch at the slightest sound in 3D. Ellena's arm hairs bristle like a forest, and Michael's otherwise small snore was a bear's roar. Perhaps it was because the danger seemed so close to home.

"Georgie, you okay?" Ellena bounced up close, gripping my hand.

"Grab the bat," I pointed to the baseball sticking out of a box in the room's corner. Another on my to-do list. Unpack. The surge of dead bodies hadn't given me time.

"Why? What's happening?" With a sharp intake of breath between her words, Ellena squeezed my hand again. Her heart was full throttle, and I hadn't meant to scare her. So I cupped her hand, and Ellena instantly calmed. I felt her relax, as if she'd been given a narcotic to knock her out. That wasn't all, though. I felt a warmth in my hand and glanced down. I could've sworn my claws slowed like I'd take her stress away.

Michael jumped upright in his seat. Eyes blazed bright yellow with claws out. I couldn't tell if he'd reacted on autopilot because his eyes looked glazed behind the yellow. Either way, his body sensed the danger, too.

"Georgie, what's happening?" Michael croaked, and the typical smoker choked.

"You feel that, right?"

"Yeah, but I sensed you."

"I think it's here."

"What, Santa Claus?"

"No, Michael, the bloody 'black widow' it's here. How can you not smell it?" I said, looking at him, confused.

"I've just woken up, and all I can smell is my morning breath. And yours, I might add."

Ellena was armed with the bat, and I'd reached the doorway first, holding out my arm to keep her back. At first, I couldn't tell where it hit—Andy's room. I didn't wait. I charged in, moving far quicker than I had yet. Glided twenty feet in a matter of seconds. He was gone...

No windows were open, and the bed had been slept in. Andy wasn't a small bloke, and it wouldn't have been easy without making a noise. They had to subdue him with toxins in his sleep—my nightmare. Then Ellena helped me drift deeper than before. I hadn't heard anything. In his place were some papers, a folded note, and a woman's sparkly black and white masquerade mask.

I could smell it all—a collection of stale aromas that included drugs and floral perfume. Panic had me paused, thinking about what to do. Ellena breezed to my side, placing the bat on the bed before slipping on some gloves. I glanced sideways in a surreal moment of 'Why on earth do you have gloves?' then I thought of Michael and how prepared he always is. Ellena was studious.

I picked up on the LSD, but it had been mixed with a stronger, far more toxic scent. Ellena's nose twitched, and I felt she didn't need our heightened senses to have at least half an idea.

"Vapor of either ketamine or Rohypnol mixed with LSD. If this lot was mixed, this was one mask used that night. Those girls wouldn't have known what was up, what day it was, much less have the strength to do anything about it. We could compare toxicology strains with the other masks."

With every word, every second I got to stand in Ellena's presence, I was falling for her more. She drove me crazy in so many ways. Not least, her brains. And an unrelenting ability to know exactly what to do at the right moments that put me at ease.

"Is that even possible?"

"If they know their chemistry as much as they've shown. Anything is possible. The question is, why now and where on earth is Andy?" That brought my attention back to the note. Far too many lately.

'In case you needed motivation. Don't worry; he's safe for now. Follow the money,'

The papers underneath, the first few, were for Edward Cornell going back years. Line after line of large transfers from the same account number. That's what they wanted us to trace. Then, clipped to that was a death certificate. A sudden picture was painted in my head. For one, I wasn't sure if it was rational enough for the rest.

'Andrea Cornell. Died 17th May 1985 tetrodotoxin poisoning,'

The mother, Andrea Cornell, died in 1985. Selene went missing on October 86 before the father, Edward Cornell, was killed in 1987, albeit mixed in political cover-ups and selling his daughter off to be experimented on. I pieced those jigsaw parts together, looking back at the bank statements.

Several transfers between £200,000 and £800,000 between the beginning and end of May 85. In 87, eight transfers between £500,000 and £2,000,000 from the beginning of October until Halloween night. Which was the last payment for a while.

A light bulb buzzed above my head. The information and the shock of Andy being taken were spinning in my head in a tumble dryer. Bit by bit, each detail dropped into place. Edward Cornell got paid to have his wife used, and it killed her. Edward Cornell was paid more for his daughter. Only she goes missing during or after. A big scene to get attention at the party then vanishes.

The only one to hardly be spoken of and hardly looked for. Someone who could be highly motivated against people like her father. Anyone who would trade blood for money. How? I had all those thoughts, but couldn't believe it was possible. By the 'Widow' taking Andy, our timescale for a plan had been forced to speed up. Now, down by one.

'1482 WALNUT AVENUE EPPING - 5 pm,'

Maybe they're a sum of parts that would eventually become a greater supernatural whole. It's not wasted on me that these bastards dangled a supposed dead relative under my nose as bait and then snatched it away again. Was she my sister? I had to know.

Once this case was over. The chips fell our way, and that holiday got approved. It was high time I donated time to embrace my origins instead of denying it. There had to be more. I had to have more family out there. Otherwise, who was I? No real past I could or would want to claim and an unknown future. Ellena was my silver lining. One I prayed to God didn't turn blood red. With her, the world seems right. We're in sync on so many levels it's scary, and I didn't want to lose that chance. No matter what was to come tonight, I had to ensure I kept her safe at all costs.

Even to my detriment. I've learnt how her heartbeat differs from others. It's not quite a murmur, but each beat didn't sound the same. Every other was slightly shallower, and when it sped up, Ellena had a sharp intake of breath. A subconscious reaction that allowed me to know if she was in danger. That image of her burnt is haunting.

Everyone had their jobs. I was in my car equipped with a few surprises as a backup. No way in hell was I going in through the front. I couldn't smell the 'widow' yet, but that didn't mean they weren't on the periphery.

They wanted us to find what they couldn't. So far, all we had was a house and a vision. A look at the sky caught the first glimpse of a dim full moon as the sun faded.

It could already be felt—a slight boiling of my blood. I stood at the corner of a mixture of light brown stone walling, black fence spikes, and more fir trees. It reminded me a little of visiting the 'Whitlock' place.

Only no self-gratifying signage. That didn't mean this place held any less danger in store for us. There were plenty of heartbeats. Livestock beat to one rhythm, human, another. A mixture of both had my arm hairs alive with electricity.

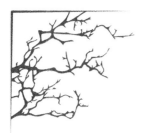

39

WELCOME INTO THE WEB

The grass crunched beneath my feet, a familiar haunting sound that had me grateful I wasn't barefooted this time. The sky rippled shades of purple-red, with the moon getting brighter by the minute. This house was largely made of brick, with only the front door and window frames from what I could see. That had even the remotest chance of being mountain ash.

I kept in the tree line, hearing a low buzzing, constant and slightly piercing. I put it down to how I heard earlier, amplified. I figured it would be somebody's electronics in the house making noise. There was plenty of cover, almost a mini forest. The further I moved, the faint aroma of 'fur' changed a little sweeter. With so many scents around, it had become harder to narrow anything down. The space to the left opened up to more of a farm, horses, pigs; you name it, I could probably see it. Plenty of frail-looking barns that didn't seem able to stand up to a hairdryer, let alone much else.

On a property like this, there was no visible CCTV. Perhaps I shouldn't have been too shocked. Not with the type of parties we believed went on here. There were several hard-wired holes and small boxed units, possibly air conditioning, in certain places around the top perimeter. If the alleged depravity was like the picture painted for us, they'd have hidden cameras inside.

Some of me had become unsure how truthful Sally had been over the events unfolding. Still, Mr Etherington was pretty adamant something bad went on. I planned to work around as much of the immediate house grounds as possible without being seen. Listen and get a lay of the land while hoping somebody screams for help. Otherwise, it's counting the heartbeats inside before a welfare check.

Until we could prove differently, we had to treat whoever was inside as potential victims in waiting. The left flank of the house appeared normal, with a few windows on top and bottom. All had curtains closed—no surprise doors on the floor or a low window drenched in mountain ash. I was close enough to get a read, but far enough to stay in the shadows. Everything seemed calm, almost therapeutic, with the early evening insects beginning to sing. A few tweets from the birds and snorts from the pigs up ahead.

My werewolf's eyes highlighted the heat patches and the electrical current running to and from, but nothing unusual. A singular, steady heartbeat was on the move inside. Nothing frantic, the plodding of somebody going about their business. I hadn't seen a car, but there was a separate three-door garage to the far right of the driveway.

It felt like an anti-climax, but with each step, my hackles rumbled. A spark down my neck that sent a brief shiver. I just couldn't see or feel why. I had made my way completely around with nothing to urge caution. The only thing to get my attention was that constant, sweet aroma within the tree spaces. Being amongst it felt hazy and peaceful. Back at the start, I stood on the pebbles and faced the front door as I had in that vision. The apprehension was building inside me. We had nothing to give us cause for alarm and had to change tactics.

'Units be aware, moving to the next phase.'

I made sure we were all on the same dedicated channel. We didn't need the constant blearing out of calls to grab attention or interfere with our communications. I had one person with a separate radio on the main channel in case I called for help. If it turned out to be a bust, the last thing we needed was to look like overkill and end in a complaint. Those things get the wrong attention, and we'd inadvertently give our intentions away.

The front door was closed—another change to what I'd seen. My hackles danced in the breeze, but still only one beat inside. I reached for the knocker with nerves rampant. A look around the porch, but there's still no camera. Could this place belong to someone important? It looked great but felt oddly subdued in terms of protection. Not even the scent of wolfsbane or mountain ash. Doubt had crept in. Had I allowed myself to be misdirected by bad dreams and visions?

The moon was slightly brighter, and I felt that pre-warning edge. So far, I have had it under control. For how long was a guessing game?

'Knock, knock, knock,'

"One minute," a well-spoken man's voice echoed in their hallway. Shoes clapped across the solid surface.

The door swung open with that same jarring creak. There stood a man in his mid-forties, dripping cigar smoke, five foot seven, with a slightly portly belly dressed in a blue-white stripy shirt and grey trousers with braces. I knew the face. The whole goddamn country knew the face. It was the bloody chancellor, Mr David Dinkley. I froze on the spot, feeling that heat bubble over deep inside.

Coming up with a plausible excuse hadn't been a problem. Staying face-to-face with the man responsible for the country's budgets and other things was different. Not to mention, he'd been a part of Sally's story from that night and the lies that followed. There was one piece of information that could've been useful beforehand. How would we have known who lived there? Though, an issue that took me back to the lack of CCTV, somebody so important and yet nothing and nobody was on guard.

"Hi" I went to speak when I heard a whisper only I would hear. 'Georgie, David Dinkley is shown to have bought the property ten years ago through a dummy company. So wasn't straightforward,' Locke's voice was bang on queue, and I couldn't have been more relieved. I didn't respond, just smiled slightly before quickly returning to what I was about to say.

"Hi, sorry, I'm a detective for the murder task force. We were just carrying out a welfare check. We're investigating a series of high-profile murders where prominent members of parliament had been targeted. So we're working through a list to warn and see each member's security to beef up," I blurted. Felt a little over-elaborate, but I couldn't get past how non-existent it was.

"Ah, well. This is a surprise. But yes, the news is like wildfire through the 'commons'; as far as I'm aware, several have upgraded drastically. The curious thing, though. It's not common knowledge who owns this house," Dinkley said with a cockney expression about him. All that talk of murder and security didn't cause even the slightest blip out of the ordinary. It didn't faze him, and that had alarm bells ringing. Anyone normal would've shown some distress. A quiver in the voice, but this guy gave nothing away.

"Well, that's why we have talented researchers. If your house had been missed and something bad had happened. It would be a travesty, and we would've failed," I said as I regained my composure and reeled Dinkley back in line a little.

"A good point. Please come in. There's a chill in the air, and we can't have our best in blue getting sick now, can we? Although I'm sure you're quite hardened to most elements by now. Oh, only you?" Dinkley still had that smug demeanour and caught me off guard. What had he implied with the element's comment? As for being solo, the next dribble of bullshit was about to trickle off my tongue.

"Well, it's not like you're an axe murderer or any kind of killer, are you? So we spread the load out," I knew what I was doing. I wanted a reaction. A throwaway comment was the best way to express my thoughts without saying it. And boy, did that wipe away the smug smile.

"Tea? Coffee?" Dinkley asked without acknowledging my comment. He didn't need to. His heart did the rest. Juddering at the mention of 'murderer' before he cleared his throat. The floors were the same white marble. A wide hallway is big enough to be a room. Almost the size of my lounge. To the left was an oak door and at least twelve small glass panes. Beside that was a wide wooden staircase. There were other doors to the right, but straight ahead was straight into a huge room. White marble continued, and furniture peeked from next to the wall.

Dinkley guided the way; all I could think about was the story told by Sally Turnage. At the doorway, I understood just how big the space was. Certainly enough for a party and to the left, fed into a red marble-topped open-plan kitchen. In the far-left corner was a dark oak door, no glass. Possibly another hallway or room, a very impressive space. Some might say it is perfect for a seedy masquerade party. I felt a little worried for the first time since Dinkley welcomed me in.

If all that happened here, what else could be got away with? Dinkley flipped a couple of switches on the wall, and the room lit up—only one enormous chandelier, gleaming in all its splendour. There must've been a window open because as we neared the start of the kitchen, I could smell the fur trees again, accompanied by that sweetness.

"So detective, any leads?" Dinkley had calmed a little, but there was no hiding the excited octave change when he mentioned 'leads'; he got a thrill from thinking I was stupid.

"I'm afraid, chancellor. I can't divulge information about an ongoing investigation. But seeing as it involves you directly. I will say there are a few things we've learned. The killer is highly dangerous and motivated," I knew my answer was ambiguous, on purpose designed to see where his mind went—hoping to instil some fear. My sixth was doing the macarena. I knew the situation was precarious, but other lives were at risk, so I had to do whatever was necessary.

"Involves me? Aren't all killers dangerous and motivated?"

"Of course, parliament. Some, I find, have different motivators. Like," Dinkley's heart spiked again. I was hitting the right cords.

"Greed? How does that equate?"

"One has money; another has more. Schemers will scheme to gain more money and power. It usually involves murder. Maybe they are not doing it themselves, perhaps have lackeys for those jobs." I remember us being shot at and the body going up in flames.

Dinkley paused. His face looked constipated, but he was probably thinking as he retrieved two cups from a cupboard. I watched intently, careful to see each movement of his hands. Carefully, he didn't try to drug me. He knew nothing and merely allowed his house to be used. Yet, the signals I was getting told me otherwise.

I could hear slight whistles of wind, and that sweet smell grew with the 'fur'; I needed another set of eyes. One watches Dinkley; the other scans the room. A detail made me curious; another light switch was inside the room, with only one button for one enormous light. The big socket had several switches by the hallway, and he flicked two. What did the other go to?

"There could be many reasons to motivate a person these days. Anything from greed, like you say, to maybe the greater good?" Dinkley tried hard to steady himself while generalising, yet he also hinted at his thought process. 'Greater good,' as if he thought creating monsters and destroying lives was of any benefit.

"Murder is murder. No good comes from that. The collateral damage is a testament to that:" With each comment traded, I got the impression he knew I may have been on to him. He attempted to justify what's gone on in some bizarre, covert way.

The strong coffee fumes were the best thing about this little chat, and so far, I couldn't see any way that led to cobbled stone floors. It wasn't like I could use my werewolf's eyes.

"Thank you," as Dinkley slid the coffee forward.

"I noticed the property seems quite vulnerable. Are you going to reconsider that, considering the situation?" Dinkley went to speak with his coffee near his chin before pausing with a slight smile.

"Oh, you'd be surprised how protected this place is. I just don't advertise it. It's the little things that go unnoticed." As he said that, his voice suddenly sounded deeper. Perhaps nature and I aren't good friends after all. That tree scent made me feel a little hazy, affecting my hearing. It had to be the full moon beaming through the window.

"It's the little things that will get you caught." I meant it, but it must have been a little on the nose because Dinkley's face dropped.

"Is that so?" again sounded so much deeper.

"The same way the little things can kill someone," my head felt dizzy, and I hadn't touched my coffee yet.

"Do you like chess detective Reynolds?" he said. What? I never told him my surname, and he hadn't looked at my credentials properly.

"Sorry, what?"

"Chess. You say the little things, but chess is a game that requires thinking of those things, but many move ahead." My hackles were on fire with good cause. I could suddenly see two tall figures at the far end of the lounge. All in black and their heads. Beasts... My heart raced.

I was stumbling back from the counter. They moved closer, and another appeared from the hallway.

"I, er..." I couldn't form my words. Too distracted, confused, and dizzy. The full moon felt different.

"What's the matter, George? Did you miss the details? The little things? Like walking through a forest of trees and being slowly drugged with LSD. Or the air con that's been kicking it into the air. Or your cup, coated in it. My dear Detective Reynolds, I'm afraid those details will get you killed," Dinkley knew. He'd been onto me from the start.

It wasn't the moon, but my head was everywhere. Those figures had multiplied and had got a lot closer. I could feel my claws trying to come.

"W... What about you?"

"I'm immune. I have been for a long while now, thanks to science. George or Georgie. I pay attention to the little things. It's my job, and I'm good at it. Money makes the world go around. This country trades in guns and ammo. Soon, we'll be able to trade in something far greater for so much more. All at our disposal, and when I'm in charge, this country will be the superpower it once was. With an unstoppable army that nobody would see coming. We'd have one for different occasions. All to make the world bend to our will,"

He was warped, yet I felt powerless, surrounded and not knowing which way was up. Dinkley pressed a switch that lit up. I was in danger at that moment. The game changed again. I smelt death. At least one constant has been my accurate sense of smell, and right then, I knew the 'widow' had arrived.

"Too much bending and things break. Besides, that's all a...a... fantasy... somebody is out for your blood." More cloaked figures entered the room. He'd admitted to LSD dosing, which could explain some of what I saw. My hackles told me some of it was real. I needed to figure out which ones, and fast. Dinkley sounded like a man with a plan.

"It's easy when you pay the right people. You need to understand, Georgie, that you are nothing but a pawn in this world, and I knew eventually the police would visit to warn me. Not all are as efficient as you or have your abilities. Yes, I know what you are. And the treat on your cup includes wolfsbane, that's slowly seeping into your pores,"

"So you paid people off?"

"My dear boy, I've paid for many things. Out for my blood? I will just pay to have them killed. Not the first time and won't be the last."

"What like to cover up a murder?"

"Small picture again. I paid to make the world keep moving, and the failures disappear. Those who stand in the way get dead. It's some,"

"Why are you saying all of this to me?"

Dinkley moved to my ear. I could barely stand. I was seeing double everything, and he sounded like a giant. He wouldn't have needed anyone to help. The air-con could blow me over.

"Because you are just a blip on the horizon of my future. Blips disappear, and so will you," he whispered. That smell of death was now mixing with the breeze of LSD, enveloping the surrounding air.

I was the fly that walked into the spider's web. Only an even bigger spider was waiting in the wings; Dinkley hadn't expected that. He saw me as the little thing. I may not play chess, but I'm tired of bending to the breaking point. And this blip had no intention of disappearing.

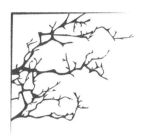

40

PRICE TAGS

The shrill ring of the phone on the wall abruptly disrupted our conversation. I took the opportunity to glance around the room.

"Hello?"

"Did he come?" The voice on the other end was familiar, someone I'd met.

"Well, well, if it isn't the Grim Reaper. Yes, he arrived as you said he would. Seems quite meticulous."

"That's great. Once it's done, get him frozen. He may be of use down the line. Could even raise the price tags." I didn't like the sound of that. I needed to recover and rid my body of toxins. Carefully, I patted my pockets, trying not to draw attention. Not that Dinkley seemed bothered.

"Speaking of which, I'll have the money transferred."

"Look at you. Getting everyone to do your dirty work." A clue: the transfers wouldn't show up as Dinkley's. He had someone else doing his bidding.

"That's how this business works if you want to sit at the top."

"Ah, well. Be careful; there isn't somebody ambitious waiting to climb over you."

"That's why I told you to learn how to play chess. That witch can barely play a game of cards. Anyway, best get on." Again, with the chess. Dinkley seemed to pride himself on being many moves ahead. Yet, his grandeur often led to mistakes.

"Sorry about that. Where were we? Oh, that's right. You are brave. Doing your diligent work, you carried out a welfare check. We discussed my fears over the corruption within and who might pull the strings I'm in the shadows. I'd uncovered these papers relating to the secretary of state for defence minister, Mr Bert Wexford, formerly a partner in crime. The papers showed money transferred to the families of the dead girls and copies of letters between him and the late M.P. Dowden, planning to cull parliament for a new regime."-

- "The killer came for me. You saved my life at your own cost, and sadly, the killer got away. Other officers will arrest Wexford, creating a snowball effect. He won't make it to the station, and all will be reshaped."

Dinkley's arrogance was astounding, thinking he'd get away with it all. He had indeed thought moves ahead but only on one side. Mentioning covered-up murder. I hadn't said who, and he spoke of the dead girls. I glanced at the moon as the sky darkened. I let it soak my face, the bright white painting my skin. I could feel the blood boiling once more.

"Dead girls?"

"Don't play dumb. The coverup and that group of girls died. Not all straight away. Wexford and Dowden had them signed up for a medical testing program, and sadly, one by one, they got sick and died, or at least soon will be." Dinkley believed his lies. I wasn't sure how much he knew about the killer.

"You have it all figured out. Even the killer?"

"Mostly. I didn't want to know the details. Trusted they would be efficient, and so far they have been." Dinkley smirked, sipping his coffee while I struggled. He didn't know the girls were the killers. That much, I was certain. His heart remained calm. He had pulled a file from a drawer when he spoke of Wexford and Dowden—prepared for an outcome that involved my death. Meanwhile, the moon felt like it was working magic, and the dizzy spells were easing.

"For someone who likes control, you couldn't even do the deed yourself." I toyed, buying time and hoping for the right 'dot' I needed. It seemed the 'Widow' wanted it too. They were biding their time. Unless, as I thought earlier, a hallucination.

"Ooh, you're after details. I will say you're taking longer than I expected. Let's just say the 1st is always the sweetest. And boy, that Francis was a sweet one. A fighter, too. I love a bit of rough me. The thrill of the hunt." The sick smile without a care. He truly saw himself as untouchable. Believing I was dying, instead, I could feel my strength returning, and then some. Just looming at Dinkley's arrogant, gurning face made me want to rip his head off.

I slipped one of Ellena's treats out of my pocket and into my mouth. I hoped her concoction would give me the extra kick to send me over the edge, even if it meant playing 'lame' until the right moment came along.

"Don't you have any shame? I listened to what the girls went through, and they were abused in so many ways."

"The real shame is our conversation will have to end. I have some business to attend to. Seeing as you're taking your time. How about a helping hand from willing soldiers?" Dinkley smiled, nodding at the tall figures. The dizziness had eased enough for me to notice they were wearing hoods like the ones seized from Mr Turnage and Dowden before the limousine blew up. The moon had steadily been recharging me—something about those last words stuck with me.

'Willing Soldiers,' the way the figures moved. Very rigid, almost robotic, but not quite. Not smooth either. He'd bragged earlier about creating an unstoppable army at his disposal. Two more came from the hallway, but I couldn't see how. There were six tall hooded figures in black clothing wearing black gloves. The earlier ones up close had been my imagination. These weren't.

Dinkley was smug like he'd been for the majority, peering over his cup. My senses livened up. Every cell, every tendon and muscle was steadily swimming in adrenaline. A chilling breeze rushed through before the chaotic shrills of the 'Widow' whipped through. One by one, the hairs on my arms shuddered to attention as a shiver rocked through my body.

Pain, anger, and ferociousness were the chemo signals of the moment. Its shriek pierced the air, causing Dinkley to pause, open-mouthed. A nice rarity, fear, was etched into the fabric of his face. Could almost hear his arsehole puckering at the thought he hadn't paid as much attention to his chess moves as he thought. My ears twitched, trying to pinpoint the noise bouncing off the walls.

"You see, Chancellor, this is the details and little things I pay attention to." Dinkley looked stunned. The six figures couldn't narrow it down either. Each drew a machete-like blade from their rear waistband. I stood on edge and prayed for a miracle. That's just me.

"This still isn't ending how you thought. You may think I'm evil, but you'll find I'm necessary." The trouble is, no evil is necessary. It's just an excuse for scumbags to use to justify them doing scumbag things. Dinkley was already taking a leaf out of Melanie's book and hadn't been arrested yet. One thing I couldn't disregard, Dinkley was intelligent. That was clear; only he'd used it for politics and crime. Some would say they are the same. What we've come up against lately has done little to show me otherwise.

The darker the sky got, the brighter the moon became, and I was soaking up as much as I could, so much so my eyes were straining. Quick flashes of red kept coming, and I'd evaded Dinkley's view so far. The black cloud finally showed itself, whipping the room into a frenzy. The 'six' lashed out with their blades recklessly, and no matter how many times they caught thin air, they just repeated their futile actions.

More alarming for me was the change in rhythm from Dinkley. He'd been racing. No sooner did he see the black cloud than he slowed. That made me question whether he knew more about the killer than he let on. Its screech was terrifying, and the board was almost set. Dinkley had it in his head. He would get away with the bad stuff he'd done. They even lined up some sacrificial lambs.

He was right. The paper trail we had so far would only prove his innocence, and if the folder contents were what Dinkley said, our task would be even harder.

"Chancellor, the world doesn't need any evil, let alone yours, but right now. That's your problem. It's here to kill you." I looked him in the eye, hoping the penny would drop. His pupils bounced to the cloud and back again. Dinkley tried to control his breathing, but confusion had jumped into the mix. The hamster in his head couldn't compute how a black cloud could kill.

"Remember, if that kills me, you don't get your chance at justice and will never learn the whispers I know. Whispers that impact you in particular. The people who want you for what you are, those who fear you and the million bad things in between will slowly become this world and yours." Dinkley pretended he was all-knowing, and perhaps he was, but others say they know about me and the world that's new to us.

Yet all that's happened is more murders and no less drama. The widow breezed around, taunting and intimidating, yet I sensed a slight confusion and disharmony again. And I could use that. It had the six chasing shadows and Dinkley battling flight or fight.

My veins throbbed, blood boiled, and the dizzy haze had gone. Between what Ellena made, which was probably slightly illegal for me to use. My petty drug dealer. Both that and the full moon. I'd reversed the effects of the LSD and Wolfsbane, but I continued to play lame while I watched Dinkley.

For a few seconds, at least. He seemed to bank on my vulnerability. I watched his shifty little eyes search around but not for an exit. His heart sped up, and I couldn't be sure what exactly. He didn't seem the sort for a gun, and it would be no use on the cloud unless he planned on shooting his only real defence. His left dropped below the counter. I heard a click. Something on springs bounced out, and he appeared to pocket something small and square, black. Hard to tell. As much as the dizziness had stopped, I still had a slight sporadic blur in my vision.

Deep down, I knew what would speed it up. Doing so would mean showing the other me and throwing caution to the wind. Whatever Dinkley slipped into his pocket must have been important. It lingered in the back of my mind as the 'Widow' whooshed past and back to the large room near three grids or air conditioning vents. All windows were closed.

I closed my eyes, and for the first time, I dared to embrace the full moon. I turned to Dinkley and opened them again. Blood red filled the space. Dinkley became a motorway of heat lines. All the veins and nerves were drenched with warm blood, and it was like a beacon—a mouth-watering appetiser. I wanted to taste it. I wanted to rip his flesh apart. My claws flew out, and my face shifted as it had earlier.

Dinkley stepped backwards. His face dripped with the fear he deserved to wear. For all the pain and bloodshed he'd caused, Dinkley deserved every nerve-shedding moment that had him ready to piss his pants. My body was on fire, and I could smell death and blood, yet none had been spilt.

Dinkley had become the fly in the spider's web and hadn't grasped it yet. A chess move that wasn't in his repertoire. The turmoil within the cloud was loud and riding. It was fuelled by unrelenting rage with one target. For now, at least. I looked around at my chessboard, the six I hadn't bargained for—Dinkley to my right and the Widow centre of the room.

A quick turn to the man of the moment. His discomfort thrilled me, and I knew it was wrong, but in the thralls of the full moon, I didn't care. He'd bragged and made power moves throughout, emphasising his ability to think so many moves ahead. I wanted to savour his expression with what came next...

"All units. Next phase now," My radio beeped loudly, echoing amidst the chaos. Dinkley looked at me, eyes bulging. The penny dropped, and so did the power.

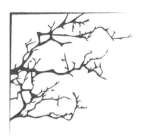

41

A DODGEY CHANCELLOR, REALLY?

The cloud froze, and everyone stopped. My eyes blazed red in the window reflection. Dinkley gulped with fear at the realisation he'd been blindsided. A loud click boomed out above, rippling through the ceiling. Motors whirred, and air thrust through. Lights rocked on, and a torrent of air flew out of the air conditioning, spraying the room with a mist that enveloped everything in its path.

"Chancellor, I enjoy the little things. I call them 'dots' and don't stop working on the problem until they connect. Today, our hand was forced, and we had to work the problem quickly to save another life. I needed all the pieces in place. Didn't factor in how many would be in your goon squad, but figured a pretentious prick like you would have a few to hide behind."

"What do you mean? But you were drugged."

"Yeah, we realised that would come if it's been the theme, especially on the masks. Walking through the trees, I smelt it and knew it wouldn't be long. But my friends, as you called them, are amazing, and one, in particular, is a genius and counteracted the effects. The room is filled with something that will help with a big reveal. I hope you're good with ghosts."

My attention turned to the widow, watching as it drifted lower. The six stepped backwards. The mass carried and got thicker with each gust of air. It pierced the black veil, spreading like a virus. I could hear their screams and squeals. I could see it slowly thickening, solidifying. Dinkley was panicking on many levels. All because he didn't know my moves or what we'd planned in the hours beforehand. The tide was turning.

"Don't just stand there. Get him," Dinkley shouted at the six. Neither looked ready.

My fangs were bared and claws ready. One after the other, they charged in their dysfunctional way. I bobbed the first swing of a knife before ripping an uppercut to the jaw that laid the first one out. I ducked in time for the next, ripping across the chest with my claws. The feel of their blood and flesh tearing was exhilarating and had my mouth watering. They dropped to their knees before a punch to their face flattened them.

I could hear footsteps running through the hallway but didn't have time to look as the 3rd came. The blade sliced across my right biceps, burning like a hot iron on flesh. I clawed at their right forearm, forcing them to drop the knife as they stumbled backwards. Another was approaching quickly; an elbow strike to one smashed into their teeth. Bone cracked and buckled; the onrushing was met with a head, but that sent them flying. Through the crowd, I clocked Michael's yellow eyes, with Ellena not far behind.

"Quick, the mountain ash," I shouted. Ellena sprayed a large jar in the air. Thick grey powder cut through the room before breaking into a mesmerising circle. Dancing a ring around the widow. It couldn't move sideways. Not for the lack of trying, a thick black mass battered an invisible barrier, sending sparks of green cascading in the air.

Bordering on a lust for more. One after the other, they all fell in painful heaps. Cries of agony rang out. My ears tweaked at each ripple. Dinkley was hypnotised by what was happening to the widow.

"That's another dot, Chancellor. Mistletoe removes all guises and lays the wearer's sins bare for all to see—time for the ghosts of your past to meet the present. The depraved damage you caused and the sick rampage were all on you. These are your sins. Look around... bask in the glory of you being a sick bastard. Come on, don't be coy now."

"How is this possible? Who is that?" Dinkley stuttered, his eyes darting left and right, looking at his options.

"The same way this is possible. A little of the 'million things in between.' You stomped into the darkness without taking a moment to appreciate the gravity of what the world hadn't seen yet. All the while, you pretended to be a righteous man hell-bent on bringing the right change to the country. Instead, all you are... Is a crook in an expensive suit."

I waved my claws as I grimaced through gritted fangs. Ellena got busy working on her next magic trick. Michael had all but laid the last one out and was busy strapping their wrists and feet with cable ties. I could hear sirens in the distance, and droplets of 'arse fell out,' sweat dripped from Dinkley's red, wrinkled brow.

"But... W... who?"

"Don't you recognise your repercussions?" The black cloud slowly dissipated, leaving behind five young girls. Grey-mottled skin and ghostly eyes appear to be in a trance. They looked like vacant shells of human beings, including Sally Turnage. Mr Etherington may have been right. What came back from that party was nothing but walking corpses with supernatural abilities that had them being controlled.

At first, I thought I'd counted wrong, but only five. Alice, who had been killed by her father, was missing. Maria, Francis, Susan, Grace, and Sally. Considering Susan had hanged herself and Francis overdosed at the party, and in a nightmarish way, they didn't seem all that bad. However, I could see the ligature marks around Susan's neck from where I stood. All were motionless and fairly lifeless. A notable absentee was Selene Cornell.

"The girls?" Dinkley exclaimed. I wasn't sure if he was play-acting or genuinely surprised. His heart jumped and displayed a gormless rabbit in headlights look.

"Don't pretend with all your self-righteous chess moves. You didn't know. A man with many fingers in many stuffed pies." I goaded. Dinkley shuffled uncomfortably. His earlier confidence about proof and lack of had just unravelled. The brag about Francis now stared at him through glazed eyes, and his fear of her torment being shared scared him.

I couldn't be sure whether there was any hope of that happening. Yet, for the time being, the widow had been slowed. A subconscious look from Dinkley at the phone as he fiddled with his pocket brought me back to that thing he had slipped in earlier.

"Well, if you think I'm in 'Check', don't count your chickens... before you bite their heads off."

"Well, there are other things I could bite the head off if push came to shove." I stepped forward to watch his body shift again.

'So, this corrupt money gets you? How much did you pay for our blood, not to mention our parent's cooperation? Did you think we had failed, died and disappeared? Or was that all you were told?'

A spooky interjection from the widow grabbed our attention. The cluster spoke in unison, but felt a little too so. Then I remembered the page in the book—a 'hive mind,' one controlling all. My earlier irrational thought came knocking. Selene. The only one without the obvious dead that hadn't made an appearance.

"Hey, who speaks for the group?"

'We speak as one. We hurt as one. Now we make them pay as one.'

"Selene? Did you all hurt as one? Or did some just get luckier than others?" I had to know. But each strobe of green against the circle made me careful not to rock the boat. Ellena looked concerned. But the cluster stopped speaking for a moment. Dinkley was acting squirrel, truth hurting, or assessing options. I couldn't get a read.

'Brilliant detective. You didn't let up after being warned, and it seems you've learned a lot since we got to massage your organs. Our pain is shared because he and his sick friends abused us. They experimented and cast us aside like rubbish because they thought we hadn't become what they wanted us to. Thanks to a rogue sympathiser, we could flip the tables. Can you imagine how it feels to have a body flooded with spider venom to wipe out a country? Not just one, either. The top five most dangerous. So, thanks to him, we have poisons instead of blood in our veins and all but the walking dead. We can operate like nothing is wrong, but together, we're so much more.'

"So why aren't you here? Maybe some are far more alive than others. Am I right?"

'Aren't you the quick study? Now hand him over, and you can walk.'

Selene's confidence put doubt in my mind. Whatever Ellena was doing, she had to hurry. Selene may be in control, but surely wouldn't be able to do it far away.

"He will pay for his wrongdoing. They all will. We won't be handing them over. Other strobes rocked out as the five began testing parts of the circle.

"Too right I'm not, and I'm afraid that pressing business needs my attention. By the looks of it, you have your hands full and seem far from having anything coherently tangible to use against me. So I bid you farewell for now."

Dinkley rummaged in his pocket; I heard a click, and the lights suddenly shot off. I still saw it in red and made a run for him. Then came a second click before an excruciatingly loud, piercing noise—Ellena's, but so much more. It was like a hot drill bit being ploughed through my brain. I couldn't hear, move, or function properly. Michael was the same. We both crumbled to our knees. Ellena was panicked, torn between seeing us or what she was doing. I barely waved the anger away. Clouds of white filled that immediate space. The next phase...

Mistletoe mixed with liquid nitrogen to incapacitate the five elements of the widow. The green strobing soon stopped, and I could see their bodies frost up.

Then, the emitter suddenly stopped. Its frequency had to be far greater than what Ellena had made. I was in agony but rapidly recovering. Michael too. Unfortunately, Dinkley was gone. My hearing slowly returned to somewhere near normal. I could hear all five girls' flesh stiffen and crackle. The power in the ash barrier was strong. I could feel it where I stood, but the extra protection may have caught the Black Widow.

I scanned the room. All windows and doors that I could see were still closed. He hadn't got past Ellena. She would've said so or heard. With my hearing, I tried to listen past all of us, seeking something different. A hint of where he could've gone. His scent carved through the air like a chainsaw. I still had it locked. Chemo signals, too, panic and heightened adrenaline, all wrapped in a tasty fear bundle.

He'd been on the other side of the counter. I jumped to where he'd stood. His fingerprint signature lingered in three places: the lit-up button, a little draw on the counter, and a small, otherwise indistinguishable recess on the lip of the counter.

My claw hovered across, and the tip felt a little movement. Beyond the noise from Ellena's spray, Michael's phlegmy lungs, and the grumbles of pain from the six on the floor, I picked up on a whirring beneath my feet. With a quick press, a group of tiles dropped, letting a whiff of a damp breeze out.

"Go, Georgie, this is in hand," Michael hollered. Caught in two minds, I looked at Ellena with my hackles rumbling and blood bubbling. The 'Widow' cluster seemed controlled, but I worried about leaving these alone. That seed of doubt lasted a minute until I heard several patters of shoe heels deep under the floor.

Looking in, there's a ladder going down about thirty feet. There was no time to climb down—a last look at the mess. Then I dropped—damp, cobbled stone floors, just like in my vision. My stomach was doing somersaults, entering the dark unknown. My head replayed everything that had happened. A saving grace this time, both Ellena and Michael were upstairs.

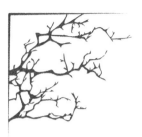

42

ENDGAME

Frantic footsteps echoed ahead in the abyss of crimson darkness. Leaks rippled down the walls, each droplet a thump between my shredded nerves. I pressed on, reaching what felt like the hundred-foot mark, senses heightened by the lingering scent of blood—aged but still vivid on my tongue. The absence of the moon's glimmer offered a twisted solace, sharpening my focus.

The clopping ceased, replaced by two heartbeats—one racing, the other inching towards death. Dinkley's fear escalated, a cocktail of anger, hatred, toxins, and impending doom swirling in the air. Selene had him, and the horrors awaiting me danced in my mind. The rack and fire loomed, scenarios I wished to avoid.

"Detective? Take me. I surrender. You've got me in 'checkmate.' I'll spill everything. Just save me," Dinkley's panicked plea echoed in the distance, the desperation tangible.

"Now it's a party. A time to kick back, laugh, and maybe slit a throat. What do you think, Detective?" Selene's voice resonated with a chilling anticipation, foretelling an inevitable end—more death.

"How about we take this to the station?" A flicker of light unveiled a silhouette—a young woman gripping Dinkley, her hand clenched around his jugular. The VHS-remembered fork-like tongue hovered over his carotid artery.

"What? Let this bastard get away with murder? He tortured Francis, experimented on us, and turned us into weapons. Paid off our parents, ensuring their silence. Someone saved us and gave us a purpose. He realised I could control the group. We made a hit list, and bodies fell—bittersweet revenge. But you know what's even sweeter? The thick bastard has been paying for the privilege," Selene revealed with a venomous calm.

"What do you mean?" I inquired, a 'dot' dropping into place, connecting the hidden strings.

"Our saviour drains this scumbag while working with us to kill his friends, erasing the evidence," Selene elaborated, revealing a sinister alliance.

A realisation struck when Selene hinted at my knowledge. The mastermind had a perfect cover, nudging corpses to decay faster.

"He has a 'dead-end' job?" I probed.

"Smart, isn't it? We kill our parents, and he transfers their money to our little slush fund for a 'bloody day' and other wheels in motion," Selene explained, hinting at a broader conspiracy.

"Other wheels?" I pressed.

"This might end here, for now, but only for now. Your claws are going to be full, Detective. This arsehole may have created us, and now we have a taste for it." Selene's ominous words hung in the air, a warning for another day.

"Well, it's an occupational hazard. Let's end this now. Let us deal with him, and we can work through the aftermath," I proposed, though deep down, I sensed the futility.

"Poor Detective, still believing in hope? Still believing in Santa? There's no saving our souls now. Good luck with the bloodshed ahead. By the way, your friend should be enjoying a rest on the steps of your station about now," Selene cooed menacingly.

Andy had been released, or so Selene claimed. Tiptoeing within ten feet, I calculated the risk, heart in my mouth, uncertain if I'd make it. Selene had two ways to end him; even if I reached, no guarantees existed. Selene smiled, her tongue swished, and in a flash, she tore through Dinkley's throat.

As her fingers shredded flesh, satisfaction oozed from Selene. Blood fanned out, painting the cobbles red as she dropped Dinkley's corrupt form. Selene held her hands aloft, blood dripping down as the jugular fell. She surrendered but had already won. Bittersweet revenge was hers, and the danger persisted.

"Selene Cornell, I'm arresting you for the murder of David Dinkley and countless others," I declared on a grander scale. We had the killers, yet the real criminal lay on the floor. In some twisted way, his death seemed an escape from justice. Painting a picture with the 'dots' became crucial, a risk worth taking.

Surveying the wider tunnel section, a room of torment from my dreams unfolded. The rack, blood-siphoning machines, and more. A camcorder faced the scenery, and a muzzle-like mask, used to secure Selene's face, rested on a table.

With the last clip in place, relief washed over. The immediate danger ceased, but uncertainty lingered. Money cycled through corrupt hands, and only God knew the plans. Escorted upstairs, Selene faced a circus of uniforms, and a relieved Ellena and Michael were not far behind. The six were gone, the girls subdued, and Selene was injected with a neuro-inhibitor and sedative for containment.

"Selene has been in control, using them as walking, murderous corpses. Some life may remain, but how much survived that night is a question for the bigger picture," Ellena explained.

"Is it over, matey?" Michael, exhausted, sought clarity.

"Mostly. Downstairs is a treasure trove, and these houses hold more secrets. This is a jigsaw we need to piece together. We've stopped the 'Black Widow,' but the rest of the pawns will come soon," I assured.

"More bad news. Welfare checks yielded more deaths, but Andy has been found sleepy and confused on the station steps," Michael shared.

"They got their revenge, but others need to be picked up. Selene hinted at it. Once this is clear, there's one more immediate stop to make," I declared, the weariness etched on their faces reflecting the nightmare endured.

A visit to the coroner's office awaited, but closure came first.

FOUR HOURS LATER, AT 29 Connaught Square, West London, I faced Mr Nicholls.

"Mr Nicholls, how the devil are you?" I greeted.

"Detective Reynolds... I am fine, thank you. How can I help?" Nicholls replied.

"Let's start by turning around and sticking your hands behind your back," I commanded.

"What? Why?" Nicholls panicked, complying.

"Because I'm arresting you on suspicion of murder, conspiracy to murder, fraud, and a million other things too long to list. Terrorism with conspiracy to bring down parliament. You do not have to say anything, but it may harm your defence if you do not mention something you later rely on in court when questioned. Anything you say may be given as evidence," I recited the charges.

Nicholls's face dropped. Another 'Dot' lined up. Finally, the other dropped, this time for the bad guys.

"I think the words you're looking for, Nicholls lad, is 'Oh, Fuck.' I just heard your arse fall out," Andy quipped with a cheesy grin.

The whole team savoured the 'mic drop' moment. Nicholls turning pale was the icing on a very bloody cake. We battled and got rattled, but the sound of handcuffs clanking closed was music to our ears. The widow got revenge, but we came for justice. The journey was far from over. Time to rest before the next body drops.

About the Author

I fell in love with writing many years ago. Then I grew up, fell in love with many other things, and had to learn how to be an adult with responsibilities. Two teenage sons later, things didn't turn out too bad, and now I have a little more free time to reunite with my first love ... I want to create a world where readers sink deep and never want to escape. A supernatural detectiverse with intriguing cases and loveable characters. Join me on this rollercoaster.

www. RyanHoldenBooks. co. uk

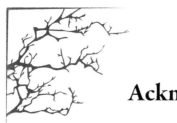

Acknowledgements

To the family and friends who sat through the countless drafts and listened to my crazy ideas, you inspire me to be better every day and with every novel I create. Thank you...

Don't miss out!

Visit the website below and you can sign up to receive emails whenever Ryan Holden publishes a new book. There's no charge and no obligation.

https://books2read.com/r/B-A-OVABB-VCBQC

BOOKS 2 READ

Connecting independent readers to independent writers.

Did you love *Black Widow*? Then you should read *The Cursed Knights*[1] by Ryan Holden!

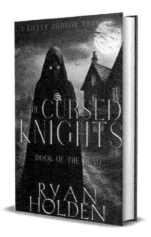

[2]

"**Demons are real, and they want your soul.**"

Gerald Ackerman is still haunted by their deaths – barely six months had passed since he lost his wife, Charlotte. Now he's hearing wailing, chilling voices.

He'd worked hard to make life seem normal for the sake of his daughters. Yet, nothing made sense, least of all the how. And why? Gerald's world shattered.

Disturbed by the constant calls to 'Let the voices in' Gerald senses a sinister tale to the two accidents. Determined to uncover the truth, he embarks on an investigation that plunges him into an unending nightmare. Even if no one believes him.

As he delves deeper, Gerald unearths a terrifying revelation steeped in the supernatural. A centuries-old curse binds his family to a faction of the **legendary 'Knights Templar,'** that veered into the realms of devil worship.

1. https://books2read.com/u/m0oXyW

2. https://books2read.com/u/m0oXyW

Way back then, some knights rebelled against the darkness, fleeing for safety only to be cursed to kill, with each victim's soul taken, sections of an ancient text needed to open the gates of hell, is revealed in **'The Book of the Dead'** while their bodies become 'demonic vessels.' Waiting for the day demons can roam the earth and rule. As Gerald's mind unravels, he's tormented by those sinister whispers beckoning him to **surrender to evil and go on a killing spree.** A way to wash away the pain.

Each revelation he uncovers further intertwines him with the reality that his wife and father were murdered. Then more bodies drop – and suddenly Gerald witnesses these crimes through the eyes of the killer. . . fuelling his fear that he might be the one responsible.

Guided from beyond the grave by his father through tapes and cryptic clues, Gerald must confront the curse head-on to break free. Embracing the disturbing truth to save his hometown and beyond.

Will Gerald Ackerman break the curse? Or succumb to the whispers and fate?

Read more at www.ryanholdenbooks.co.uk.

Also by Ryan Holden

The Detective Reynolds series
Burnt Blood
Murder on the Waterway
Black Widow
Secrets in the Bones
The Cursed Knights

Watch for more at www.ryanholdenbooks.co.uk.

About the Author

I fell in love with the idea of writing many years ago. Then I grew up, fell in love with many other things, and had to learn how to be an adult with responsibilities. Two teenage sons' later, things didn't turn out too bad, and now I have a little more free time to reunite with my first love... ❤ I want to create a world that readers sink deep in and never want to get out. A supernatural detectiverse with intriguing cases and loveable characters. Join me on this rollercoaster.

Read more at www.ryanholdenbooks.co.uk.

Printed in Great Britain
by Amazon

37128530R00148